SEXY Dirty COWBOY

ELLE THORPE

SEXY DIRTY COWBOY

DIRTY COWBOY #3

ELLE THORPE

For all the women in their small town era.

1

WHITNEY

"*W*hy don't detectives wear uniforms?"

I cast a glance over my shoulder at Karsten watching in the mirror while I applied my Chap-Stick. With the balm smeared across my lips, I rubbed them together before turning to flash my badge at him. "Because they give us these nifty little things in order to identify ourselves. No need for a uniform."

Karsten gripped me by the hips and pulled me toward him. His mouth twisted into an exaggerated pout. "But you'd look so good in a uniform, babe. Your ass…"

His palms slid down my hips and around to cup the cheeks of my butt.

"Is still pretty good, even in a pair of jeans?" I cocked one eyebrow, challenging him.

"Damn straight." Another squeeze and a swat to my behind reminded me he'd always loved my body, even though I wasn't a tiny delicate woman. I'd never lost my curves, despite the amount of exercise I had to do in order to pass my department-mandated physicals.

Outside, a horn blared, and I craned my neck to see out the window. Mia sat behind the steering wheel in the police cruiser we used when we had no need to conceal who we worked for.

Karsten cringed and peered at his watch. "Doesn't she know what time it is? The neighbors will complain."

I laughed, capping the ChapStick and tossing it back onto the bathroom vanity. "To who? The police?"

Karsten shrugged, his cheeks pinkening a little. It was a bit adorable. So I grabbed his hand, and he followed me down the stairs. It was technically my house, but Karsten had lived here almost as long as I had, so I never really thought about the fact it was my name on the mortgage.

From within neatly aligned picture frames, hanging in the hallway, images of the two of us smiled back. Photos of our travels and accomplishments were mixed in between photos of Rusty, the dog we'd adopted. No kids yet, but they wouldn't be far behind. I wanted them. Desperately. I'd felt my biological clock ticking every day since I'd turned thirty. Now at thirty-two, the ticktock was making a bit of a racket, reminding me constantly I wasn't getting any younger. I just had to convince Karsten we didn't actually have all the time in the world, as he kept proclaiming.

We reached the front door, and Karsten leaned around me, opening it so I could leave. But when I stepped out onto our porch, he tugged my hand, spinning me back to face him. Before I could say anything, he pressed his lips to mine, hot, hard, and branding.

Despite the fact the streetlights lit up the evening enough that Mia would be able to see us, I kissed him back. Like I always did. It didn't seem to matter where he wanted me. It could be in the privacy of our own home, in a park as we jogged together, or on our darkened porch while my partner waited for me to start our shift. I always responded. He had some weird sort of pull on me, which made me forget I was normally a Sensible Sally. I'd never been one to lose my head over a guy, but Karsten had swept me off my feet two years ago and hadn't put me down since.

His tongue invaded my mouth, and he walked me back to the wall. A brief flex of his hips against mine told me we should have started this earlier.

The horn blared again, and I pulled away from my man with a groan, peering over his shoulder at Mia.

"Quit making out like you're sixteen-year-old virgins on prom night!" Mia yelled through the open car window. "Or at the very least, make me a bag of popcorn while I watch the free porn!"

I choked on a laugh and shoved Karsten away.

He rolled his eyes at Mia's antics. "Seriously, you need to talk to her about appropriate neighborhood behavior. If Mrs. Toadley next door corners me in the morning and bites my head off because Mia disturbed her cats, I'm not going to be happy."

I burst out laughing at his all-too-serious face, and eventually, his pressed-together lips widened into a smile. I kissed him lightly and skipped down the steps. "See you tomorrow," I called over my shoulder.

He lifted his hand in a wave. A lingering glint of heat in his eyes sent a shiver down my spine. I yanked open the passenger seat door and climbed inside with the hugest grin on my face. Maybe I'd ask Janice if I could leave early tonight. If I could get home before dawn and slide into bed before Karsten's alarm went off, we'd have a whole hour of naked time before he needed to be at work. He was going away for work again next week, so I wanted to make the most of the time we did have together.

Mia shook her head, and with a quick blind spot check, she guided the cruiser into the suburban street. "You guys make me sick. You're really *there*, aren't you? In that honeymoon phase where it's all kissing and sex and hot, stolen glances when you think no one is watching. Or even when you *know* people—your partner specifically—are watching. When are you going to get over that?"

I shrugged. "It's been two years. Maybe this is just what we are? I don't see it stopping anytime soon."

"Ugh. As I said, sickening. That phase lasted three months with Lucas and me."

"So push him up against a wall before he leaves for work?" I side-eyed her. "Works for me."

"Yeah, I noticed," she grumbled.

Mia and I had been partners for years, though, so I knew her complaints were in good fun.

"What are we doing tonight, anyway?" I asked, steering the conversation away from how physical Karsten and I still were. "A fraud case or something, right?"

Mia made an affirmative sound in the back of her throat. "Wilson and Stavos are meeting us there at twenty-one hundred. We drew the short straw. Everyone else is at the rodeo, bringing in the ex-gang member."

I blinked. "From the rodeo?"

Mia hit the blinker to maneuver the car around a

sharp left turn before answering me. "All I know is that he's a professional on the bull riding circuit now, but seems he was once mixed up with the Kings of Chaos Motorcycle Club. Some cold case they got a new lead on."

I nodded, running through the facts in my brain. I'd heard bits and pieces about the case but hadn't paid a lot of attention since it wasn't assigned to me. I wish it had been. Sounded a hell of a lot more interesting than what we had to do tonight.

Mia's chatter about her kid's softball game filled the time it took us to drive to the suburban home of our target. I let out a long, low whistle when we stopped the car outside a sprawling, two-story mansion. The lawn was perfectly neat, interrupted only by gardens full of flowers and a rock path that led to the painted wood door. Lights glowed in the downstairs windows, and I heaved a sigh. It was so beautiful on the outside, but it just went to show, you never knew what people did behind closed doors. Did the other people on this street know their neighbors were embezzling money? Did they suspect that underneath the good morning smiles, lay someone who cared so little for the law that they would break it, just so they could have all this material wealth?

"You've got that look on your face again." Mia glanced at me. "The one where you seem disappointed by what we're about to do."

I shook my head. "Not just disappointed. Angry, too. We have laws for a reason, you know? I just can't stand when people don't respect them."

"You and me both, girl. But let's just get this done, huh? I want to get back to the station. Lord knows we have more interesting cases to work on."

She wasn't wrong there, and Wilson and Stavos were already out of their car and waiting for us. Mia locked our cruiser, and we took the lead, the two uniformed officers trailing behind. I liked being in control, even on something as mundane as this. Mia rapped her knuckles across the door, and after a moment's pause, a woman appeared in the doorway. Dim light spilled out around her pajama-clad form, and a young baby in a onesie sat propped on her hip.

Mia flashed her badge and handed her a folded piece of paper.

"What's this?" the woman asked, struggling to unfold it with her one free hand.

"It's a search warrant, Mrs. MacIntosh."

"For what?" Her fingers gripped the door tighter, her knuckles turning white with the effort.

"Ma'am," I said gently, aware she had a child with her and unwilling to upset him. "Please. You need to let us in."

With clear reluctance, she opened the door wide, and we all traipsed through. The baby's gaze followed me curiously, and my heart skipped a beat at the sight of his pudgy little hands, grasping at his mother's sleep shirt.

Mrs. MacIntosh caught me staring and tucked him tighter against her chest. "I don't know what you're searching for. Don doesn't bring his work home."

I ignored that statement. It didn't matter whether it was true or not. We had another team at her husband's office, doing exactly the same thing we were. We were merely covering all bases.

"Where is your husband right now, Mrs. MacIntosh?"

"Away. For work." She smoothed her palm over her

son's back in a calming motion that seemed more for her benefit than for his.

The little boy twisted in her grasp and gave me a gummy smile that I had a hard time not returning. But I needed to focus on his mother. Not the fact my ovaries were squealing with delight.

"We'll get out of your hair as soon as possible. Just sit over there, please." I pointed to an armchair. The woman turned stiffly and walked the few steps to where I'd indicated. She sank down onto the cushions, worrying her bottom lip with her teeth.

"You ready, Whit?" Mia asked with one foot on the bottom of the staircase that led to the second story.

"Yeah, I'll be right..." I narrowed my eyes at the framed photo on the table beside where Mrs. MacIntosh sat. I didn't know what it was about the image that had caught my attention. Perhaps it was the familiar blond flop of hair...

I picked up the frame, blinking hard. Three people, enjoying what looked to be a picnic smiled back at me. Two of the people were Mrs. MacIntosh and the baby currently gurgling on her lap. And the third...

I thrust the photo into Mrs. MacIntosh's face. "This man." The words came out squeaky, and I cleared my throat and tried again. "Is he your brother?"

Though from some place deep inside me, a place where a whirling current of unease now swelled, I knew what her answer was going to be.

"I don't have a brother. That's my husband, Don."

With those few words, my world tilted on its axis. The current turned into a tidal wave and dumped a load of lies, secrets, and betrayal right on top of my head.

"What's going on?" Mia asked, coming up beside me.

Limply, I passed her the photo.

Her gasp of shock washed over me, but I barely heard it. I spun, searching the walls of the house, and wondered how they weren't the first thing I'd noticed. To my left, another family portrait hung. This one more formally posed. But it was still his eyes. His smile, staring back at me. A familiar leather jacket was slung over a coat rack. I stalked toward it and fingered the cuff on the sleeve, knowing when I turned it over there'd be a smudge of red paint from when we'd painted our bedroom.

Our bedroom. In the house *we* shared.

But apparently, I wasn't the only one Karsten shared a bedroom with.

All the late nights. All the business trips. I mentally pulled each one apart and put them back together in their true form. He hadn't been late. He hadn't been away. He'd been here.

Nausea rolled my stomach. Stavos asked what I was doing, but Mia shushed him, while everything I'd known for the past two years fell apart. My gaze bounced around the room, trying to imagine Karsten walking these floors. Watching TV on that couch. Making dinner in that kitchen.

Making love with *his wife* in the bedrooms upstairs.

With horror, I stared at the baby. He was the baby I'd wanted for years. The one Karsten had said he wasn't ready for.

Now I knew why. Karsten was never going to marry me. Never going to give me a baby. Because he already had all that.

With someone else.

My nausea boiled into anger. "Your husband is away for work?" I asked Karsten's wife.

"I already told you that."

"Give me your cell phone," I demanded.

Mia put a hand on my arm. "Whit, no. You don't need to do this."

But I did. I needed it like I needed air to breathe.

"Your phone!" I barked.

The woman fumbled to pick it up from the table. The baby was no longer smiling. He buried his face in his mother's shoulder as she held the phone out to me.

"Don, right? That's your husband's name?" I asked.

She nodded, confusion written all over her pretty face.

Don. Seriously? At least when Karsten made up an alias, he picked a cooler name. Was Don short for Donald? Donatello? What did it fucking matter? It was short for lying, cheating asshole. I scrolled through the woman's phone until I found his number and hit the 'call' button.

It only rang twice. "Hey, sweetheart. I was just thinking about you."

I snorted on a harsh, bitter-sounding laugh. I didn't say anything, just letting the long pause drag out.

"Belinda?"

"*Not* Belinda," I bit out.

Another moment of silence, then, "Whitney?"

My lips twisted into a cruel smile. "Ding, ding, ding. We have a winner."

"Whit...fuck. I can explain."

"Can you, *Don*? Can you really? I don't think there's

any need for that. I think it's pretty obvious what's going on here."

To my surprise, Karsten—Don—whatever his name was, burst into tears. I pulled the phone away from my ear and stared at it like it had just sprouted horns. Tears? What the actual fuck? Was this seriously the same hot alpha boyfriend who'd pushed me up against the wall just an hour ago? I'd never seen Karsten cry in two years, but when I put the phone back to my ear, great gulping sobs echoed down the line.

I ground my molars together. Did he think I was that stupid? That he could cry, and I'd somehow feel sorry for him? His tears had the opposite effect on me. I wanted to put my fist through the drywall. You know, since his face wasn't handy.

"Please don't say anything to my wife. I love you. I swear. I'll talk to her. I'll tell her it's always been you. She means nothing to me."

I let him continue, wheedling his way through the call, begging, crying, whining to me about how he'd make it up to me. How he'd leave her. How she trapped him with the baby.

That was the last straw. I looked into Belinda's big brown eyes, just like her son's, and prayed to God her son was more like her than he was his father. And then I hit loudspeaker.

"I never loved her, Whitney. I swear it. Just come home and I'll make it up to you. I'll do anything, everything! We can go away together. Maybe we can make that baby you've been wanting. It'll be just like when we first started dating, and we'll just put all of this behind us."

Belinda's eyes filled with tears, and she stood to face

me. On the loudspeaker, Karsten carried on, his words now unheard by both the women who'd loved him. *Loved*. Past tense.

"You didn't know about me?" his wife asked, ignoring her squawking husband.

I shook my head. "I swear it. You didn't know about me?"

A single tear spilled down the woman's cheek. "No." She glanced around the big house. "What the hell am I supposed to do with all of this? We're married. We have a child."

I focused on her son, and though the walls inside me were breaking down, threatening to collapse my strong outside façade, I forced my words to sound determined. "You take your son and raise him to be a better man than his father is."

Then I held out the phone and let her have the honor of hanging up.

2

REM

"What's with the cowboy getup?"

I cast a sidelong glance at the man sitting slumped against the opposite wall of the holding cell. His blond hair fell in red-rimmed eyes, and I wondered if he'd been crying. Or maybe he was high. "I'm a bullfighter. I was working when they picked me up."

The man quirked an eyebrow, and leaned in, resting his forearms on his knees. "Oh yeah? You ever get bucked off?"

I shook my head. "Bull *fighter*. Not bull rider."

He squinted, small lines creasing the skin either side of his eyes. "So, what? You're like one of those guys who waves a cape around and stabs the bulls with a sword?"

"What?" I snapped. The guy was beginning to annoy me. I'd already had the shittiest fucking evening possible; I didn't need his dumb-ass questions on top of it. "I don't hurt the bulls. Just distract them while the rider gets out of the way after a buck off."

He shrugged, losing interest, and went back to slumping against the wall.

Whatever. I probably should have just said I was a rodeo clown, since that's how most people recognized my job. But I didn't have the patience to explain further anyway. I just wanted to get the hell out of this cell, go back to my hotel, and have a few beers with the rest of the guys. I knew my arrest was probably putting a downer on their big night, and that sucked. The Las Vegas bull riding finals had been all but over when the cops had swarmed the arena and dragged me out of there in handcuffs. That had been hours ago, and I was still waiting for my one phone call. Or bail. My brother, Abel, would be out the front somewhere, demanding I be released. I knew that. But I hadn't heard a peep from anyone since they'd shoved me back here.

I took my hat off and ran my hands through my hair. Probably wouldn't do Abel any good. I knew he'd front the cash for my bail if they let him, but he wouldn't understand why bail probably wasn't on the cards for me tonight. He didn't know about all the messed-up shit I'd done in my past.

I'd known it would come back to bite me. Would have preferred it hadn't happened with thousands of screaming rodeo fans watching, but that wasn't exactly something I could change now. I groaned, wondering if I'd even have a career to go back to when I did finally get sprung from this place.

From outside our cell somewhere, a door opened and closed. Footsteps echoed down the corridor, and eventually, a woman appeared in our line of sight. Her jeans molded to her thighs, and her fitted, button-down shirt was professional but still kind of sexy. It skimmed her breasts, and the open top button gave the tiniest hint of cleavage. She clipped her key card back onto the belt loop of her pants and strode through the cell-lined corridor like she owned it.

I tracked her movements, my gaze drifting over long legs and the swell of her hips. Fuck me. She was a knock-out. Long blonde hair scraped back into a simple, no-nonsense ponytail. Full pink lips held slightly parted, not smiling, but not clamped tight either. Curves for days, shown off to perfection, even in her understated outfit.

Her shrewd eyes missed nothing, and when her gaze landed on me, I realized I could die a happy man, staring into those aqua-colored orbs. She barely lingered a second, though, and all too soon went back to focusing on wherever she was going.

"Whitney!" The man beside me yelped. He flung himself toward the bars of our cell, rattling them. He reached through, fingers outstretched.

The woman—Whitney, apparently— took a step back, deftly moving out of the man's grasp, and stared him down.

"Behind the bars, prisoner," she barked out.

Huh. Interesting dynamic. I sat back and watched, wondering what the story was there.

I didn't have to wait long to find out.

"Baby, please. Let me explain!" my cellmate whined. "I need you. You gotta get me out of here." A sob, which frankly sounded like a crock of bullshit to me, burst from his chest, and tears leaked down his dirt-smeared cheek.

I rolled my eyes. Somebody hand this guy his Emmy.

To my surprise, Whitney hesitated. *Oh, hell no.* She

wasn't seriously buying this bullshit routine? They obviously knew each other. But if she was on one side of the bars, and he was on the other, something had gone down.

Her face softened, and she stepped closer.

The man's tears abruptly stopped. "That's it, baby," he cooed to her so sweetly, it made me want to check my teeth for cavities. "You know I'd never do anything to hurt you. You're my girl, right?"

Whitney let him reach through the bars once more, and this time, she allowed him to tuck a strand of loose hair back behind her ear.

An irrational surge of something that felt suspiciously like envy rose in me. Lucky bastard, getting to touch her. She pushed the side of her face against his hand, like she'd been missing his touch. My stomach rolled.

"Karsten?" she said, closing her eyes.

"What do you need, Whit? Anything, I'll do it."

With lightning fast movements, she reached through the bars and grabbed the guy by his junk. I widened my eyes then winced, my own balls shriveling, when she yanked hard and then...twisted. Oh God. The woman was vicious.

The howl my cellmate let out echoed off the high ceilings, and I had to bite my lip to keep from laughing.

Whitney's eyes went so bright I could have sworn they glowed from the fire burning behind them. "I don't need anything from you, Karsten." She hissed the words into her wailing lover's ear. "Ever again. Your shit will be on the lawn, in fucking flames before sunrise. So don't bother coming by to pick it up. If they ever let you out of here, that is. Which I hope they don't. You can burn in Hell for all I care. Asshole."

I wasn't sure whether to laugh or scrape my jaw up off the floor. With a final yank to Karsten's family jewels, she released him and stalked away, like a woman on a mission.

I watched her go with a grin. Holy hell. She was the hottest thing I'd ever seen, and the display of power did nothing but turn me on. I stood and pressed myself against the bars, watching her until she disappeared through another door and out of sight.

Damn.

Karsten lay at my feet, writhing on the dirty floor in the fetal position. "You fucking bitch!" he screamed after her.

Irritation prickled at the back of my neck. "Watch your mouth," I growled at him.

He stared up at me, still clutching his probably mangled man parts. "Or what, *cowboy*?" He drawled the last word, so it sounded mocking and condescending.

I shook my head. What. The. Fuck. Ever. With a quick look to make sure no one was watching; I leaned down, getting in Karsten's face.

Instantly, he realized he'd made a mistake. "No, wait!"

Too late. I swung my arm back before letting my fist fly, straight into his nose. It made a satisfying crunch beneath my fist, and pain exploded through my knuckles. Fuck! It had been years since I'd thrown a punch, and I'd forgotten how much it hurt. Dammit!

But Karsten howling on the floor, this time clutching his busted nose, was worth it. Douchebag deserved the pain. I shook out my fist and slumped back against the cell wall.

It took a long time for someone to come check out

what Karsten was yowling about. I'd had enough time to think about what I'd done, and to realize it probably wasn't my smartest move. What with already being in jail, I didn't need an assault charge added on top of whatever else it was I'd done to land my ass here. But I couldn't bring myself to regret it. I didn't like when men hurt women. And Karsten had obviously hurt Whitney. Though she was doing a fine job of looking after herself, I didn't think the big guy upstairs would judge me too harshly for the punch.

The police, who had probably watched the whole thing on monitors, might be a different story, though.

They dragged Karsten off to the infirmary with blood drying on his chin, and I waited for the inevitable trouble I had to be in. But the two uniformed officers who took Karsten didn't say anything. And then it was just me in the cell, with nothing to do but listen to the distant sounds of other prisoners breathing, talking, or snoring. I stifled a yawn. I had no idea what time it was. I didn't wear a watch, though they probably would have taken it off me even if I did, and the cells were lit solely by artificial light. There weren't any windows to tell me if it was night or day, but my body clock was telling me it was the early hours of the morning.

Deciding that being alone in a cell was the best time for a nap, I laid out on the bench and put my hands behind my head, covering my face with my hat.

The cell door slid open. "Remington James? Let's go."

I cracked open an eye. Whitney stood by the open cell gate. I pushed to my feet, fighting back a grin, and it occurred to me I just might follow this woman anywhere she wanted to lead me.

REM

Sweat trickled down the back of my neck, but I refused to tug at my collar. They likely kept the interrogation rooms uncomfortably warm on purpose, but I wasn't going to give away that it was getting to me. Or that the room was tiny and airless. Or that I'd been claustrophobic for years, ever since my first stint in a jail cell.

I tried to breathe deeply, without actually showing that I was. I kicked back in my chair, crossing my legs at the ankle, folded my arms across my chest, and attempted to keep from hyperventilating. I wanted to suck deep lungfuls or maybe put my head between my knees. But I couldn't show weakness. That was something I'd learned back when everyone called me Viper instead of Rem.

I raised one cocky eyebrow when the door opened and a burly-looking detective with a beer gut and a double chin strode in.

"I'm Detective Lorrel," he declared in a deep baritone

that suited his physique. He was a big guy: tall, broad, and dressed neatly, so he carried his extra weight well. He was an imposing force, even if he had let himself get soft around the middle. He'd pulled out a seat, before I noticed he wasn't alone.

Whitney's gaze met mine, and I straightened. I took off my hat, swiping my fingers through the tousled lengths of dark hair, and put it down on the table between us. I thought I saw her give me the tiniest of nods—perhaps acknowledging I'd punched her ex-boyfriend? Who knew? I was probably imagining it. She took the seat next to the big man, and I dragged my eyes off her, not wanting to make her uncomfortable.

Lord knew I was uncomfortable enough for everyone. The presence of two extra people in the shoebox of a room only made my chest tighter. What I wouldn't have given for a glass of water or one of those paper fans that little old ladies used when their churches were too warm.

"Remington 'Viper' James," the detective mused out loud, shuffling some papers on the table while Whitney looked on silently.

"Just Rem now, actually. Dropped the Viper bit a long time ago."

"So we've heard. Keeping your nose clean on the WBRA tour. Nicely done."

"Thank you, sir." I didn't love kissing ass, but hey, if playing the part of the polite, law-abiding citizen got me out of here, then I could suck it up.

"Shame you can never outrun the sins of your past, though, can you?"

My stomach sank.

He picked up a single sheet from the pile of papers

and read off it. "Son of David 'Crow' James, who is currently serving twenty-five to life in maximum security for crimes committed with his motorcycle gang. And then you went and made Daddy proud, by becoming the vice president of the Kings of Chaos MC for three years. Walked right into his footsteps there, didn't you? What a good boy you are. Oh look, a five-year stint in the clink for weapons and drug-related crimes..." His bushy eyebrows rose as he glared at me over the top of the paper. "Sound about right?"

I balled my fingers into fists; opening up the knuckle I'd split on Karsten's nose. "You missed the part about how I was released early and turned my life around." My gaze darted to Whitney. "Clean as a whistle ever since."

If she cared about what I said, she didn't show it. Shame heated my cheeks. I wasn't proud of my past. But it had happened. I'd grown up with the club after my father had landed himself in jail, when I was just a kid. Abel's mother was smart and got him out. But mine was a club woman through and through. She'd never wanted a kid and did the bare minimum as a mother. The bare minimum meant keeping me alive and little more. The Kings of Chaos had been the only life I'd known. And I'd followed them blindly.

Until I didn't.

I wasn't the same guy anymore. And I'd spent the last five years on the outside, making a new life for myself. One that was law-abiding. One I was proud of. One far, far away from everything I'd been before I went to jail.

"New evidence has come to light. A body was found in the scrub off Eastend Road."

I stiffened before forcing myself to relax. "What's that got to do with me?"

The detective leaned in, running two fingers over the five o'clock shadow on his flabby cheeks. "Dental records told us it's Leon Crawford. With a bullet hole through his skull. Name sound familiar?"

He knew it did, though I'd never known Leon by his given name. He'd always been Two Knot to the club. There was no point lying. "Yeah, I used to know Leon. Everyone did. He was pres of our rival club, The Devil Red MC. So what? I didn't kill him."

The man shrugged one shoulder. "Maybe you did, maybe you didn't. All I know is, we have evidence that says you could have. Evidence that puts you away for what?" He looked over at Whitney.

"Hmm?" she said distractedly, as if she hadn't been listening.

"What's the minimum term for murder these days?"

"Oh. Minimum twenty-five years. More likely for life."

A wide smile spread over the detective's face. "Fancy a reunion with your pop, Viper? I'm sure he's been missing you."

"You're full of it," I gritted out. "I want my lawyer."

Detective Lorrel ignored me. "We just needed the body, kid. We've already got the bar fight footage from the night Leon went missing."

He threw a photo on the desk in front of me and stabbed it with his meaty finger. The image was grainy, but sure enough, there I was, plain as day, wearing my Kings of Chaos cut, with blood literally on my hands. My old president, Miles Mitchell, by my side.

Detective Lorrel was enjoying this entirely too much.

I could practically see him tripping over his words in excitement, like a little kid, desperate to tell their parent all about the amazing thing they'd done. Detective Lorrel was exactly the same, only his excitement was over telling me exactly how much evidence he had against me.

"I'd argue that this photo says you and Miles Mitchell beat the shit out of Leon in the Lonely Daisy Bar, and then—oh look!"

I almost rolled my eyes at how joyous he sounded.

He threw another photo down in front of me. This one was of me and Miles and dragging Leon's body out a side door. "You two carried him off to Eastend Road and put a bullet in his head. Nice! Right? And oh, wait, here's the best bit! Dashcam footage of your club van at the scene of the crime, plus a whole bar full of people who can testify that you two were the last people seen with Leon alive. You certainly had motive, what with Leon's crew encroaching on your territory, trying to smuggle in on your weapons trade. So let's see now. That gives us motive, means, and opportunity. Need I continue? Because I can. I can go all night." He patted the folder he hadn't even touched yet. It could be fake; but with my history, there was every chance he wasn't bluffing.

Fuck. Fuck. Fuck. I stared down at the images and felt like I was time-warping straight into the past. The sounds and smells from that night came rushing back. Glasses breaking. Women screaming. The rhythmic slap of fist against flesh and the metallic tang of blood in the air...

"You're going back to jail, James. Ain't a judge alive who'd turn down the chance to nail a Kings of Chaos member to the wall. You guys have been notoriously slippery. But not today." He sat back like the cat who ate the fucking cream.

"I'm not going back," I said quietly. And I meant it. I couldn't go back to jail. Give up bull fighting, and my friends, and the brother I'd only just gotten back? No. Fuck that. I wasn't wasting the rest of my life, rotting in a tiny cell, with the walls closing in on me for something I didn't fucking do.

"Leon was alive when we pulled him out of that bar," I insisted. "I didn't kill him. I helped Miles put him in the van, but that was it." Then I'd gone back to the clubhouse and gotten blind drunk. The next morning, Miles had bragged to all of us about putting a bullet in Two Knot's head and burying his body in the scrub on Eastend Road.

I hadn't said anything back then. And I wasn't going to say it now.

Detective Lorrel shrugged. "Does it matter? All the evidence together? Looks pretty bad. You and Mitchell will both take the fall."

I pushed to my feet, only to be yanked back down the by the handcuffs that bound me to the table. "I didn't fucking kill anyone!"

The detective chuckled. "Sit down, sit down. Don't get your knickers in a twist."

Easy for him to say. He wasn't the one being wrong-fully accused of murder. I sat down hard and turned to Whitney, willing to plead my case. "I've done a lot of bad shit in my life, but I didn't do this. I swear."

She didn't respond. There was a blankness in her eyes that told me she was here in body but a million miles away in her mind.

"Not gonna be pretty for you on the inside, huh? You

didn't have too many friends in there back then, when you were doing time. Still don't by my count. Plenty of enemies, though."

I ground my teeth. He was right. Half the Devil Red MC were on the inside, because they were all dumbfucks who didn't know how to get around a parking ticket, let alone a serious crime. They were sloppy and lazy; mostly small-time drug pushers who'd gotten in over their heads. But we'd come up against them enough that I knew they were vicious and bloodthirsty. What they lacked in brains, they made up for in pure psychopathic brawn. And if they thought I murdered their pres?

"I'll die in there," I said sullenly, dropping my chin to my chest.

The detective nodded, like this fact didn't even bother him. "Yeah, you probably will. Or..."

I lifted my head. "Or what?"

He pulled a pen from the pocket of his shirt and flicked the lid off. It skittered across the table, landing in front of Whitney. "It's not you we want, James."

"Who?" I croaked out, mouth parched. My words were tinged with desperation, and I knew it looked weak, but I was beyond caring. I'd built this good life, where I wasn't the bad guy who small children shied away from when they saw me on the streets. This life where people respected me, and where I had a job protecting guys who had come to be my family. I could feel it all slipping away.

But if there was someone else they wanted...

He pointed to the photo again. "Give us Miles Mitchell, and we'll give you your freedom."

The room spun around me, bile rising in my throat. "You might as well have just asked me for the moon."

Miles Mitchell. The name sounded so sweet and innocent. I'd bet when his parents named him that, they thought he'd grow up to be an accountant. Perhaps a schoolteacher.

The reality couldn't be further from the truth. Miles 'Smoke' Mitchell was the Kings of Chaos president in everything but name. In theory, my father still held the title of pres, but Miles had been my father's right-hand man. And for a reason. There was nothing Smoke wouldn't do. He had no lines. No boundaries. No morals. He wasn't the sort of guy you wanted to be on the wrong side of.

When he'd become the stand-in pres, the Kings of Chaos MC had dissolved into exactly what it stood for... chaos. As his VP, I'd thrown myself right into the middle of it. And I still couldn't escape.

"I can't rat on Smoke. I wouldn't even make it to the trial. I'd be dead within twenty-four hours. It's impossible."

"Leaves you in a sticky situation then, huh?"

Was this guy for real? Did he think this was funny? This was my life he was talking about! I lurched toward him again, which did nothing but make the metal around my wrists cut deep into my skin. I barely felt it.

"Look, kid. I like you. I've seen you on the WBRA. I'm a big Kai Hunt fan, so I've seen what you can do. Let me make you a deal."

I didn't bother answering. The ball was entirely in his court, and he knew it. "Witness protection."

I jerked my head up. "What?"

"Or rather, a safe house. Until the trial. Then witness protection afterward, if it's deemed you need it."

I squinted at the man like he'd spoken a different language. "How the fuck did we go from you trying to pin a murder on me to witness protection?"

His eyes narrowed. "Despite who your father is; you're a little fish in a big pond, James. I'm a big man, and a little fish like you won't even tide me over 'til supper. I want Miles Mitchell. Give him to me. Everything he's ever done, that you stood by and watched. Say it all at trial, and I'll give you your freedom."

"So, what? I just give up everything? For how long? Weeks? Months?"

"You've done it once before."

"My brother is in my life now! And I have a job I actually like!"

The detective folded his arms on the table. "You're going to lose them all, one way or another. You can lose them for a few months, while we prepare for trial. Or you can try your luck in front of a judge and *hope* he believes you weren't the one who put a bullet through Leon's skull."

I gazed down at my wrists in cuffs and shook my head. I no longer had any loyalty to the club. They'd chewed me up and spat me out. I'd already taken the fall for them once, and I'd barely made it out with my life. I didn't owe them squat. I didn't want to leave my life for months either, but when the alternative was taking my chances with a judge and jury...that idea didn't fill me with confidence. I had a history. No matter who I was now, who'd I'd been back then could drown me. What choice did I have?

"What's it gonna be?" The detective sat back and

folded his arms over his chest. "Tattle on the old crew or do your time?

"I really don't like you all that much, you know?" I said as straight-faced as possible.

From the corner of my eye, I saw Whitney's mouth twitch, as if she wanted to smile. I chanced a glance at her and realized she was watching me. Heat rolled down my spine as our gazes collided. Damn, she was beautiful. And I'd bet she didn't even realize it. Had that dumbass Karsten told her every day how stunning she was? Because he should have. Hell, I'd barely met the woman and I wanted to lean in, brush her hair away from her face, and whisper into her ear exactly how her eyes and the curve of her lips made me want to write her a fucking poem. Not that I would, because that just wasn't my thing. But her beauty had me considering it, nonetheless.

I dragged my gaze back to Detective Lorrel's. "You'd tell my brother where I am? He'll be beating down your door every day if you don't."

"No details, but we'll tell him you're safe."

"Fine. But I've got one condition."

The big man leaned forward and steepled his fingers beneath his chin. "Oh really? This should be good."

4

WHITNEY

"Thanks for letting me sit in on that one," I said quietly to Hank, as we left the interrogation room. "I just needed a minute."

The older man took off his reading glasses and tucked them into his shirt pocket before regarding me with a worried look. "You're welcome. But you can't hide out with me forever."

I groaned and scrubbed my hands over my face. "I know, I know. But I just can't be around Mia and everyone else. Not yet. I'm so embarrassed."

Hank stopped, and his pudgy hand grasped me by the shoulder. "What do you have to be embarrassed about?"

My mouth dropped open. "Are you kidding me?" I held my hands up and started ticking things off on my fingers. "One. I very publicly find out that my live-in boyfriend, of two years, is actually married with a kid. Two. I then handle that scene like a jealous girlfriend, forgetting any semblance of professional conduct. Three. Said ex-boyfriend is in a jail cell downstairs for crimes he's very likely guilty of, all of which I didn't even have an inkling of. All very embarrassing when you're supposed to be a lead detective!" Heat flushed my face, and I buried it in my hands.

Hank stepped in and put his arms around me, patting me awkwardly on the back. "Well, I suppose when you put it like that..."

I stifled a laugh and slapped his broad chest. "Stop it! You're supposed to be on my side!" I'd always liked Hank. His sense of humor amused me, and he'd become somewhat of a father figure to me over the years we'd worked together.

"I'm always on your side, kid."

I peered up at him, remembering he'd called Remington James the same thing. "Did you realize you called both me and that probable murderer by the same nickname?"

Hank's bushy eyebrows pulled together. "Did I?"

"You called us both kid."

He shrugged and gave me a nudge in the direction of the roll call room—the one place I didn't want to go. It was filled with workspaces for every cop and detective who worked in this building, and even in the wee hours of the morning, it would be bustling with my colleagues. Colleagues I'd really rather avoid, at least until the end of my shift. I needed to go home, run a hot bath, and *not* cry over that douchebag Karsten. Or Don. Stupid fucking name for a stupid fucking man, who didn't deserve my tears.

"Only an hour left of shift," Hank said, holding open the swinging doors for me. "Then go home and get yourself some sleep. It's not as bad as you think."

But when the two of us entered the busy room, an immediate hush fell. I stopped abruptly, heads turning in our direction, each of them staring directly at me.

Hank let out a soft whistle. "Wow, yeah, okay. Maybe I was wrong. It is that bad."

I glanced back at him with wide eyes. "I'm removing you from my Christmas card list."

Hank faked insult then clapped his big hands together. "Okay, okay, people. Nothing to see here. So Whitney's boyfriend was leading a double life and she had no idea? Could happen to anyone, right? Go about your business and quit your gawking."

I wanted the floor to just open and swallow me whole. "*Not* helping!" I hissed at Hank and scurried away to my desk, grateful it was in the far corner of the big room.

"Sorry!" Hank called after me, but I was already sliding into my seat and tucking my chair behind the room dividers that would block me from most of the room.

Not from Mia, though.

Her sympathetic brown eyes shone across the desk from me.

"Argh, God. Not you, too. Stop it. Please."

Mia held her hands up in surrender. "I didn't say anything."

"You didn't need to. It's written all over your face and in those big doe eyes you're giving me. I'm fine. Just mortified."

Unlike Hank, Mia didn't try to make me feel better. "Yeah, I get it."

I shook my head, feeling so damn stupid. "How didn't I see any of this coming? I'm a detective, for Christ's sake.

I should have seen the signs. Hell, I should have done a background check!"

Mia tilted her head to one side. "I didn't suspect anything either, and I've known him just as long as you have."

"Yeah, but you didn't sleep in his bed every night. You didn't share a house with him. I probably should have caught on when he continually refused to talk about getting married. Of course he didn't want to get married! He already had a wife. Who needs two wives?"

Mia didn't answer. Probably because I was babbling nonsense. "Ugh, dammit, Mia. I'm sorry."

"Would you stop apologizing for him being a lying asshole? This isn't on you. You were a woman who met a man and fell in love. That's all. There was no need for you to go looking for a problem where there shouldn't have been one."

Hot, angry tears welled in my eyes, and I blinked hard, trying to keep them at bay. When that didn't work, I changed tactics and remembered the way it felt to grab Karsten by the balls and bruise his manhood the way he'd bruised mine. Or bruised my...ladyhood. Whatever.

"Did you hear Karsten was taken to the infirmary?" I whispered to Mia.

She frowned. "For what?"

"Not entirely sure. Might have been the damage I did to his junk. Might have been the fact his cellmate had a shot at him after I left him writhing on the floor."

I couldn't bring myself to feel any sorrow for the fact Karsten had taken a beating. I didn't know why his cell-mate—Remington— had done it, but I was grateful to him nonetheless. His motives for punching out Karsten had to be entirely unrelated to me, but it still kind of felt like Remington had had my back. Even if he didn't know it.

A shadow fell over Mia and me before she could even reply.

"Detective? A word in my office, please?"

Sergeant Janice Minor's imposing glare made it clear there was no point arguing. Mia and I both stood, but the sergeant shook her head in Mia's direction. "Just Whitney."

I fought back a groan. Janice spun on her heel without another word and weaved through the maze of desks, back to her own in a private office at the front of the room. Her big glass windows overlooked everything that went on. It also meant everyone would be watching me get my ass handed to me. Just great. When would this horror of a night ever end?

"It won't be as bad as you think," Mia whispered as I passed. "There isn't much of our shift left anyway. She wouldn't have delayed it this long if she was truly upset with you."

I gave her a tight smile. "I hope so."

I lifted my chin and strode after my boss. Mia was right. I might have let myself fall into Karsten's web of lies, but it was an honest mistake. Karsten was a con man. I'd been naïve. Too trusting. It wouldn't happen again. Janice would understand.

Ignoring the whispers, I slipped into her office and closed the door quietly behind me.

"Pull the blinds, too."

"Uh, okay." I did as I was told, then took the seat opposite the solid wooden desk.

The older woman folded her hands neatly on top, studying me with shrewd eyes. There was a reason she'd risen so quickly to the rank of sergeant. She was whip smart, ambitious, and missed nothing. She'd been a hell of a cop in her day, so Hank said. And she was a good, fair boss. I hated I'd let her down.

"Please just let me say how sorry I am," I started before she had a chance to speak.

The woman shook her head. "You don't need to be."

I sat back in my chair, surprise making my movements jerky. "Oh, okay. Then why am I here?"

"I'm putting you on the Remington James case. I believe you're already somewhat familiar with it?"

I blinked, though I supposed I should have seen this coming. I couldn't continue to work on Karsten's case. Not when I'd been personally involved with him. I pulled myself together. "Of course. I understand. Yes, I know the basics. And I sat in on his interview with Hank just now, so I know he agreed to testify against his old club members."

Janice nodded. Her dark, curly hair had been pulled back into a no-nonsense braid that fell over one shoulder. It was shot through with gray, but for as long as I'd known her she'd never dyed it. She wore minimal makeup, only mascara and a little blush that highlighted the apples of her dark-brown cheeks. She had to be in her fifties, but you wouldn't have known it. If it hadn't been for the gray in her hair, I would have assumed she was only a year or two older than me. I'd often wondered if that was why she kept the gray, proving she wasn't as young or inexperienced as she might have looked.

"So you'll know then that Remington James will need to be escorted to one of our safe houses?"

"Ah," I fumbled. "Yes, sure. I hadn't really thought about it, but that makes sense. Do you want me to organize someone to handle that?"

Janice sighed. "No, Whitney. I want *you* to handle it. Personally. It should only be a six-week assignment. We're hoping to get an early trial date."

It took a moment for her words to sink in, but when they did, mortification rushed through me. "What? No. Come on. You're giving me babysitting duty?" Because that's exactly what sitting at a safe house in God knew where, would be. Hours and hours of sitting around, doing absolutely nothing. A first-year rookie could do that job. Shame flushed through me. "Is this my punishment for the Karsten...ah, Don MacIntosh debacle? I already told you I was sorry. I know I should have seen what Karsten—dammit, Don—was doing."

Janice held up a hand in a stop motion, cutting off my protests. "Whitney, you're one of my best detectives. But why would you think your own boyfriend was guilty of something like this? If there'd been signs, you, of all people, would have noticed them. Of that, I'm one-hundred-percent sure."

"Thank you," I said quietly, a smidgen of weight lifting off my shoulders. "Your respect means a lot to me."

Janice nodded. "And you still have it. But that doesn't change the fact you're doing this assignment."

"But—"

I shut up when Janice gave me the evil eye.

"If you were any other member of my team, I would have insisted you take some personal leave after something like this. But I know you. And I know you'd go crazy sitting at home by yourself."

She wasn't wrong there. As much as I didn't want to be at the station right now, the thought of going home to my empty house and having to see all the things that reminded me of Karsten...our photos. His clothes. Our bed. That was the last thing I wanted to do. Hanging around there for a few weeks of forced personal leave sounded like torture. I didn't have family nearby. I didn't even have any real friends besides Mia and my other colleagues. Outside of work, Karsten had become my life. A mistake, I realized. Too late now, though.

"So consider this assignment your personal leave. You'll still be working, but you'll get a change of scenery and some fresh air." Her expression softened. "It'll be good for you, Whit. I know you have a tough exterior, but speaking as your friend, rather than your boss right now, at some point, that exterior is going to crack, and you're going to realize what you've lost tonight. You need time to process that. And this assignment will give you time."

I didn't agree. Not at all. But I didn't need to be reminded of my place again. I respected Janice too much to continually speak out of turn. Whether I liked babysitting criminals was irrelevant. I straightened my shoulders. "Where am I taking him?"

5

WHITNEY

"Clothes, toothbrush, deodorant, sneakers..." I mumbled as I flew around my bedroom. My bedroom. Not ours. Not anymore. Anger bubbled up inside me when I noticed the framed photo on my bedside table. I picked up the wooden frame. It was a photo of Karsten I'd taken six months earlier. He was gazing into the camera, giving me that look I'd always found so damn attractive. His 'let's go to bed' expression, I'd always called it. Funny how, not even twenty-four hours after his betrayal had come to light, it now did nothing for me. He just looked stupid. Were those supposed to be bedroom eyes? Ugh. Gross. I contemplated throwing the photo across the room, imagining the satisfaction of it hitting the wall and the sound of glass breaking. Maybe a piece would stab him right between the eyes. In the photo. Of course.

But the private car picking me up for the trip to the airport was going to be here any minute, and I still hadn't finished packing. How was I supposed to pack for a six-week trip when I didn't even know where I was going? The details were top secret until we were in the air. Even from me. The only person who seemed to know was the pilot. And he had no idea who he was transporting or why. It was all more hush-hush than I'd been anticipating. I'd assumed we'd just stay in the local Las Vegas safe house. I didn't know where it was, but I knew we had one. But apparently this case was higher profile than I'd realized.

That made me feel a smidgen better about babysitting a fully grown man for the next few weeks.

A horn honked outside, and I yelped, throwing the photo facedown on the dresser and shoving the last few items of clothing into my already heaving suitcase. I opened the window, spotting the black town car parked outside my house, and yelled, "Coming!" to the driver. The windows were blacked out with some very illegal-looking tint, but I supposed that didn't apply when you drove a police-issued vehicle.

After swearing and yanking so hard on the suitcase zipper that I was surprised when it didn't break, I finally got my luggage under control and dragged it down the stairs behind me. Rusty wandered over, and my heart damn near ripped from my chest as I took in his big soulful eyes. "Yeah, boy," I said, kneeling to pull his little body into a hug. I rubbed my fingers through his red-brown fur. "This sucks. I know. I'm going to miss you. But Mia is coming to pick you up later tonight, and you're going to have a little vacation at her place, deal? You love it there. She's got those expensive shoes you like chewing. Not like my dirty old sneakers."

Rusty whined, and I knew I had to wrap up this

goodbye before I burst into tears. "Be good." I planted a kiss on his silky head and opened the front door, letting myself out before closing it on the other side. Fucking Karsten. None of this would be happening if it weren't for his lying, cheating, asshatty face.

The suitcase wheels clicked over the paved path, and the driver opened his door at my approach. He took my belongings, putting them in the trunk.

Tired and emotional after saying goodbye to Rusty, I didn't feel like talking. So instead of taking the front seat, I slid into the back.

"Hi," a deep voice said from inside the depths of the car.

"Oh, holy fuck!" I yelped. My eyes adjusted to the dim interior, and I eyed the man sitting on the other side of the plush leather seats. I sighed, recognizing his deep-brown eyes.

Remington James reached out a hand to steady me but then pulled it back without actually making contact. Smart man.

"Sorry. They picked me up first, and I thought I should leave the front seat for you."

I nodded curtly and went to open the door again, right as the engine started up. I could have asked the driver to stop, but a sudden wave of exhaustion rolled over me, and I just didn't have it in me to move again. The seats were cool and smooth, and perhaps I could get a quick nap in on the way to the airport.

"It's fine," I said stiffly.

Remington nodded, and I closed my eyes, leaning my head back on the seat. The car pulled away from my house, leaving all the memories I'd shared with Karsten behind. A little more of the weight from my shoulders freed itself. Maybe Janice had been right. Maybe this assignment would be exactly what I needed. A little time away. A little space from real life. Maybe I'd even get to work on my tan. And I'd brought my knitting. Maybe I could actually get a piece finished while I was sitting around, waiting for absolutely nothing to happen.

That was a better attitude to have. Think of this as a vacation. I hadn't had one in such a long time.

"I'm Remington, by the way," the man said, interrupting my thoughts. "Rem. Nobody calls me Remington. Except my mom. And I don't really like her."

I cracked open one eye.

"And you're Detective Whitney...."

"How did you know my name was Whitney?" I asked, ignoring the unspoken question in his words. I hadn't introduced myself to him when I'd sat in on his interrogation with Hank. Had I? I'd been so out of it. The last twenty-four hours were a complete blur.

Rem shifted on his seat, so he was facing me. "Your, uh, boyfriend? He was my cellmate."

I twisted my head, suddenly interested. "Karsten was talking about me?"

Rem's lips pressed together. "Not exactly."

I narrowed my eyes, reading into Rem's expression. "What did that cretin say?"

Rem sighed. "He called you a fucking bitch."

To my surprise, it wasn't anger that spewed from my mouth but laughter. And it just kept rolling. I laughed until Rem awkwardly joined in and then I laughed until tears streamed down my face. I was overtired. Obviously. And perhaps losing it a little. But the thought of Karsten laid out on the floor in the fetal position, whining about how I was a bitch, just made my day.

Abruptly, Rem's laugh cut off. "I hope you don't mind I slugged him one for that comment."

I stopped laughing, too, and raised an eyebrow. "That's why you hit him? For me?"

Rem shrugged. "I hit him because he called you a bitch. I don't like when men speak about women like that." Then he gave me a sheepish grin. "Plus, he's kind of an annoying prick."

I laughed again, but this time it was tinged with sadness. I turned away from Rem and stared out the window instead.

Rem didn't try to say anything further. We arrived at the airport, and he got out of the car, pulling both sets of luggage out of the trunk before the driver could. Then he waited on my cue.

Right. Get the criminal on the plane. He might not be in cuffs, and we might have shared a laugh in the car, but I had responsibilities now. I wasn't going to screw things up any further. Back to business.

I went to take my suitcase from Rem.

He wouldn't let me. "I don't mind."

"I'll carry my own, thank you." This time when I reached for my bag, he let me take it, and I led us to the flight gate Janice had told me to go to. An attendant nodded at us, and I showed her my badge and ID. She stepped aside to let us on the plane.

Rem let out a long, low whistle as we stepped through the doorway. "Not exactly your run-of-the-mill passenger airplane, is it? Is this where my tax dollars go?"

We edged our way down the center of the plane and I

glanced back at him over my shoulder. "You mean, you pay tax on all your gun and drug deal money? Huh. Who knew?" My voice dripped with sarcasm.

I didn't want to let on to Rem, but I was a bit in awe of the plane, too. I hadn't been expecting a private ride. Comfortable seats lined the narrow space on either side, each one given plenty of leg room, and I suspected they might even recline into a sort of bed. There was nobody else on the plane, except for a neatly dressed flight attendant who stood next to a beverage cart. An overenthusiastic, red-lipsticked smile curved her lips. It made me wonder about the safe house we were headed to. Maybe this really would be a vacation in a swanky, government-funded house. With a little luck, maybe there'd be someone serving drinks there, too. Thank you, Janice.

After putting my luggage in the overhead compartments, I settled down into a seat. I stared out the little round window at the tarmac and other planes taxiing down runways in the distance. It was a big airport, bustling with ground vehicles and support crew in high-visibility vests.

The engine started up with a roar, and I signaled to the flight attendant, who trotted forward eagerly, all too willing to hand over packets of salted peanuts and crackers. I glanced longingly at the bottles of wine in ice buckets, but since I was here on official business, I couldn't indulge.

Rem however, had no such qualms. "Glass of red wine, please," he said, flashing the woman a blinding smile that took both of us by surprise, if her slight hitch in breath was anything to go by. I couldn't blame her. Whoa.

I'd noticed Rem was a good-looking man. Of course I had. I might have just been dumped and in no mood for men in general, but I wasn't blind. Beneath his brown leather jacket, a white T-shirt stretched across his broad shoulders. His legs were thick and encased in jeans that fit snuggly around his ass. Not that I'd been staring on purpose, but it had been hard to miss as we'd navigated through the crowded airport. His jaw was stubbled with dark bristles, and it was evident he'd spent a lot of time outside during the summer, because his skin was still a golden tan.

All very nice features.

But that smile... My stomach gave a little flip-flop, so I turned away, staring out the window once more while I got myself under control.

The steward chatted to him eagerly while she poured him his wine. "It should be a lovely flight," she said. "Weather is supposed to be great. Will you be staying in town when we get there? The crew is booked in to stay at the—"

A surge of something that felt suspiciously like jealousy took hold of my tongue. "You know he's a convicted criminal, right?" I cut in. "Did five years. Probably murdered a man." I turned back around just in time to see the young woman's mouth drop open. Her gaze darted between Rem and me before she corked the wine and scurried to the back of the plane.

Rem raised an eyebrow at me. "That wasn't very nice."

"Not here to be nice."

He shrugged. "Well, this will be a fun six weeks." He picked up a laminated emergency procedures card from the back of the seat in front of him and studied it for a moment, then put it back down. "I was telling the truth when I said I didn't do it, you know? I've done my time for the crimes I did commit. But I didn't murder anyone."

I tugged on a pair of headphones and a sleep mask. "Yeah, yeah. That's what they all say." I'd been awake for too many hours in a row to fight off sleep any longer. Figuring my 'prisoner' couldn't go anywhere when we were thirty thousand feet in the air, I found some classical music and let the sounds of Beethoven lull me off to sleep.

Sometime later, a weird snorting noise woke me, and I groaned as my back protested movement. One earbud had already fallen from my ear, and I pulled the other out while shoving up my sleep mask at the same time. I stretched my arms above my head, twisting from side to side to crack my neck, and stood to glance around the empty plane.

Through a sleepy fog, I slowly became aware of somebody watching me, and remembered I wasn't entirely alone. I glanced sharply to my left and met the dark-eyed gaze of my flight mate. Rem's eyes twinkled with amusement.

"What?" I asked, trying not to show how self-conscious his gaze made me. He really was too hot to be a criminal. He was still as fresh and put together as he was when we'd stepped onto the plane. And I probably looked like death warmed up. Not that it mattered. Rem could have been the sexiest man alive, willing to give me the world, and I still wouldn't have been impressed. After Karsten, men could all go to hell. Even the sexy ones.

He shrugged, all too much like the boy next door with innocence in his expression. "You snort in your sleep."

I recoiled, scrunching up my face. "What? No, I don't!"

He shrugged nonchalantly and went back to reading the magazine on his lap, but his mouth turned up in the corners.

"You're laughing at me!"

He chuckled but didn't lift his gaze. "I'm really not. But you do snort."

With dawning horror, I remembered it had been a snorting sound that had woken me. Could that have been me?

Heat flushed my cheeks. Wanting an excuse to turn away from him, I rifled aimlessly through the back pocket of the seat in front of me. "Mind your own business, prisoner," I mumbled.

Rem's only response was another chuckle, which I chose to ignore.

Realizing that there was nothing of interest in the pocket, I leaned over toward the window and lifted up the shade. Bright sunlight flooded in, temporarily blinding me, forcing me to rapidly blink before I could focus again. "Oh, hell no!" I gasped, covering my mouth. I took in the scene outside. A vast expanse of untouched lands and mountain ranges loomed, getting bigger by the second. The plane seemed to be slowing and gradually descending. "No, no, no!"

"What?" Rem asked. He unclicked his seat belt and stood, leaning over me to peer out my window. "What is it? I don't see anything."

"Exactly!" I groaned. I put my hand on his chest and pushed him back toward his own seat. "Quit crowding me and sit in your own seat, would you?" I flinched at the contact. His chest was entirely too solid beneath my palm. Karsten wasn't one for the gym, so while he'd been slim, he hadn't been muscled. One touch of Rem's pecs, even through a jacket, told me that Rem's body was nothing like Karsten's.

Rem moved slowly but did as he was told. When he was back in his own seat, I pulled out a department iPad and opened my email. At the time the flight had taken off, I hadn't received any of the paperwork for this assignment. But now, hours later, it was flooding my inbox. I hadn't even heard my email notifications, thanks to the music I'd been listening to as I'd slept.

I tapped the first email and closed my eyes as I took in the word *Wyoming*. "You've got to be kidding me."

Rem craned his neck across the aisle.

I glared at him. "Do you mind?"

His expression fell slightly. "Sorry. Just wanted to make sure you're all right. You seem upset."

"I'm fine," I snapped. Then I softened my voice a little, because he really hadn't done anything wrong. "I just wasn't expecting to be landing in *Wyoming*. Most of our safe houses are in cities."

His grin turned wide. "That was my one and only condition to testifying," he said proudly.

"What was?"

"That I be sent to the country while we wait for the trial. I don't mind the city when I'm just passing through, but I need wide open spaces if I'm staying in one place more than a night or two."

I gawked at him. "You could have gone to a dozen different safe houses in a dozen different cities. And you willingly chose *Wyoming*?"

He frowned. "Why do you keep saying Wyoming like

it's burning your tongue? And why are you acting like this is news to you? You were right there in the interview room when I told the other detective where I wanted to go."

Oh.

I had been there. In body anyway. But my mind had been a million miles away, lost in thoughts of Karsten, and his wife and his baby son. Dammit. That's what I got for not paying attention. A one-way flight to the middle of freaking nowhere.

"Never mind," I mumbled.

"Not a fan of the country?"

I glanced over at him. "Is anyone?"

He just stared at me. When I didn't respond, he spread his arms and pointed his fingers back toward his chest.

"Yeah, yeah, you are. Good for you, cowboy. I forgot you have the hat and everything," I grumbled, going back to my iPad and my overflowing inbox.

One email title caught my eye, so I nudged it with my finger. And nearly dropped my device. "I'm going to kill Janice."

Rem glanced down the aisle to where the steward sat. "Did you hear that? Maybe it's not me you should be scared of." He was smiling again, but this time I knew better than to look directly at him. I didn't need the distraction.

He sighed. "Lord, you're a grump. What's the problem now? Too many trees outside? Too much fresh air?"

I scowled at him, then shoved my iPad in his face. "This actually."

He squinted at the small screen, but I jerked it away

before he had a chance to read it. He threw up his hands in frustration. "How quick was I supposed to read that email, Whitney?"

"Detective Nicholson to you."

Pink crept up his neck. "Fine! Detective Nicholson then. Are you always so nitpicky?"

"I'm not nitpicky. You're just being disrespectful."

"Do you really want me to call you Detective Nicholson for the next six weeks?"

I folded my arms across my chest. "Well, no, actually. That's what this email is about. Apparently, for the next six weeks, I'm no longer Detective Whitney Nicholson. I'm Mrs. Whitney Washington."

He let out a low whistle beneath his breath. "I feel for your fake husband. Or are you widowed? Did you nitpick him to death? Poor fake bastard."

I glared at him. "I guess we'll see. *Mr. Washington*. Because apparently, we're married."

6

REMI

The plane touching down onto the tarmac at Jackson Hole Airport took me by surprise. I'd been too busy gawking at Whitney to even realize we'd arrived. "Come again?" I choked out.

When she held her iPad out to me, I snatched it from her hands, and this time she actually let me hold it long enough to read the email displayed on the screen.

Your alias is Mr. and Mrs. Washington. Your new IDs have been sent on to your accommodations and should be there within two days.

"Well, that's not happening," I said with a laugh. "Remington Washington? What kind of drug addicts were my fake parents to give me a name like that?"

Whitney shoved her iPad under her arm and unclipped her seat belt, not bothering to wait until the plane had come to a complete stop. She grabbed her bag, leaving mine above her head. "You're telling me. At least you aren't Whitney Washington."

I followed suit and pushed to my feet, reaching up

into the overhead compartments to pull out my luggage then followed her toward the door of the plane. "It could be worse. If your middle name started with W you'd be WWW. We could call you World Wide...or perhaps just Web, for short?"

She stopped, spinning around in the narrow aisle to glare at me.

I stifled a laugh, knowing letting it loose would only annoy her further. I had to spend six weeks with this woman. I didn't really want to be on her bad side. Even if it was kind of fun to mess with her. She was cute when she was angry.

Her eyes burned with indignation, and when she shoved her hands on her hips, something dawned on me. I burst out laughing. "Your middle name starts with W, doesn't it?"

"No!" She speed-walked down the remainder of the aisle, dragging her suitcase behind her.

When we reached the door, I thanked the attendant who stood to one side, trying to be professional but giving me as wide a berth as the walls of the plane would allow. She looked ready to run screaming from the plane at any minute. "I really didn't kill anyone," I assured her.

The woman's eyes went so wide that white showed the entire way around her irises. "It's not my business," she squeaked out. "I won't say anything. I swear."

"Shot him right in the head with a nine millimeter," Whitney called back, in the dry, sarcastic tone I was beginning to associate with her. "Boom!"

"Whitney!" I hissed. What the actual fuck? Was she trying to send the poor woman into a nervous breakdown?

I could have sworn I heard Whitney chuckling. Dammit. The woman was something else.

Giving up on reassuring the attendant that I wasn't there to do her any harm, I hurried across the tarmac, catching up with Whitney as she made it inside the airport terminal. She was biting back a grin but losing the battle.

Instead of being annoyed, though, I smiled. If this had been any other situation, I might have thought Whitney was deliberately trying to nix my chances with an attractive woman who had seemed interested in knowing what I was doing for the night.

"So, *Web*. What's your middle name? Wait, let me guess. Willow?"

She rolled her eyes. "No."

I hoisted my backpack onto my shoulder. "Okay, okay. I bet your parents were *Peter Pan* fans. Wendy."

"Wrong again, Mr. Washington. But you weren't too far off. My awful middle name is because my parents had a weird obsession. It's Winona."

My brow furrowed, and I tried to think of what obsession would lead to calling your child Whitney Winona. "As in, Winona Ryder?"

Whitney nodded.

"Your parents had a strange obsession with...shoplifting?" That was the only thing I could think of that Winona Ryder was famous for.

Whitney snorted, and I laughed. Her snort cracked me up. "*Beetlejuice*. They had—have—a weird thing for that movie. She was in it."

"That's weird."

"Very. Can we go now? And quit calling me Web."

"Aye, aye, Captain."

"Detective."

"Whatever."

It was going to be a long six weeks if this kept up.

Her eyes narrowed, and she straightened her shoulders, standing a little taller. The laughter that had pulled at her lips just moments earlier disappeared.

"Come on, let's go find our ride. Stay close, okay? There's a lot of people here. And even if you aren't in cuffs, you're still in my custody. Got it?"

I got it. Playtime was over, apparently. I trailed her through the airport, until we found a uniformed man holding a sign with our names on it. Our fake names, that was.

Taylor, our driver, was a man of few words, and after a few attempts at engaging him in conversation, I gave up. Whitney raised the partition that separated the front and back seats, saying we needed to discuss our covers, but then she'd gone quiet, too. She stared out the window at the late afternoon sun rapidly sinking toward the horizon. The little sighs she made grew more frequent and urgent sounding, as our driver took us farther and farther into the country.

I almost felt sorry for her by the time Taylor navigated into a private road. But my excitement over the property we were approaching outweighed any other feeling. I shifted to the middle seat, trying not to notice that my arm brushed Whitney's in the process. She noticed, though, and edged away so a small gap was established once more.

Ignoring her, I hit the button for the divider and peered through the windshield. An older style farmhouse came into view, and my mouth dropped open. It wasn't huge but it was everything I loved about country living. There wasn't a person in sight. "If that's our safe house, I hope the trial is never called. I could happily live here forever."

"Don't even joke about that," Whitney snapped.

"Touchy much? It's a beautiful place, have a look."

Taylor maneuvered the car along the paved road that formed a circular drive, taking us right to the steps of our accommodation. The main house loomed in front of us, and I eagerly pulled the handle on my door, sick of sitting after the plane and car rides. The door opened, and I got my first breath of clean, fresh, country air.

It was the first proper breath I'd been able to take since I'd been arrested, and I sucked in greedy lungfuls like a man who'd been starved of oxygen.

"Oh Lord!" Whitney wailed. "There's rocking chairs on the porch!"

She wasn't wrong. Three wooden rocking chairs with patchwork cushions sat abandoned on the wooden porch. By the wooden door. Of the wooden house.

"They like wood out here, huh?" Whitney stated.

"Were you expecting some modern feat of engineering? Amongst all the rolling hills, green pastures, and mountains in the distance?"

She didn't answer me. Ugh, city girls. Not that I was one to talk. I was, in theory, a city boy, too. I'd grown up with bright lights and bustling sidewalks. All I'd known was noise and chaos. But ever since I'd gotten out of prison, the city made me miserable. The air always felt too thick, too polluted. The smells were too strong. The sounds too loud. That need to get out of the crush of people was what had led me to the country and eventually to the rodeo.

The screen door banged open, making me twitch, and a pretty blonde woman came out onto the porch. Her boots were dusty below a pair of faded jeans, and she'd tucked a plaid, long-sleeved shirt into the waistband.

"Welcome!" she called, striding across the porch and down the stairs to greet us. "I'm Scout Wilden. Good to have you here."

Whitney moved forward and held her hand out to the other woman. "Whitney Nic—"

I coughed loudly, and Whitney shot me a look before she realized what I was doing. She turned back to Scout. "Whitney Washington."

"I know," Scout said simply, taking Whitney's outstretched hand and shaking it. If she noticed Whitney's slip up, she didn't say anything. "We've been expecting you." She turned her gaze on me. "Hello, Mr. Washington. Lovely to meet you."

I gave her a genuine smile. "Just Rem, please." Mr. Washington made me sound like I was a hundred years old. Scout couldn't have been that much younger than I was, and the Mr. tag didn't sit well with me. How did I go from Viper to Mr. Washington? Neither name fit.

Scout nodded. "Okay, well, let's get the two of y'all settled." Scout took Whitney's bag from the ground where Taylor had deposited it and strode down a dirt driveway that led around the side of the big house, pointing out various features along the way.

"Horse barn...cow pastures...bull pen—" Scout glanced back at us, her smiling expression morphing into something more serious. "Do not go near that one. That bull is a mean old man. You don't want to be stuck in an enclosed space with him."

On the contrary, my interest was piqued. I leaned in closer to Whitney and tried not to be offended when she stiffened. "How much does she know about us?" I whispered.

Whitney frowned. "I'm not entirely sure, so until I do know, keep your mouth shut."

"Fine." And I would, but I'd also be checking out the ranch's bulls at the first opportunity.

We walked for a good ten minutes, and the main house was getting smaller and smaller in the distance behind us when Whitney interrupted Scout's introductory monologue to ask, "I'm sorry, but why are we dragging our luggage all the way out here? Aren't our rooms in the house back there?"

Scout stopped in front of a row of small, square cabins. At the far end, the remains of an ancient tractor sat rusting like a museum piece. The constant mooing of cows made up a background chorus, and Scout looked entirely at home amongst it all. A smile spread across her face. "Oh, no. The main house is only three bedrooms, and they're all taken up by me, Gage, and Grandpa."

"Gage?" I asked

"My brother."

"Right."

Scout pointed behind her "That's your room."

She stepped over the single stair and straight onto a rickety porch that squeaked beneath her weight. Eagerly, I followed behind. Inside, the little wooden cabin wasn't anything fancy. Wood-paneled walls. Bare floors with only a faded rug to cover them. A large bed sat to one side of the kitchenette, and two armchairs faced a small TV screen. A grin pulled at my mouth. I instantly loved the cozy room.

"Where's my room?" Whitney asked from the doorway. "Is it one of these other cabins?"

Scout's eyebrows furrowed. "There's only one room. You're married..."

Whitney shook her head, staring at the solitary bed in the room. "No, we're not."

"Whitney!" I hissed.

"Your surnames are the same," Scout said, a frown creasing her forehead.

I opened my mouth, but Whitney cut me off.

"We're brother and sister."

I swiveled around and squinted at her. *What the hell?* I mouthed. She was going totally off script, and I now had no idea what to say.

Scout seemed confused. "I'm really sorry. I must have got my wires confused somewhere."

Whitney waved her hand around. "That's fine. If you could just show me to my room, though..."

A pink color tinged Scout's cheek. "We don't have any other rooms...well, there is one in the back of the barn, but it's currently full of horse tack and..."

Whitney was shaking her head. "No, that won't do. We need to be together."

Scout seemed even more confused by that response. I couldn't blame her.

Deciding to salvage the situation before Whitney blew our covers entirely, I dumped my backpack on the bed. "This room is fine, for both of us. Really. My little sister over there can take the bed, and I'll sleep in one of the armchairs."

"I could get you a blow-up mattress. I'm sure one of the guys has one. They go camping a lot."

I smiled charmingly at her. "That'd be great. Thank you."

Whitney looked annoyed. I glared at her meaning-fully. I didn't want her to blow this. Who knew where we'd be sent if she screwed this up. "Come on, sis. It'll be just like when we shared a room as kids."

Scout's frown dissolved into a smile. "Gage and I shared a room when we were kids, too." Then she wrinkled her nose. "Wouldn't want to share with him now, though. You two are obviously closer than we are. That's nice."

I strode over to Whitney's side and put an arm around her shoulders, giving her a squeeze. "*So* nice."

Whitney elbowed me sharply when Scout turned her back. "You saw what I did to your cellmate yesterday, didn't you?" she murmured beneath her breath. "Keep it up and I'll do it to you, too."

I fought back a laugh, but I dropped my arm.

Stunningly beautiful. Smart as a whip. And could bring a man to his knees. In more ways than one. But I didn't want to be on the floor because Whitney had ripped my balls from my body. When I got down on my knees in front of Whitney Nicholson, I wanted it to be for very different reasons. Ones that didn't involve pain.

Quite the opposite, in fact.

7

WHITNEY

*D*arkness fell early around the tiny cabin in the middle of nowhere. And so did the temperature. I shivered violently when a draft whipped beneath the door and wrapped its icy tendrils around me.

"Snow on the breeze," Rem murmured, going over to the window and staring out. "Hope you packed warmly."

"Of course," I huffed, though I frantically thought through the things I'd stuffed in my suitcase. I'd packed for winter, but had I packed for a Wyoming winter? I didn't like the idea of venturing into town to buy warmer clothes, with a witness I was supposed to be protecting in tow. One who might be recognized. The thought of blowing our cover and being moved to a safe house in the city was appealing, but I could never knowingly put someone in danger like that. So I'd have to make do with whatever was in my suitcase.

I rubbed my arms briskly, trying to ward off the chill. Rem strode across the room to the fireplace. He knelt on the rug and pulled kindling and matches from a basket by the side of the old stone hearth. Within moments, he had flames licking along a pile of wood, a glow lighting up his profile in the darkening room. The glow danced across his strong jaw, his dark eyes seeming paler than they really were. He really was incredibly attractive. In other circumstances, I might have been pleased to be sharing a room this small with a man that attractive.

Rem glanced over, catching me staring at him. I dropped my gaze to my hands. He chuckled and stood, then moved away from the fire, brushing his hands on the back of his jeans.

As he passed the bed where I was sitting, he said quietly, "I don't know you very well. But if you look at your real brother the way you were just looking at me, your fake parents might get a little concerned."

My mouth dropped open, and heat flooded my cheeks. "What?"

He shrugged. "Just sayin'."

"Cocky much?'

He shook his head. "Just calling it how I see it." He sat on the bed next to me and flopped onto his back.

I inched away, suddenly flustered by the nearness of him. I sat stiffly on the very edge of the mattress, as far away from him as I could get without falling off the bed.

He twisted his head to watch me. "No need to be embarrassed. You were checking me out. So what? I checked you out the moment I saw you. Of course, you've made this whole thing a whole lot more difficult by telling Scout we're brother and sister. If you'd just run with the married thing, we could be..." He shifted, forcing the springs in the mattress to squeak suggestively.

I pushed to my feet and glared at him. "That is *not* on the table."

He laughed, tucking his hands beneath his head. I refused to let my gaze drift to show I'd noticed how his biceps popped in that position.

"Could have been on the table, if we weren't brother and sister." He jerked his head toward the tiny kitchen table behind me. "I'm sure it's stronger than it looks. It could take our weight."

I picked up a pen and threw it at Rem's face. He snapped one hand from behind his head and caught it before it could bean him between the eyes. I blinked, surprised at how quick his reflexes were. That pen should have bounced off his forehead for sure.

"You get quick when you're being chased by eight hundred pound bulls every night," he stated, reading my expression correctly.

"I'm sure that's not the only thing you're quick at." I smiled sweetly. Satisfied I'd gotten in the parting retort, I grabbed my bag and took the entire thing into the bathroom with me. I pretended I didn't hear Rem's deep chuckle from the other side of the door. And I pretended that parts of me weren't warm and tingly from our little back and forth bantering session.

Shucking my clothes and dropping them to a pile on the scuffed bathroom tiles, I stepped into the shower and turned on the cold water. I let it fall into my heated face, before cranking up the hot water as far as it would go. It took a good minute for me to warm up, but I stood there under a spray that wasn't hard enough for my liking, for a good fifteen minutes, until the water ran cold again. Only then did I smile to myself and step out. Would serve Rem right if he had to have a cold shower. I chuckled to myself, imagining his yelp of surprise when his shower ran cold after only a minute or two. Petty, but hey. I was going to have to keep myself occupied somehow over the next six weeks. Torturing Rem seemed like an entertaining way to pass the time.

8

REM

I was still chuckling to myself when the squeal of the shower pipes stopped ringing through the small cabin. The bathroom went quiet, and I imagined Whitney rifling through her suitcase, looking for something clean to wear to bed.

I wanted to be in there doing the same thing. Not necessarily with her. Not yet, anyway. But I'd felt some sort of sexual undercurrent in the way we'd been bantering back and forth all day, and I'd pushed it that much further when I'd called her out on sizing me up. I knew I was putting her on the spot, but I'd wanted to see how she'd react. And I hadn't been disappointed. She hadn't denied it at all. Just called me cocky. I could work with that.

Much to my disappointment, though, human needs outweighed my desire to flirt with my pretty blonde bodyguard any further tonight. A shower and bed were higher on my priority list. But Whitney had been in that bathroom for an exorbitant amount of time. I'd lived in cabins just like this one. Without even testing it, I could guarantee there wasn't an ounce of hot water left in the tiny heater. I'd have to wait a good hour or so for it to heat up again.

So instead, I decided to give Whitney some space, hopefully to stew on the sexual tension between us. I pulled on my jacket and slipped through the door, onto the wooden porch. Outside, the sky still held the very last of the day's light, but stars already twinkled. So many stars. I sucked in a breath of cold air and really just let myself feel that I was back where I loved being most in the world. I loved the applause and showing off for the crowds at the rodeos, but the country held my heart. And I wanted to find it again. I might not have asked for this time away, but I could make the best of the situation and use it to my advantage. I'd use the time to reconnect with who I was now. Not dwell on who I'd once been.

A lilting guitar riff floated back to me on the cold night air, and I wandered down the steps, following the soft tune until the glow of a bonfire stopped me. A branch snapped beneath my feet, and the melody stopped. Three sets of eyes stared in my direction.

I raised one hand awkwardly. "I'm Rem," I called. Then jabbed a finger in the direction of the cabin. "I'm staying in that cabin there, with my...sister."

A young guy with shaggy brown hair curling around the nape of his neck crossed the gap with his hand held out. I met him in the middle and shook his hand firmly.

"I'm Oliver," he said with an easy smile, then motioned for me to follow him back toward the firelight. "That's Gage." He pointed to the man on his left, who was probably roughly the same age, in his late twenties.

Gage's cowboy hat shadowed his eyes, and when he stood to shake hands with me, I realized how tall he was. Well over my six feet. The man should have been playing basketball or strutting a catwalk somewhere, not sitting around a fire in the middle of nowhere.

"Good to meet you. Rem? That's your name?" Gage asked.

"Remington. But yeah, just Rem. Please."

Gage nodded. "My sister told me we had some new tenants. Good to meet you."

"Ah, Scout's your sister, then? She mentioned you when she brought us out here earlier."

Gage sat back down in his spot by the fire, his smile broadened into a grin. "Not too many other Gage's around here."

"Not too many Remingtons either," the third man said in a low, gravelly voice.

I twisted in his direction.

He studied me carefully. "Dane," he said eventually, identifying himself. His shrewd gaze darted back and forth across my face while he sipped his beer. "I know you," he said, his eyebrows pulling together as he tried to place me.

Shit. Perhaps it had been a risk, asking to come to a country town, where the locals might have seen me on the rodeo tour. But it wasn't like I was recognized all that often. In fact, I could count on two fingers exactly how many times I'd been approached by a random stranger who knew who I was. And both times, I was with guys from the tour. Bull riders. They were recognized first, and I was an afterthought. Abel and I had a growing fan base, sure. But out of all the millions of people in the world, there were probably less than ten thousand people who would recognize me without my WBRA uniform on. It'd be just my luck one of them would be sitting right in front of me, when I was supposed to be lying low.

I forced my words to sound casual, hoping I could bluff my way out of the situation. "Nah, don't think so. I've never been through this area before. Beautiful, though," I said, changing the subject. "How many acres do you have here?" I asked Gage.

Dane let it go and went back to drinking his beer, but I could feel the weight of his gaze. It made me uncomfortable.

"Too many to count." Gage laughed. "Property has been in the family for longer than anyone can remember. Each generation has bought more and more land, it seems. Roaming free seems to run in our blood."

"And you both work here? Or are you family, too?" I cast a glance between Oliver and Dane. I was interested, but the questions served a purpose, too. If I was the one doing the asking, then I wasn't the one doing the answering. And until Whitney and I worked out exactly who knew about us, and who we could trust, it was better if I said as little as possible. Lord knew I wasn't particularly good at keeping my feet out of my mouth, but giving up who I really was could mean putting a target on my back. I was certain that once the Kings of Chaos knew I was set to testify against their leader, they'd come looking for me. It seemed unlikely they'd find me on a property that was a thousand miles from Vegas, but it wasn't worth taking a stupid risk either.

Ollie paused with his beer bottle halfway to his lips. "Me and Dane are hired hands. Our cottages are next to yours. Gage lives up in the main house with Scout and Gramps. I've been here two years. Dane's been here—"

"Forever," Gage cut in.

Dane snorted on a laugh. "How old do you think I am?"

"Ancient," the two younger men answered in unison.

He made a face at them, and I used the distraction to cast a gaze over him. He was older than the other two, for sure, his rough skin and lines at the corners of his eyes giving away that he was no longer in his twenties. But I doubted he was much older than I was. He did give off a more experienced vibe, so I could kind of see where Gage and Oliver were coming from.

"You want a beer, Rem?" Oliver asked, reaching into a cooler beside the log he was sitting on. He held the can up to me, firelight glinting off the aluminum can.

"Hell, yes. Thank you." I bumped beers with Ollie before sitting beside him. "You guys have a lot of work at the moment?"

Gage nodded. "Always. There's a never-ending to-do list. It's even bigger lately because we have a cattle drive coming up. Got to bring in a herd from the far pastures before it gets too darn cold. We should have done it weeks ago, but we've just had too much going on and haven't had time or the bodies to do it. Food will be scarce up where they are in a few weeks, so we gotta get on it."

"Need any help?"

Gage cast a glance at me. "Aren't you here on vacation?"

I shrugged. "I get bored easy. Got too much energy."

"Can't pay you."

"Didn't ask you to."

Gage's smile widened. "Scout said you're from the city. You even ride? We like to take the horses, but I suppose you could take one of the quad bikes."

"I ride. Don't much like bikes, either." *Anymore*, I added silently.

Gage nodded eagerly. "Nice. You'll fit right in here, then."

I could already hear the lecture I was going to get from Whitney, but the idea of an old-school roundup was too good to pass up. Riding all day, sleeping under the stars at night, eating food you cooked over an open fire— it was about as far away from running drugs and weapons with the club as possible. And that was exactly why I wanted to do it. Perhaps, with a little luck, Whitney might see I was a whole lot more at home on the back of a horse than I was on the back of a motorcycle. That was the Rem I wanted to show her. She saw me as a criminal. I wanted to show her the man who rode horses, worked hard, and dodged bulls at rodeos.

"Rem!" Whitney's voice carried faintly above the crackle of the fire. Then a string of foul-mouthed curses rang out, and Ollie burst into laughter.

"My sister, ladies and gentlemen," I deadpanned, but I was fighting back my own laughter. "She's going to be horrified you all heard that."

Ollie shook his head. "Ain't nothing wrong with a woman who knows how to curse. I'm so turned on right now that Dane might find me in his bed tonight, for lack of other choices." He cracked up laughing, continuing even when Dane shot out a hand and pushed Ollie off the back of the log. He hit the dewy grass on his ass, but it didn't seem to bother him any. They were obviously used to ribbing each other, and no one took it personally.

The camaraderie between them made me miss my brother. But that only strengthened my resolve that I'd made the right decision. If all went to plan, I'd see Abel in a few weeks. When the only alternative was seeing him through the bars of a jail cell, there was no alternative.

Ollie sobered as he climbed back onto his seat. "Seriously, though, she single?"

Hairs prickled at the back of my neck. It was a simple enough question and one I knew the answer to. Yet I found myself hesitating over the words. Ollie was an attractive guy. And I didn't want him going after Whitney. But I couldn't say that. Not without looking like I was the one with incestuous thoughts. Damn her for saying we were brother and sister. I would have been a whole lot happier saying we were married.

"Rem!" Whitney's yell came again. She sounded ready to roast a man alive. She was pissed with a capital P.

"Better go. Thanks for the beer," I said, pushing to my feet, grateful to avoid answering questions about Whitney's personal life.

Gage and Ollie raised a hand in goodbye. Dane didn't say anything, and I shrugged, turning on my heel and walking away. The sounds of footsteps crunching over twigs and stones followed me.

"James, wait," Dane said.

I turned to face him, surprised that he'd followed me. "Yeah?"

He raised an eyebrow, and it dawned on me I'd blown our cover without even realizing it. I'd responded to my real name and given us away. Fuck! I knew I'd be no good at this.

Dane narrowed his eyes. "I don't know what's going on here, but I know who you are. I don't know why you're using some other name, but I'm guessing it's got something to do with your arrest in Las Vegas the other day."

"You watched that, huh?"

"The WBRA finals? Yeah. I watched it. Lot of folks round here like the rodeo. I happen to be one of them."

"They know who I am?"

Dane shrugged. "Might. Didn't take me long to work it out." He eyed me. "That gonna be a problem?"

I nodded. "People can't know I'm here. Could be bad, for everyone."

"You got people out for you?"

I let out a long sigh and decided to just be straight with him. Couldn't hurt now, he already knew who I was. "Fucked if I'd know, man. I hope not. But it's a possibility."

A dark expression passed over Dane's face. One I couldn't decipher.

"I just need to know if I can trust you to keep this to yourself? Or do I need to go pack my shit and get out of here?"

Dane mused on that for a moment. "You serious about coming on that roundup? And helping out here?"

I nodded.

"And you won't go sniffing around Scout?"

"Why would I..." I tilted my head to one side. "You got something going on with her?"

Dane's look turned sharp. "You leave her alone."

"Scout's honor," I joked, holding up three fingers in

salute. The smile fell from my face when Dane didn't smile back. I dropped my hand back to my side. "I'll stay away from her."

"Fine then. I'll keep your secret."

A rush of air left my chest in relief. "Thank you."

He nodded briskly and turned to go back to the other two, who were getting more drunk by the minute.

"Dane?"

"Yeah?"

"Why? You don't owe me anything; why would you keep my secret?" Maybe he wouldn't in the long run, I had no reason to trust him yet, but the man seemed sincere. I was curious about his motives. Knowledge was power, and if I knew why he was willing to keep my true identity to himself, then more power to me.

Dane shook his head, a shadow covering his eyes as he lowered his head. "That's a story for another time."

9

WHITNEY

"Where the hell have you been?" I demanded the minute Rem sauntered back in the door. I eyed the beer in his hand and sniffed at the smoke scent coming off his clothes. It didn't smell like cigarettes, though. I narrowed my eyes. "Have you been at a bonfire?"

Rem grinned. "Yeah, I met some of the ranch hands, and Scout's brother, Gage. Had a beer with them." He held up the beer can. "Well, half a beer anyway, before you started hollering for me."

My fury mounted. "Are you serious? You can't just wander off by yourself! I was ready to pull my gun and go searching for you—with wet hair and everything!"

He snorted on his laughter. "Oh, horror. Not with wet hair!"

I scowled at him. "You're an asshat. I could have caught pneumonia."

"Or you could have caught a good time? You could

have come and had a beer with us. Listened to Ollie play the guitar. Smiled a little perhaps?"

God, the man was infuriating. "That's not what we're here for."

He rolled his eyes. "Okay, well, six weeks is going to feel like a lifetime if we never leave this cabin and never speak to anyone else. Especially if we're still pretending to be brother and sister. All that alone time could be a whole lot more fun if we weren't."

"We are," I gritted out.

"Your loss. I'm going for a shower." He grabbed a towel from the pile Scout had left on the table and locked himself in the bathroom.

I opened and closed my mouth a few times like a startled fish, as I tried to come up with a smart retort, but when the water turned on, I knew it was a losing battle. Much to my disgust, he'd gotten the last word.

Dammit. I hated that.

With nothing better to do, I wandered around the small cabin, trailing my fingers over the wooden panels. An old-school telephone—the kind that had a cord—was mounted to one wall, and I smiled at the piece of nostalgia I remembered from my childhood. I picked the receiver up and held it to my ear, remembering all the hours I'd spent with one of these things tucked beneath my chin, chatting with girlfriends, or with Torrance Orthing, the one boy who'd asked for my phone number during high school. To my surprise, a dial tone purred on the other end.

Without thinking about it too much, I punched in the numbers of Mia's cell phone and waited.

"Who's this creeping on an unknown number?" Mia demanded without even saying hello.

I cracked up laughing. "It's me."

"Whit! Oh my God, should you be calling me right now?"

"Probably not."

"Janice would kill you if she knew."

I laughed. "Highly likely. But I needed to talk to you."

"Aw, you miss me already? The biker cowboy not amusing you with his wit and sass like I do?"

"Nobody amuses me with wit and sass like you do."

"Damn right. I saw that man's mug shot, though. He might have something I don't have."

I leaned back on the wall and eyed the still closed bathroom door, trying not to think about the fact Rem was naked on the other side. "Oh yeah? What's he got that you don't?"

"A giant man schlong."

I choked on a laugh. "You could tell that from his mug shot?"

"Girl, I got a gift. That boy is fine. And I guarantee, his man meat is long and thick. Just the way you like it."

"Stop. You have no idea how I like my meat. Man, or otherwise."

"That's what you think. Don't you remember that work Christmas party where you blabbed your big mouth about Karsten—"

"Ugh, don't say the K word. Is he still in lockup?"

"Yeah, last I heard."

"Good. I hope he rots."

Mia paused. "How you doing with all of that?"

I sighed and let my head thunk back on the wall. "It's

weird. I know it was only two days ago, but so much has happened since then that it feels like a lifetime."

"Did you have a cry yet?"

"No! And I won't. He doesn't deserve it."

Mia paused.

"He doesn't, Mia!"

"Not saying he does, but you thought you were going to marry that man and have his babies. Even if he turned out to be a no-good ho, that's still gotta hurt."

"I'm fine."

"Okay. Well, is it too soon for me to suggest you get yourself a sandwich with a helping of Remington James man meat?"

"Oh my God, you're the worst. Yes, it's too soon for that! Not that I'd go there with him anyway."

"Why not?"

"It's against protocol, for one."

"You mean the protocol you just broke by calling me."

Yeah, that'd be the one. "Shut up, Mia."

"Nope. I want to know why you wouldn't go there. You got something against broad shoulders and cocky grins? I heard he's a bull rider, too. So I bet he's fit as fuck."

"Bull fighter."

"What's that?"

"Rodeo clown?"

"Ugh. Not so sexy."

I laughed. "See? Now get off the Remington James train and come back to Whitney world. How's Rusty?"

"Perfect. Sweetest dog in the whole world, and I probably won't want to give him back in six weeks."

"You're giving him back. And if Karsten gets out, that son of a bitch goes nowhere near him, capiche?"

"Of course. He steps a foot on my property and he'll be met by the barrel of my gun."

"My best friend is a badass."

"You know it."

"Will you let me know if he makes bail? Just call me on this number. It's the phone in our cabin."

Mia made a choking noise. "Excuse me, what? *Our* cabin? You don't have separate rooms?"

A rattle on the bathroom door alerted me to the fact Rem was about to emerge. "Gotta go, Mia. The meat is coming out of the boiler."

"What? What does that even mean?"

I didn't really know either, my sass game was not as strong as Mia's, evidently, so I just hung up. A cloud of steam escaped the bathroom, and through it, Rem appeared like some Greek Adonis, wearing nothing but a towel. Immediately, my gazed rolled down over his pecs and abs to the trail of hair that ran from his navel below the white fabric tucked around his waist. My gaze lingered on his covered area for the briefest of moments before I forced myself to look back up into his face.

He was laughing.

Damn Mia for making me think about what he was packing beneath that towel.

"God, you're annoying," I huffed.

"And you're beautiful," he replied, without missing a beat.

I paused, shock ricocheting through me. Warmth spread through my blood, all of which seemed to be rushing south to my lady bits. It took me a long moment to recover enough to speak. "Inappropriate."

"Why?" His brows furrowed together, and he appeared genuinely confused.

"You know why."

"Because we're 'brother and sister'?"

It infuriated me even further because he did air quotes with his fingers. "That, plus a million other reasons. I'm unavailable. And even if I was available, I have a code of ethics. I can't date a prisoner."

"I'm not a prisoner."

"Fine, I can't date a criminal then."

Rem folded his arms across his chest. I was sure he knew how it made his biceps pop. Goddamn him. He was deliberately goading me.

"I'm not a criminal either. And who said anything about dating?"

I barked out a laugh. "Oh, that'd be right. I should have known you'd be the love 'em and leave 'em type." Heat rushed to my face, and I hoped like hell the room was dark enough that he couldn't see my pinking cheeks. I turned away and busied my hands, pulling clothes out of my suitcase and refolding them to place neatly into the chest of drawers by the bed.

Every muscle in my body went stiff as he moved in behind me. The fresh scent of him filled my nostrils. Soap and water plus clean, naked—oh so naked—man. I closed my eyes, internally yelling at my traitorous body for responding to his nearness. What the fuck was wrong with me? Just a day ago I'd had a man I'd thought I was in love with. How had I gone from that to being completely turned on by someone else?

Because you want to get back at Karsten, a voice whispered in my head. I pondered that thought for a moment.

It did give me a sick sense of satisfaction that Karsten was in a cell somewhere, while I had a very attractive man making it known he might want more than just my official protection.

Rem's warm breath misted over the back of my neck, goosebumps rising on my skin. I tilted my head to the side slightly, an invitation for him to move closer, and heard his sharp intake of breath. His chest and abs lightly pressed against my back.

Then I rammed my elbow straight back into his stomach.

A cough of surprise burst from his lungs, and I swung around with a self-satisfied grin on my face. "I told you. Inappropriate."

He clutched his stomach, wheezing as he tried to catch the breath I'd knocked out of him. I waited for his retaliation. Any moment now he'd call me a bitch, storm away, and that would be that. The boundaries between us would be clearly established again, and this whole back-and-forth, flirty-what-the-hell-ever, would stop.

Just like I wanted it to.

Right?

My momentary indecision was forgotten as Rem straightened, grasping his towel that had slipped dangerously low on his hips. I fought to keep my eyes from the V lines of muscle running either side of his hips. Oh Lord. *Boundaries, Whitney*. Professional boundaries. That was what I was trying to establish here, and I couldn't do that if I kept wondering about his salami.

"Good thing I like it rough," he drawled. Then he winked, dropped the towel, and slid into the bed completely buck-ass naked.

"Oh hell no." I slapped a hand over my eyes and spun around before I could catch a true glimpse of what was beneath the towel. "Put some pajamas on! And get out of my bed!"

His voice dripped with smugness. "Our bed. Scout never came back with that air mattress."

"Then you can sleep in the armchair." I dared to turn around and was thankful—sort of—the blankets covered his nakedness.

He had his hands linked behind his head, though, his arms and chest looking entirely too tempting, his wide shoulders filling way more than just one side of the bed.

He grinned. "No good for my back, Whit. Grab the light, would you? I'm tired."

I gaped at him. "You're a nightmare."

"And by nightmare, you mean dream come true? Want me to warm your side of the bed up?"

"I'm not sleeping in there with you! Especially not naked you!"

He rolled over onto his side, his damn smug grin making me want to slap him. "Then I guess you're in the armchair." He closed his eyes, faking sleep.

I gritted my teeth. Goddamn him. He'd gotten the last word. Again.

10

WHITNEY

*I*n the early morning sunlight that bathed the room in soft yellow tones, I stretched my hands above my head and stared at the ceiling. The exposed *wooden* ceiling. Right. Still in the cabin in the middle of nowhere, then. Yesterday hadn't been a bad dream. But at least I'd slept like a log. I ran my palms over the soft sheets—not exactly a luxurious silk, but warm flannelette that felt snuggly.

Sheets.

What?

I sat up and looked down at myself. Sure enough, the sheets were fitted to the bed. And I was in it.

That wasn't where I'd gone to sleep. After my disagreement with Rem, I'd reclined the armchair closest to the fireplace and made the best of things with a cushion and blanket I swiped from the end of the bed. I was too stubborn to even ask Rem for a pillow. But now, that armchair was occupied by an oversized man. Wearing twice the amount of clothes I'd last seen him in.

I picked up a pillow and threw it as hard as I could at his head.

"Oof," he mumbled, pulling it away from his face and blinking at me sleepily. "Bit late to offer me a pillow, don't you think?"

"How the hell did I get in this bed? And don't tell me I sleepwalk, because just like I don't snort, I also don't wander around while I'm catching Zs."

He stood, moving stiffly to the fireplace. The fire had died down during the night. He winced as he knelt in front of it, one hand coming to his lower back. "I moved you. I was never really going to let you sleep in the armchair. But you crashed so hard and so quickly that I didn't even get a chance to tell you I was just messing with you."

"Oh." That was pretty much the last thing I'd expected when I'd gone to sleep last night, mumbling beneath my breath about all the ways I could get him back for being a bed hog. I had no idea how he'd managed to move me without waking me. I had absolutely no recollection of it. But I had been exhausted. "Well, thank you," I said grudgingly. "That was good of you."

He glanced over his shoulder at me and grinned, that devilish glint back in his eye. "My pleasure."

"Why are you looking at me like that?"

He shrugged. "I was naked in that bed. Now you're in it..."

I whipped another pillow from beneath my head and threw it at him.

This one he caught easily and tossed it back before he returned to messing around with the fire. What was it with guys and fires anyway? Why couldn't they ever just leave them be? Deciding I didn't care enough, I got out of bed and grabbed some workout gear from the dresser. Ducking into the bathroom, I did my business and got dressed quickly. When I emerged, Rem had his shirt off—again—and was rubbing some sort of cream into his back.

"You got a thing for not wearing clothes?" I asked.

"Only when you're around."

I ignored him. "Get dressed. We're going out."

"It's barely six, and it's freezing outside."

"Don't be a baby. We're going running."

He frowned. "What if I don't run?"

I folded my arms across my chest. "Well, you will by the time we go home. Let's go. Get your shoes on."

He shook his head. "Go without me."

"Nope. Told you last night. You can't just go off on your own."

"I'm not. You are."

"Same difference. Where I go, you go."

He raised one eyebrow. "You're not going to let me out of your sight for the entire time?"

"That's my job. To protect you. Can't do that if you aren't running right alongside me." I picked up one of his sneakers from beside the pile of things spilling from his suitcase. It was big. Hmm. Maybe Mia had been right about the size of his junk last night. I drew my arm back to throw it at him, but he crossed the room so quickly I barely saw him move. He plucked the large sneaker from my hand.

"What's with you and throwing stuff at me? You a baseball pitcher in your spare time or something?"

He moved in so close we were practically touching. I gulped, hating that I might have liked it. "No. I just enjoy using you as target practice. Your head is like this massive blinking bull's-eye to me. Perhaps if your ego was a little smaller, your head would be, too. Now quit stalling and get dressed."

I pushed past him and opened the door, letting the crisp morning air blast into the warmth of the cabin. Holy hell. It was cold out there. And running in it suddenly seemed like the worst idea possible, but I wasn't going to change my mind now. I put one leg up behind me to stretch it, then the other, and was halfway through my regular pre-run stretching routine when Rem finally made it outside, still dressed in the sweats he'd slept in, but with his sneakers laced up. He jogged down the steps and started along the trail we'd walked with Scout last night.

No way in hell was I going to let him lead.

Abandoning my stretches, even though I hadn't completed them, I took off after him, catching him as we passed the last identical cabin in the row. I pulled ahead a few steps, but he caught me quickly, so we were shoulder to shoulder once more. I inched ahead again, and for a second, I thought I had him, but then he put on a burst of speed and caught me. We followed the trail, past the main house and the barn, and while I might have liked to go a little more slowly so I could take in how pretty everything looked, I couldn't fight my competitive nature long enough to do so. We ran into the woods behind the house, jostling for the lead.

"You know you're smiling, don't you?" Rem ribbed.

I shot a glance at him, then arranged my mouth into a taut line. "I was smiling because I enjoy running."

"Nope, you were smiling because you think you're beating me."

"I am beating you," I deadpanned, making sure I was a few steps ahead. My chest heaved with the effort of talking. Sweat rolled down my spine, and I wished he'd shut up.

The early morning sunlight was dappled by the trees, the air fresh and clean. And quiet. So very quiet, you might even call it peaceful. Normally my runs consisted of blaring horns, car engines, and dodging pedestrians on the street. Not to mention the fact the air I sucked in was full of exhaust and pollution. The cleanness of the air here almost burned my lungs.

The path opened up from dense trees, to a round clearing with a stream running through it. Rem skidded to a stop. He bent over and rested his hands on his knees, breathing hard.

A thrill ran down my spine. "Giving up already?"

He nodded. "Yeah. You win. I need a minute."

A giddy satisfaction rolled through me, and I had to stop myself from skipping back to his side.

He flopped on the grassy bank, propped himself up on his hands, and gazed out at the rushing water. "Did you even realize there was a stream winding through the woods?"

I shook my head. "Perhaps I would have heard it if you hadn't been puffing and panting so much."

Rem side-eyed me. "Are you this mean to everyone? Or just me?"

"Just you," I replied with a grin.

He laughed. "Right."

I plonked down on the ground beside him and stretched the muscles I'd pushed too hard. Rem just stared out over the water. After a moment, I couldn't stand the silence anymore. It was too strange. Too foreign. And anyway, there were things we needed to discuss.

"Listen, so I went through the paperwork that was sent over. And we need to be careful with our covers. The only person here who knows who we really are and why we're really here, is the grandpa. Apparently, this place has been used as a safe house before, for low-key cases, but the department had it written into his contract with them that he wouldn't disclose any information about anyone they sent out here."

Rem's eyebrows pulled together, a frown forming between them. "Nobody else knows? Not even Dane?"

"Who's Dane?"

"One of the ranch hands. He's older than Gage and Ollie. Been around longer by the looks of things."

I shook my head. "Any reason why you think he might know more than they do? If the old man has told a ranch hand, he might have told others, too. We might not be safe here, and he's in breach of contract."

Rem shrugged. "No. It's fine. I just got the impression Dane was the lead guy around here. Seems pretty switched on."

I quit stretching and folded my legs beneath me. "Introduce me later, okay? I'll check him out."

"With your super detective powers?"

The words could have sounded condescending, but Rem's warm smile let me know he was just ribbing me.

Despite what I'd told Mia last night, about not being interested in Rem or men in general, I did sort of like when he teased me.

Not as much as I liked teasing him, though. "Yep, with my super detective powers. I'm Velma. Which makes you Shaggy."

Rem barked out a laugh. "Can't I at least be Scooby Doo?"

I grinned and pushed to my feet again. I started to walk away, but at the last minute I held out a hand to him. He looked up at it, surprise clear in his expression, before his gaze drove higher, meeting my own. For a moment, I thought he might ignore me. But then his warm fingers wrapped around mine, and my palm zinged into tingle town.

Shit. That wasn't good.

I helped heft him to his feet and then dropped his hand as quickly as I could. "Race you back," I yelled, taking off in the direction we'd come.

To my surprise, his heavy footsteps caught me in seconds and then passed me. I sprinted, putting every-thing I had into catching him, but Rem's long legs ate up twice the distance mine did. I realized with a jolt that he'd been going easy on me.

"Dammit, Rem!" I yelled to his back.

His laughter floated back, but he'd disappeared from view, leaving me in his dust.

I'd tie his damn shoelaces together next time.

11

REM

I didn't beat Whitney back to the cabin by all that much. I'd barely had time to sit down on the wooden steps and get my breathing under control before she ran down the dirt path in front of the cabins. I forced my lungs to inflate evenly and slowly, instead of gulping the air like I had been a moment earlier. She might be a good six inches shorter than I was, but she was faster than I'd given her credit for. I'd had to run full-out the entire way back in order to beat her.

With one sneaker off, I set to work on the laces of the other. Whitney stomped up the stairs beside me.

"Good run?" I called out sweetly.

She opened the screen door so hard it bounced back off the wooden wall. I winced as the doorframe protested with a crack, but I couldn't keep the grin from my face. "Don't bother having a shower," I called without turning around.

"Why not?"

"Because we've got work to do."

Whitney stomped her way back onto the porch and glared at me, but it was impossible to take her seriously. She was too damn cute with her hair all plastered to her face, her cheeks pink, and fire in her eyes. I just wanted to kiss her. "You know I just want you all the more when you're riled up and angry, right?"

She threw her hands up in the air. "Are you deliberately goading me?"

"Yep. Didn't your parents ever teach you that boys pick on you when they like you?"

She rolled her eyes and gestured between the two of us. "Never gonna happen. Whatever you think this is, it's one-sided. I don't want a man who acts like a boy anyway."

I lifted one shoulder, then went back to tugging off my shoes. "If you say so. My boyish charm is already rubbing off on you, Whit. I can see it."

Her foot shot out but stopped short of actually kicking me. Instead, she nudged me with the sole of her shoe. I deserved a kick, though. I knew it. But damn, she made it too easy. She seriously was hot when she was angry. She was hot when she was happy, too. And when she was sleeping, or when she was worried. Basically, the woman was just plain beautiful, no matter what mood she was in. Despite the fact she was always cranky with me, I was beginning to get glimpses of who she might be, beneath all her prickles and walls. And I was intrigued.

But I also wasn't going to sit around in this cabin with her all day, while we waited for one of my old club members to hunt us down. I doubted any of them had ever heard of Two-Creek Plains, Wyoming. The odds of them finding me out here were slim to none, and certainly not worth wasting six weeks' worth of country living on. I planned to enjoy every moment I had here, before I went back home, testified, and then got on with my life.

"I'm going up to the main house to find out what needs doing. The guys said they've got a lot going on before the roundup next week. Put that in your diary, by the way."

"Put what in my diary? What the hell is a roundup? And what makes you think I'm going on one?"

I pushed to my feet and faced her, enjoying the way she had to tilt her head back to look up at me. "A roundup is where we'll ride horses out to the far ends of the property, to bring back the cattle. Nothing better than riding under the sun during the day, then sleeping under the stars at night. You'll love it."

"I won't, because we aren't doing that."

"You go where I go, right?"

She shook her head. "Wrong. You go where I go."

I folded my arms across my chest. "Well, I'm going to muck some stalls out. Or mend a few fences. So come if you like, or don't. But I want to help. And I think deep down, you want to as well. They need the extra hands, and I don't think you're the sort of woman who's afraid of getting her hands dirty."

"I'm not!"

"Great, so get your jeans on and let's go." I drew my hand back, pretending I was going to slap her on the ass, the way I would have a horse.

She glared at me. "You slap me, and I swear to God, Remington James, I will end you."

I tucked my hand into my pocket and strolled inside

ahead of her. "Noted. I'll save the ass slapping for when we have less clothes on then, huh?"

The look she shot me should have set me on fire. Except all it did was make blood run straight to my dick. Because within her glare, there was something more. Something that might have been desire. I tucked that tidbit away for future use.

*G*age had been more than happy to hand over the task of cleaning out the horses' stalls to Whitney and me. Whitney had been less happy. But to her credit, she didn't moan about it. Simply threw me another death glare, which I was beginning to think of as her love language, and grabbed a pitchfork from the entrance to the barn.

"Oh," she whispered when the horses heard us coming and stuck their heads over the stall doors. She stopped in front of the first horse and a raised a tentative hand toward his head. "He's so much bigger than I expected."

I smoothed my hand down the animal's shiny neck, then scratched him behind the ears, smiling when he made a delighted snickering noise. "You didn't realize how big they are? You don't ride?"

Whitney shook her head. "No, not at all. City girl, born and raised. Never been near a farm animal in my life, unless you count the mobile petting zoo at my niece's birthday party a few years back."

"Baby chickens and perhaps a lamb?"

"Got it in one."

"Lame," I deadpanned, then winked to show her I was joking. She slapped me on the arm anyway. Which was fair enough. I clipped a lead to the horse's bridle and opened the stall door.

Whitney skittered out of the way. "Whoa, what are you doing?"

"Getting the horse out? How did you think we were going to clean his stall with him in it?"

"Good point."

"Want to lead him?"

"Nope."

I held the rope out, despite her protests. "Come on, we need to get you riding so you're ready for roundup next week. That's going to be a problem if you can't even lead the horse."

"I can lead it. I just don't want to."

I gave her a look.

"Fine," she huffed, taking the lead from my hand. "What do I do with it now?"

"Him, not it. He's a stallion."

Whitney leaned over and took a glimpse at what the horse had going on at the tail end. "I see that. Fine, what do I do with him?"

I clipped a lead to the brown mare in the stall next to Whitney's horse and led the placid girl out. "Just follow me."

We led the two horses outside the barn and over to one of the nearby training arenas. The fence served well as a place to hitch the leads, and I showed Whitney how to tie a knot that wouldn't come undone before we were ready to bring the horses back. Then we got stuck into the real work of cleaning out the dirty straw and putting it into wheelbarrows. For a long while, the two of us worked in silence, and I enjoyed the familiar, manual labor I hadn't done much of since joining the pro bull riding tour. There was a simple peace in doing something so monotonous. It was a task I'd done hundreds of times when I'd worked on the ranch, and I liked the time it gave me to just be.

Whitney, on the other hand, seemed twitchy.

"You okay?" I asked her eventually.

"Yeah, it's just...it's so quiet here. I'm not used to it."

"Want me to annoy you some more then?"

She shot me a warning look. "No. But I do want to know more about you. We haven't really discussed how we actually came to be here, and I'm interested. How did you get involved with the gang?"

I sighed. "It wasn't a gang. It was a motorcycle club."

"Not much difference from where I'm standing."

"I can see how you might think that."

She dug her pitchfork into the straw, gathering up a large mound, then carried it to the rapidly filling wheelbarrow. "Tell me why it's not like that then. What drew you to them? A love of bikes?"

I shook my head. "No. I grew up with the club. My dad was the pres—president. My mom was a club slut."

Whitney wrinkled her nose at the term.

"Yeah, I know, it's not a nice word. I wouldn't normally use it, except it does accurately describe my mother. And my father for that matter. The two of them weren't exactly choosy with who they slept with."

"You sure your dad is your dad, then?"

I shrugged. "Truthfully? Not really. But he claimed me

as his own. Maybe he just wanted an heir. But he claimed Abel, too—he's my brother. We have different moms."

"I've got a brother, too," Whitney mused.

"You two close?"

"We were as kids. Less so now. We haven't had a falling out or anything. He has his life; I have mine. He never liked Karsten."

I made a face at the mention of her ex.

"What?"

"Your ex is a dickwad."

"Yeah, I know. But I don't want to talk about him. Tell me more about your brother and the club."

I leaned back on the side of the stall, and Whitney did the same thing on the opposite side. I liked having her complete attention on me. Her brown eyes shone with intelligence and interest, and I could practically see her detective mind working, lapping up the information I was providing to her.

"Not a lot to tell. Abel's mom was never a lifer. She got him out, took him across the other side of the country when our father went to jail."

"Smart woman."

I nodded. "Abel is smart, like her. Or maybe he's smart like our old man."

"You think your father is intelligent?"

I nodded. "Very. He did a lot of bad shit, for a very long time. And he taught a lot of other men how to do that same bad shit and not get caught. He might not be book smart, but he's got brains."

"He's in jail now, though, so he screwed up at some point."

I nodded. "But he left a legacy of bad people behind him."

"You being one of them," she said quietly.

It wasn't the first time someone had realized I wasn't a good guy. But it was the first time that realization had come with a jolt of pain. It irked me that she thought I was still that same man.

"I'm not a bad guy. Not anymore."

Whitney's expression didn't change. "You did five years, Rem. You pled guilty. And now the only reason we're here is because you were involved in a murder. I'm not trying to be a bitch, really, I'm not. But I live by facts. Those are yours."

Shame crept over me. It was always there, in the back of my mind. But in the years since I'd been out of jail, I'd done everything in my power to turn things around. I knew I couldn't erase the past, but I could change my future. That was what I concentrated on every day. "I didn't do it."

"So you've said."

"You don't believe me?"

She shrugged. "Honestly? Not really."

I winced at the stinging truth of her answer. "Are you scared of me, then? Of being alone out here with someone you think is capable of murder?"

She pondered that question for a moment, then shook her head. "I'm not scared. I took the case without really knowing much about you. But I'm not scared of you."

Relief rushed through me.

"But that doesn't mean I think you're a good guy either. Once a criminal—"

"Always a criminal." I sighed and ran a frustrated hand through my hair, tugging at the ends of it. "That's a very black-and-white way of looking at the world."

Her gaze laser focused. "I see guys like you all the time. You get out of jail, you go straight for a little while, but inevitably, you land up back where you belong."

Frustration morphed into anger. "And where I belong is back in jail? Right?"

She was wrong. I was nothing like the man I'd once been. I was never going to be that man again. And fuck, I didn't owe her shit. She didn't have to believe me. I went back to pitching straw and horse shit out of the stall. Seemed fitting for my sudden change of mood.

"Rem, I—"

The jarring sound of a cell phone ringing jolted me out of my head. "You have your cell on still?" I snapped. Mine had been taken off me before we'd even boarded the plane.

Whitney fished the buzzing device from the back pocket of her jeans. "No, it's a burner phone. Untraceable. Only my boss has the number. I need to answer this."

I made a sweeping gesture with my hand. "Go right ahead. I'll endeavor not to break any laws while you're gone."

I ignored the sharp look she gave me. Stupidly, my feelings were hurt. I hadn't really expected to become friends with the woman assigned to watch over me while I waited for the trial, but I liked Whitney. We'd been teasing each other and flirting for the past day and a half, and I'd truthfully thought, at some point in the next six weeks, things might become more than friendly. Hell, I knew I wanted it to be something more. The woman was fiery and sexy and smart. She was a perfect ten in my book. It hurt to realize I was a negative number in hers.

"Detective Whitney Nicholson," Whitney said into the phone, in lieu of saying hello.

I turned my back on her and grabbed the wheelbarrow, uninterested in hearing any more of her conversation. I pushed it toward the door, blocking out her voice. I'd keep my distance, now that I knew where we both stood. Stop the flirting. Stop the banter and the joking around. I'd get a list of jobs to do from Gage and I'd bust my ass for the next six weeks to get everything they needed done. The harder I worked, the less time I'd have to think about Whitney.

I'd just reached the barn door, when a scream ripped through the barn.

"No!" Whitney howled. "No!"

Around me, startled horses neighed and whinnied in a unified frenzy, shifting and kicking in their stalls, but they became a blur as I raced back to Whitney's side. She'd slumped down onto the hard wood floor I'd just cleaned off. Her skin was pale, her eyes blank.

With my heart thumping, I scanned her for any sign of injury, scanned the immediate surroundings for danger, then finally, focused on the phone, listing from her lax fingers.

"What's happened?" I asked carefully, slowly, as if she were one of the horses that needed taming. "What's wrong?"

She didn't answer. Just stared blankly at the phone. But when I picked it up and held it to my ear, the line was dead.

12

WHITNEY

"Here, drink this." Rem nudged a mug of steaming tea into my numb fingers before sliding into the seat next to me. He folded his arms on the little wooden table in our cabin and waited.

I raised the mug to my mouth with shaking hands and took a gulp of the scalding liquid. It burned my throat as I swallowed, but the warming sensation it left in its wake was pleasant. Especially considering how cold I was. I craved the warmth and willed it to spread throughout the rest of my shocked body.

I knew Rem was still waiting for me to explain what had happened out in the barn, but I was still trying to process it myself. All I'd managed to do since I'd answered that call was allow Rem to bundle me into an old truck he must have borrowed from one of the guys, and let him drive me back to our cabin.

I glanced over at him. His jaw was rigid, his eyebrows drawn so close together in a frown that he may as well have had a monobrow. The thought amused me, but the muscles in my face didn't attempt to form a smile. They were as frozen as the rest of me.

After several more minutes of silence, Rem let out a long breath. "Where's your gun?"

That snapped me out of my daze. "What?"

Rem laid his hand out on the table, palm side up as if he expected I'd just willingly hand my weapon over to him.

"I'm not giving you my gun, Rem."

"Then start talking. I don't want to push you, but right now, I'm really fucking worried. The way you screamed..." His face morphed into an expression of pain. "If something's happened, or someone is after us, I need to know." He leaned in and took one of my cold hands, rubbing it briskly. "Please, Whit. Talk to me."

I opened my mouth to tell him he didn't need to worry about me, but all that came out was a moan. I shoved my chair back, dropping my head, and bracing myself on my knees. "I think I'm going to be sick."

Rem inched over and smoothed his palm between my shoulder blades in long, slow movements, while I tried to get my pounding heart and roiling nausea under control.

"It's Mia," I whispered.

"Who's Mia?"

"My partner. On the force. She was attacked last night."

I wasn't sure if Rem's sigh was out of relief or frustration, but I didn't question him.

"Is she okay?"

I finally looked up at him, but that was a mistake. His handsome face was so full of concern and compassion it broke whatever little reserve had been holding me together. My face crumpled, and a sob burst from my chest. I shook my head hard. "No, I don't think so."

Rem moved his chair closer until it was touching mine, and then the palm on my back turned into an arm around my shoulders. He pulled me in.

I resisted, knowing it was unprofessional to let him comfort me, but then Janice's words on the phone echoed through my head. *Induced coma. Life support. Might not make it.*

I let Rem's strong arms hold me up as I fell apart. Heaving sobs ripped from my chest while I cried into his shirt.

"Ssssh," he soothed, over and over again. "She'll be okay."

But he didn't know that. I tried to jerk away, but he held me tight. I struggled in his arms, pummeling his pecs with my fists. "You can't say that, Rem! You don't know! She was beaten half to death! They found her body, broken and battered in an alley, just a block from her home! Someone attacked her in her very own neighborhood. How? Why? Just because she's a cop?"

My mind whirled through all the hundreds of cases we'd worked, trying to think of someone who would have done this to her. But I couldn't come up with anything. I couldn't remember the last case we'd worked on, let alone all of the ones from the past few years. There were too many names, too many faces.

Rem grasped my face between his palms. I stilled under his heavy gaze.

"Stop," he commanded. "Everything is going to be okay."

"You don't know—"

"I know it because I've been there. I've been the one in the induced coma. And I woke up. I don't know Mia, but if she's half as amazing as you are, then I know she's strong enough to heal from this." Pure conviction shone in his eyes, and I let myself slump a little farther into him. I wanted to believe him. So much. Because the thought of Mia not making it through this was inconceivable.

My gaze flicked up to Rem's, and I drank in the strength in his expression, letting it refill my well. It had taken a beating. "She's got a son," I whispered. "And a husband. Or an almost husband. They never got married because Mia is so stupidly stubborn and she never wanted to, but Lucas always did. They need me."

Rem's gaze dipped to my lips, then turned tortured before he spoke. "Then let's go. We'll get you on a plane tonight."

I shook my head. "Can't. My orders are to stay put."

"They can't force you to stay here."

"They can if I want to keep my job." I loved my job. I needed it like I needed air to breathe. It was all I had now. Guilt roared through me. I wanted to be at Mia's side. Every muscle in my body screamed to get on the first plane home. But the sergeant had been very clear with her orders. I was not to move until they had more information on the attack. "The sergeant said I could be in danger if I came back. They want to find whoever did this before I return."

Rem's hand slid to the back of my neck and squeezed gently. I stared up into his eyes and saw nothing but compassion and kindness. It was almost too much to bear. "What if she wakes up and I'm not there? What if she *dies* and I'm not there?" I whispered the questions my brain couldn't stop asking.

Rem's face was so close to mine his breath misted over my lips. "She won't," he whispered.

I inched forward, so the gap between our lips became nothing more than a wisp of air. It was wrong, I knew, to be drawing comfort from him the way I was. But I needed it. He was there, and he was strong and whole while I felt small and broken. "I need..."

"What, baby?" he whispered. "Tell me what you need."

Baby.

I jerked away, blinking hard, the spell shattered into a thousand pieces.

Rem dropped his hand from my neck and sat back, confusion painted all over his too handsome expression. "What's wrong?"

I shook my head. "Nothing. It's just..." Everything. We'd been about to cross a line, one there was no coming back from. It didn't matter what I needed in that moment. It was a line that could be the end of my career if we were found out. My God, why was my own judgment so blinded when it came to men? I hadn't seen the whole thing with Karsten coming, and now I was about to make another stupid decision, with a different man. My lips tingled, still feeling the effects of being so near to Rem's. All it would have taken was for me to lean in and his lips could have been on mine, helping to erase the swirling vortex of images in my head.

I already knew one kiss wouldn't have been enough. Not with a man like Rem.

I let out a long shaky breath and tried to control the

rise and fall of my chest. How had I gotten to this place so quickly? I needed space. Air. "I need to run," I murmured.

Rem nodded. "Okay. I'll get my shoes."

I shook my head. "No, I need to run alone."

"But..."

I gave Rem a look that begged him not to call me on the fact I'd just this morning told him I couldn't go anywhere without him and vice versa.

He sat back down in his chair. "I'll be here when you get back," he said quietly.

I didn't say thank you. I didn't even glance his way. I knew if I did, the resolve I'd found in the last few minutes might evaporate entirely.

13

REM

*O*ver the next few days, Whitney and I fell into a routine. Running in the mornings, farm chores during the day. Dinner in our cabin or by the bonfire with the other guys and Scout. Then we fell into bed—me on the air mattress I'd fished out of Gage's camping gear—and let darkness take us until the sunrise. She'd loosened the reins a lot, since that day she'd first gone running by herself, but I stayed close to her side at all times, more because I wanted to than because I had to.

On the Sunday, a week after we'd arrived, we slept late. Gage had strict rules about not working on Sundays, and Scout had invited us to brunch at the main house. So we slept until the sun was well on its way to the highest point, then strolled down the path we usually ran.

Whitney had dressed up, and her flowing skirt whipped around her legs in the crisp breeze, capturing my attention as it flowed free, then stuck tight to her shapely calves.

"Quit staring at my ass," she drawled from her position a step or two ahead of me. She always had to lead, and I'd learned to let her. It was where she felt comfortable, and safe, and after the drama with her friend Mia, I knew she needed to feel in control more than ever. But the remark took me by surprise. That flirty tone she'd had on our first few days together was back. I'd missed it, though I'd understood she hadn't much felt like bantering, what with her friend so badly injured.

"You could walk behind and look at mine instead?" I quipped.

She shook her head, but her step was perky this morning. Her gait unhurried and relaxed, nothing like the angry, jerky motions she'd been making for the past few days.

"What's gotten into you?" I asked, a smile pulling at my lips. It was good to see her emerging from the storm cloud she'd been walking under since she'd gotten that phone call.

She turned around and walked backward, so we were facing each other. Cattle pens lined the path through this section, hundreds of cows milling around either side of us, their mooing noises and animal smells filling the air. "I spoke to my sergeant this morning while you were in the shower. Mia is doing better."

"Yeah?" I asked, genuinely pleased, because it pleased her. "That's so great. She's awake?"

Whitney shook her head. "No, still in the induced coma, but the doctors say that everything is good. She's as stable as she can be. They might try to bring her out of it later this week."

Her backward steps veered slightly off the path, and I lurched forward, grabbing her arm, right as Sampson the bull slammed his eight hundred pound body into the fence right beside us.

Whitney skittered closer to me, and I wrapped an arm around her, even though I knew there was no chance of the bull getting through the fence and hurting her.

"You're such an asshole!" Whitney swore in the bull's direction. "You do that every time I walk past!"

"He does?"

She nodded, still glaring at the beast that eyed her lazily while he munched on feed. "Haven't you noticed?"

I hadn't but I was well used to grumpy bulls. I steered her away from her Mexican standoff with Sampson. "Come on, I'm starving, and I can smell bacon."

"I'd like to turn him into bacon," Whitney mumbled.

I snorted.

She rolled her eyes. "Or hamburgers. Whatever. You know what I meant."

I did, but I found it funny anyway.

She elbowed me and stomped off toward the house again.

I threw Sampson a salute, and caught up with Whitney on the garden path that directed us to the main house. It led us through a neatly tended lawn with rock-lined flowerbeds, that admittedly were lacking in flowers at this time of year. But there wasn't a weed to be seen. Somebody was obviously a master gardener. A short fat garden gnome with a bulbous nose stood guard of the empty soil. I shuddered just looking at the weird little statue.

Whitney followed my line of sight and laughed. She bent over and picked up the gnome from the dirt, turning him over in her hands, studying his sun-faded expression with a smile.

"Horrible things," I muttered, trying to move around her.

"What? Why? I think he's cute."

I shook my head. "They're worse than clowns. Or those creepy elves that parents put on shelves for their kids at Christmastime. He's looking at me."

She held the gnome out, playfully shoving him in my face, and I backed up a few steps. She laughed. "Remington Washington," she said, choosing to use my fake name, I assumed because we were in the vicinity of other people. "Don't tell me you're scared of gnomes?"

I wasn't scared. I just didn't like them watching me with their beady eyes. I didn't get to answer, though. An angry shout interrupted Whitney's fun.

"You put Mr. Lolly Golly back where you found him!"

Whitney's eyes widened as we both turned to face the angry old man who yelled at us from the porch.

"Have some respect and quit touching things that don't belong to you!"

Whitney blinked, stunned at being told off. I was, too, but I recovered quicker and turned to her with mock anger on my face. "Yes, Whitney. Put Mr. Lolly Golly back. He's not a toy. Right, sir?"

I sidled up to the older man, and he nodded at me briskly. We both faced Whitney who stared at us, red cheeked. Her mouth opened and closed a few times, like she was trying to form words but couldn't actually spit anything out, while I tried to fight back the laughter threatening to explode out of my throat. I got the feeling Whitney had been a goody-two-shoes all her life. It was clear she wasn't practiced at getting out of a scolding.

I had no such problem.

Whitney shot me a filthy look, then addressed the older man beside me, who had to be Scout and Gage's grandpa, though neither of us had met him yet.

"I'm awfully sorry, sir," she apologized. "It won't happen again."

The older man crossed his arms over his chest. "See that it doesn't." Then he turned, opening the porch door. He glanced over his shoulder at me. "You can call me Gramps. Everyone else does."

"Thank you, sir. I mean, Gramps." I reached out a hand, and the older man shook it. He cast a final disapproving glare in Whitney's direction, then disappeared inside the house.

I couldn't help it. My laughter couldn't be concealed a second longer. I laughed so hard my stomach ached.

Whitney punched me hard in the pec as she stormed past. "You totally dumped me in it!"

"I know. And it was great."

"I hate you."

"Nah, you don't."

She pushed past me and into the darkness of the house, but not before I saw the curve of her smile.

She *so* didn't hate me. How could she? I was charming with a capital C.

Slightly high on that information, my steps lightened. I followed her into the house and through the living room. Taxidermy animal heads hung from the walls, and the brown leather couches were old and cracked in some places. But the room was warmed by a fireplace, and the smells of a cooked breakfast wafted through the air. My mouth watered.

"You made it!" Gage called. He, Dane, and Ollie all sat along one side of a huge dining room table. The old man sat at the head, still scowling in Whitney's direction.

"We did." I slapped Gage's outstretched hand and nodded to the other guys. "Where should we sit?"

Gage tipped his chin in the direction of the empty chairs across the table.

"I'm going to go find Scout," Whitney said, leaving me alone with the men.

I watched her go. Her ass seriously did look so good with nothing but a thin piece of fabric covering it.

When I turned back, Dane was watching me curiously.

"What?" I asked him.

"You two are close, huh?"

I paused, remembering he thought we were brother and sister. Fuck. I'd already completely blown my own cover with him; I didn't want to blow Whitney's as well. I shook my head and played it off. "Yeah, I guess. The bull scared her on the way in; I just wanted to make sure she was okay. Hey, did you watch the game last night?"

Dane didn't answer, but thankfully, Ollie jumped in, chatting about the three-pointer Dan Wisle had thrown, saving me from further interrogation. I nodded and laughed when appropriate, but my gaze kept drawing back to Dane. Every time, he was studying me intently.

The skin at the back of my neck prickled. There was something off about the way he scrutinized people that had me uneasy. I got the impression nothing slipped by him.

"I'm going to check if Scout needs any help," I said, pushing back my chair, needing to escape Dane's intensity.

His gaze burned a hole in my back the entire way, and I vowed to be more careful around him.

The kitchen was down a short hallway, and Whitney's laughter floated back as I made my way closer. I paused just before the doorway, letting the melodic sound of her laughter fill me.

"So, about Rem..." Scout said, lowering her voice.

I'd been just about to enter the room when the mention of my name had my foot hovering in midair. Instead, I leaned back on the wall, out of sight, wondering what Scout wanted to know.

"Mmmm?" Whitney asked. "What about him?"

The sizzle of frying bacon was louder back here, the aromas stronger, and I willed my stomach to not give away the fact I was eavesdropping on the women's conversation.

"Is he single?"

The clatter of a plate being dropped met my ears, and I dared a glance around the corner. Whitney stared at the pile of toast that was now on the floor.

"Shit, sorry. I'm so clumsy. Um, yes. He's single."

I ducked back out of sight, grinning to myself.

"I thought so," Scout said, "but I just wanted to check before I made a move."

My grin widened. I knew it. I really was charming with a capital C.

"He's gay," Whitney deadpanned.

My mouth dropped open.

"Oh, he is?" Scout questioned.

I shook my head hard. "*So not gay!*" I mouthed to the empty hallway.

"Yep," Whit said, in a matter-of-fact tone. "Very gay. Loves cock. Big ones. Huge cock monster."

My jaw hit the floor.

"Oh wow. I had no idea. That's cool. I'll tell him about Rusty Joe's then. That's the local gay bar. I'm sure he'll find all the...ah...cock, there."

Oh hell no. I walked into the kitchen. "What's everyone talking about in here? Roosters? I heard someone say cock." I turned to Whitney and gave her a meaningful glare. "I'm sure that's what you were talking about, wasn't it?"

She smiled widely. "Totally." She winked at Scout.

I held in a groan. The woman probably thought I was in the closet now. For fuck's sake. I was going to kill Whitney.

Scout glanced between the two of us, then picked up a tray loaded high with all sorts of heart-attack-inducing breakfast foods. "The guys are going to be beating down the door in a minute. I'm going to get this stuff out to them. Meet you two out there?"

Whitney nodded. "I'll just make some more toast then I'll be right out."

"I'll help." I flashed my most blinding smile.

The moment Scout was out of earshot, Whitney leaned her back against the pantry and burst into laughter.

"I'm a cock monster now, Whit? Really?" I hissed, but I was laughing, too.

She lifted one shoulder, her eyes full of mischief.

I couldn't help it. I stepped toward her and planted

my hands either side of her on the pantry door, caging her in. She could easily duck beneath my arm if she wanted to. In fact, I expected it. Held my breath while I waited for it. But she didn't move.

Her grin widened. "Hey, for all I know, you are gay. And that's what you get for eavesdropping."

"You knew I was there?"

"Of course I did, I'm a cop, remember? I'm well aware of my surroundings, and you don't do quiet well. Scout might not have noticed, but your footsteps are heavy, and that obnoxious cologne you're wearing can be smelled a mile away."

She wasn't the only one well aware of her surroundings. My gaze flickered over the planes of her face, and if I'd thought she was beautiful when she was angry, she was stunning when she laughed. My feet had a mind of their own. They inched forward. Closing the gap between us more steadily by the second, until she had to crane her neck back to look up at me.

Something charged passed between us. A spark of electricity so hot and powerful it tried to knock me off my feet, but the magnetic force of Whitney drew me in.

"I'm not gay," I murmured. I swallowed hard, fighting the allure of her.

Her gaze darted to my lips, then lower, scorching a path over my chest and down my abs to the instant erection straining against my jeans.

"No?" she whispered back distractedly.

"No."

She licked her lips, leaning in an inch, and my blood surged. Fuck, she took my breath away. Tension and anticipation coiled in every muscle, while I tried to hold myself back from closing the gap between us. A physical ache pushed me to go to her. To lay my lips on hers and kiss her until her knees went weak and the need I had for her eased.

I'd never wanted a woman so badly in my life.

"We shouldn't," she whispered, darting a look over my shoulder at the kitchen door.

She was right. Someone could walk in at any moment and completely blow our cover. But, fuck. I didn't care.

"That just makes me want to do it all the more." I dropped one hand to the side of her face, running my fingers to the back of her neck, and pulled her closer. Her breath danced over my lips, driving me crazy. I fought to keep control. "Say no, Whit. Say no, and I won't kiss you."

She didn't utter a sound.

My lips crashed down on hers.

Sweet heaven. That was exactly what Whitney's lips tasted of. Sweet like the maple syrup I suspected she'd stolen a taste of. And pure, golden heaven.

I pushed my body into the softness of hers, and her mouth opened, inviting me in. She moaned, and I hushed her with my lips. But not before that sound caused my dick to ache. I ground on her, our mouths moving in perfect unison, our tongues tangling.

I slid my hand down her arm and over the curve of her hip, drawing her tight, our kiss deepening. My head spun, and my heart pounded. I knew I should stop. The others were just down the hall, but my head was gone, and my heart was already trying to follow it. I was so lost in Whitney's kiss and the feel of her body against mine that nothing was going to make me pull away.

"Rem, stop," she murmured

Except that.

I broke away from her mouth with an all too loud groan, forcing my lust-filled eyes to focus on her. "Shit. Sorry. Are you okay? I thought…"

She shook her head. "Yes. No. I don't know. I…"

"Want to do that again?" I asked hopefully.

She rolled her eyes, but then her gaze drew back to my lips.

"You totally want to do it again," I teased.

She shoved me away. "Do not."

"Do."

"How old are you, twelve? Gah! Okay. I give you credit. You're a good kisser. For a criminal."

My smile fell.

So did hers.

"Rem…"

She might as well have thrown a bucket of cold water on me. "That was a cheap shot." I ground my molars. I couldn't keep doing this. This flirting, but then reminding me constantly that to her, I was never going to be anything more than a man who'd once made mistakes.

I picked up a jug of orange juice, hating that my fingers shook. "I'm going to prove it to you, you know. I'll show you."

"Show me what?"

Determination punctuated every word. "I'm going to show you who I really am."

14

WHITNEY

*I*t took multiple nights in a row, of dreams filled with guilty feelings, before I looked up on the internet what that meant. Unfortunately, it meant exactly what you'd expect. Feelings of guilt in dreams meant that you felt guilty about something you'd done in real life.

Stupid website.

I didn't want to feel guilt over what I'd said to Rem after he'd kissed me. The man *was* a criminal, after all.

But after almost two weeks of living together, and getting to know him, nothing about him set off my detective Spidey senses. In fact, everything about him set off senses of a completely different kind.

The man was hot. There was no other way around it. And handsome. Nice. He'd been sweet and kind to me after I'd found out about Mia's attack. Dammit, he was kind of funny, too. Karsten the douchebag had never made me laugh, and at the time, I hadn't thought anything of it. But Rem made me laugh every day, without even trying. His constant teasing was clever and smart, and he took my insults as well as he dished them out. The entire thing just made him all the more appealing.

He made me happy.

But ever since our kiss and me calling him a criminal, all of that had stopped. He wasn't exactly giving me the cold shoulder, but it was clear I'd hurt him, and he was licking his wounds.

I felt like shit about it. But I hadn't apologized. Because I was a bitch. But also because I didn't know what to say about the kiss that had rocked me to my very core. I'd never felt a kiss all the way down to my toes like I had with Rem. In that moment, that kiss had erased all the reservations I'd been clutching at so tightly.

I wanted to do it again.

Then I'd gone and run my stupid mouth and now I didn't know how to fix it. I didn't know if I *should* fix it. So he'd kissed me and my head had spun. It didn't mean anything. Maybe I wouldn't be fired for hooking up with a witness I was supposed to be protecting, but I doubted Sergeant Minor would be impressed if she knew. I didn't need to compromise my professional integrity because his lips shot heat straight through my body. Admittedly, that heat went straight to a place that had some achingly overwhelming needs, which only flared when he was around. Some needs I imagined he'd be really good at taking care of, if his kiss and the bulge in his jeans was anything to go by. But I was a strong, independent woman. I was perfectly capable of taking care of those needs by myself.

Which was what I needed to do right now. I squirmed beneath the pile of blankets on my bed and squeezed my legs together, trying to find some relief, without actually putting my hand down the pants of my pajamas. Rem was asleep on the air mattress at the bottom of my bed, and I couldn't just, *do that*, while he was only a foot or two away. Especially not when it would be his face I pictured as I did it.

Heat rushed to my cheeks. Fuck. This whole situation was a mess. And we still had four weeks left to go. I rolled over, shoved my face into the pillow, and groaned as quietly as possible.

"You awake?" Rem's voice came in the darkness.

I froze. "I thought you were asleep."

That chuckle Rem always did when I was a smartass only worsened the ache between my legs. Dammit. If I didn't know better, I'd swear he did it on purpose.

"Can't sleep with your squirming all around over in that bed, making the springs squeak while you moan into your pillow. What are you doing up there anyway? Sounds like..."

Oh my God. I'd die if he said it.

"...the bed isn't very comfortable."

I nodded quickly, even though he couldn't see me in the darkness. "Got it in one."

He threw back his blankets and stood, crossing the room to stand by the headboard. I gazed up at him, clutching the blankets around my neck and hating that he slept bare-chested, even though it was so cold at night. His pecs were so defined, his abs so chiseled, and that trail of hair that led beneath his sweatpants was just begging for me to follow it and find the hidden treasures beneath.

"What are you doing?" I asked, my voice oddly husky.

"It's late, go back to bed." The heat between my legs pulsed, probably in disappointment that he was so near, and yet instead of inviting him in, I was sending him away.

"Can't sleep either. I want to show you something." He put one knee on the mattress and perched on the edge.

"Now? It's the middle of the night?"

"Yeah, now. It's been bugging me since that day...in the kitchen."

I swallowed hard. "Oh." Apparently, we were talking about it whether I was ready to or not. "Look, Rem, I'm sorry—"

But the words died on my lips when he cupped the side of my face and stroked his thumb over my mouth. I closed my eyes, relishing the featherlight touch and hating that I wished it was his lips instead.

"I don't want your apologies. I need to show you for myself. Get dressed and come with me. Please. I'll go get changed in the bathroom so you can have some privacy."

His voice was so earnest, and I watched as he disappeared into the bathroom, the door closing behind him softly. I didn't think twice. I slipped from the bed and opened the top drawer. The tips of my fingers brushed over a lacy thong that had no practical value out here, when we were looking after animals and fixing fences all day. But for a moment, I contemplated putting it on. Just in case. Then I shoved the thong aside, grabbed my regular clothing, and raced to get dressed before Rem left the bathroom.

"Decent?" he called out, ever the gentleman.

"You're safe," I said.

We sat silently on the bed, side by side, putting our boots on.

At the doorway to the cabin, Rem paused, grabbing my coat from a hook and held it out so I could shrug into it. Butterflies rioted around my belly when he lowered his head, his lips brushing my ear. "Do the buttons up, it's cold out."

I shivered, but it wasn't from the temperature. It would have been so easy to just turn around. I was practically already in his arms. One step, one bold move, and we could be kissing again. But after what I'd said, I didn't even know if that was still what he wanted. So instead, I remained rigid until he opened the door, and chilly air blasted us both in the face.

The night outside was bright. A fat full moon and a universe full of stars put on a dazzling show. There was plenty of light to see by, even though it was after midnight. Rem set a brisk pace, and I matched him as we strode along the dirt track we'd run each morning. The cows were quieter than normal on the other side of their fences.

"We're not going cow tipping, are we?" I whispered, not really sure why, since there was no one but Rem and the cows to hear me.

Rem grinned. "You know that's not really a thing, right? Cows sleep on their bellies. They only doze on their feet. So they wake up at any little disturbance."

I nodded. "Sure. I knew that."

Totally didn't know that.

"We're here," Rem said, stopping suddenly. He pulled his jacket off and dropped it to the ground.

"We're where?" I cast my gaze around the darkness.

"There's nothing here. Except Sampson and his girl-friends. And put your jacket back on! It's freezing!"

Rem shook his head and strode toward the bull pen, leaning on the fence. I scurried to his side but stopped short of touching the enclosure. I peered into the dark-ness. "Is that asshole bull asleep?"

As if he knew we were talking about him, Sampson's big body appeared from the dark depths of his pen, a pissed-off snort blowing through his nose. I took another step back.

Rem grinned. "It's on."

He clapped his hands once, and Sampson eyed him, pawing at the dirt.

"Move back!" I hissed. "I think you woke him up, and he does not look like a morning person. Or a morning bull. You've angered the demon."

"I'm counting on it." Rem reached through the fence, unlocking the gate.

Without thinking, I sprinted to his side and grabbed his arm. "Are you insane?"

Rem's dark eyes shone with determination. "No. I know what I'm doing. It'll be fine." He tried to slip into the pen, but I dug my fingers into the tawny muscles of his forearm. His long-sleeved T-shirt was tight enough to be a second skin. He had to be freezing.

"You can't go in there."

But Rem's eyes took on a glint I'd never seen before. Pure determination rolled through his body, morphing his expression. "I have to. I need to show you who I am."

"Who you are is dead if you step in that pen!"

"Do you trust me?" Moonlight danced over his features. Features I'd really come to like in the past two weeks. I didn't want to see them pulverized into the dirt just because he was trying to prove something to me.

"Yes," the word fell from my lips before I could even really consider how true it was. He'd given me no reason not to. The man I'd gotten to know in the last two weeks didn't match the man on the rap sheet. "I do. But please don't do this. I'm sorry for what I said. I really am, I'm just not good at admitting when I'm wrong. You don't need to do this to prove anything to me, I swear. This is overkill."

Rem lifted one shoulder. "Maybe. But this is who I am now, Whit. And I've missed it."

With that, he slipped into the pen, latching it quietly behind him.

My stomach sank.

Sampson wasted no time. He charged at Rem from the far side of the pen, apparently no longer sleepy, but a whole lot pissed off that someone else was in his space. My mouth dropped open when Rem ran straight for him. Sampson's hooves sent chunks of dirt and grass flying, while Rem's strong thighs took the force of his own heavy footsteps.

My stomach churned. "God, no," I yelped, the words coming out strangled. The two were on a collision course that could only end with Rem being mowed down by a bull the size of a truck.

Rem pumped his arms, putting on a burst of speed. Sampson lowered his head, deadly horns pale in the moonlight. I cringed away, waiting for the inevitable crack of bones and cries of pain.

But it didn't come. Rem sprang into a Superman-style leap over the bull and landed in a roll on the other side.

"What the fuck just happened?" I whispered,

completely confused at how Rem had just managed to launch himself over a bull like he could freaking fly. Shock taking out my legs, I sank down to the dewy grass.

Rem wasn't on the ground long. He was a feat of athleticism, springing back to his feet. His laughter wafted across the silent night. "It's okay! It's called freestyling. We do acrobatic type tricks around the bull. It's an extension of what we do in the rodeo. There's a competition and everything."

"You've lost your mind," I said weakly.

My throat tightened as Sampson realized he'd missed his target and turned around for another shot. He bellowed out his frustrations and hurled himself at Rem.

But Rem was quicker. He dodged and weaved and spun around Sampson, using the bull's weight and slower response times to his advantage. Sampson put his head down and charged, but Rem side-stepped then leaped up on the fence right in front of me, just barely out of Sampson reach.

"I see who you are now," I choked out. Nausea turned my stomach.

"You do?" His chest heaved, but the lunatic had a grin from ear to ear, and something wild in his eyes. He was on an adrenaline high. No doubt about it.

I nodded. "You're insane. Completely and utterly insane."

He frowned. "Wrong answer." He jumped back down into the dirt.

I groaned.

Sampson eyed him more warily this time.

Rem clapped a few times.

"Are you trying to get him to kill you?" I squeaked out.

"Quit pissing him off!"

"Not until I show you."

Sampson had had enough chitchat. He ran hard at Rem.

My heart pounded.

Then Rem turned his back on the beast. And winked at me. Fucking winked!

"Rem!" I yelled, surprised my mouth still worked. Because the rest of me was completely frozen by fear.

But he didn't budge. Just stared at me, with a charging bull closing the distance between them. His mouth moved, and I thought he might have said, "Watch," but my blood was echoing so loud in my ears that I couldn't hear a thing. Sampson closed in; his horns lowered and ready to pierce through Rem's back. Yards turned into inches in the space of a second, and then Rem was flying through the air.

"No!" I yelled. He'd been hit. Gored. His body thrown through the air like a limp Muppet.

Then his legs tucked in. His head tilted back, and the movement became a controlled backflip that would have scored well at any gymnastics competition.

Until the dismount anyway.

He landed on his knees and flinched in pain, but got back on his feet anyway, running to the fence once more before Sampson could catch on to what had happened.

I scrambled to my feet and ran over to him, climbing the other side of the fence so we were face-to-face. I'd seen enough. I was going to pull him out of that pen myself if I had to and give him a piece of my mind while I was at it.

"Hi," he said, all cheek and wide grin.

"Don't 'hi' me!" I yelled.

"What should I do then?"

"Kiss me."

My reply shocked me as much as it shocked Rem. But then my lips were on his, all my fear and worry and guilt and regret over the way I'd acted pulsing through the places we were joined. My fingers digging into his shoulders. His palms on my hips. My lips, urgent against his.

He froze, but then he was kissing me back. Hot and hard and fast. Pulling me closer, urging me on.

Relief poured through me. He was fine. Safe.

And he was kissing me. Holy shit. He was kissing me again.

My heart rate accelerated, but this time, it wasn't nervous energy. His kiss made my heart pound in a way that was a million times more pleasant than when I'd been watching him risk his life to prove he wasn't the man I thought he was.

I yanked my head away. "Dammit, Rem! That was fucking stupid, and I hate you!"

I slapped his chest, but he caught me by the wrist and pressed his lips to mine again. The fire went out of me, and I sank into him, trusting he was strong enough to keep us balanced atop the fence. We kissed fast and hard until it turned softer and sweeter, and my head spun in dizzying circles, fueled by adrenaline and the pure masculinity of the man holding me in his arms. The whole world around us disappeared. There was no Sampson. No moon above us. No rustle of the wind through the trees. All that existed was me and him.

And the single gunshot that splintered the blissful moment into pieces.

15

REM

I've never jumped a fence as quickly as I did the moment that gunshot rang out. I grasped at Whitney's jacket, ready to pull her down with me, but she was quicker than I was. By the time I landed on the safe side, Whitney was already crouched, scanning the surroundings.

"I didn't bring my gun!" she hissed.

I turned to her, wide-eyed. "Do you think you need it?"

She gave me a look as if I was the most ridiculous person on the planet. "Well, yeah, Rem! If someone is shooting at us, we might want to be able to shoot back, don't you think?"

"I don't want to be having a shoot-out here! There's innocent people in that house, and down in the cabins!"

She crept along the fence line, moving us deeper into a shadow. "Well, let's hope it doesn't come to that, huh?"

My mind whirled a million miles an hour. If it was someone from Kings of Chaos, my old crew, they would have sent Shooter. But if they'd sent Shooter, I'd be dead already. That shot would have blown right through my skull, and probably Whitney's, too. Shooter didn't miss. Missing was more the style of the Devil Red MC. They didn't have guys who had army training like the Kings did. Still, even a fool with a gun was a dangerous fool.

"It sounded like it came from the house," Whitney said, her gaze trained in that direction. "Shit. I think there's someone on the porch."

Hunched over, she scooted closer. I followed tight, sticking close to her back.

A bright spotlight suddenly lit up from the porch of the house. We both froze.

"Who's out there? If you're a cattle rustler, stealing my animals, you can get on out of here. First shot was a warning. Next one won't be."

"Oh my God," Whitney said, choking on a laugh that sounded tinged with relief. "Mr. Wilden?" she called, louder this time. "It's just me, Whitney, and Rem. Your tenants?"

She relaxed back against the fence slightly and faced me. "Shit. Here I was thinking it was an entire MC we were going to have to deal with. Turns out it's an eighty-year-old man with a gnome collection."

"What are you kids doing out there?" he yelled. "Get away from that bull before you get yourself killed. Damn city folk!"

I was surprised he wasn't shaking his fist. "Crap. We're in trouble. I think I would have preferred to face down an MC than Scout and Gage's grandpa."

We both stood slowly, with our hands up, and the spotlight bounced over to us. The light blinded me, and I flinched away, blinking rapidly. The screen door slammed, and Gage and Scout both came out, firing questions at their grandfather, all of which he ignored, and stormed back into the house.

"What the fuck, Rem?" Gage called.

"Nothing, man. Go back to sleep. We were just taking a walk and we startled your grandfather. Sorry about that."

Gage shook his head. "Too tired for this tonight." He switched off the spotlight. The screen door slammed again as he and Scout disappeared back inside.

"Maybe we should go back to bed now?" I suggested to Whitney.

"You think?" she said with a laugh. "I can't believe you just nearly got us shot!"

"Um, I believe it was you who nearly got us shot."

Whitney turned incredulous eyes on me. "How do you figure that? You were the one in there, riling up a bull!"

We walked back along the path toward our cabin. I'd left my jacket on the grass in all the commotion, but I'd get it in the morning. I should have been cold. Snow wasn't far off, but adrenaline kept me warm.

"I was not riling him up. I was showing you what freestyle bullfighting is. And you loved it."

Her mouth dropped open, and she stopped to face me. "I loved it? How do you figure?"

"Because you kissed me," I said smugly. "And that's also why it's your fault. If we hadn't been standing there kissing, no shots would have been fired; no old men would have been angered. Seriously, Whitney. You're like a drama magnet." I could barely keep my laughter inside.

"You're completely insufferable, you know. If anyone is a drama magnet, it's you."

"You kissed me."

"Are you just going to keep saying that?"

I shrugged. We were nearing the cabins, and light poured out of ours. I frowned but then shrugged it off, not wanting to miss a chance to tease her. "I might just keep saying it until you kiss me again."

To my surprise, she moved in, rose on her toes, and brushed her lips over mine. I grabbed at her, wanting to deepen the kiss, but she skittered away, laughing. I chased after her until I caught her hand, right as we got to the row of cabins. I circled my fingers around her wrist and then slid them down until our fingers were entwined. She looked up at me in surprise, but a slow, shy smile spread across her face. Fuck, she took my breath away. She was letting me hold her hand and kiss her. Despite the fact we'd been shot at, I didn't think I'd ever had a better date in my life.

"Well, this is interesting," a voice said in the darkness.

Whitney dropped my hand and skittered away so quickly that if my palm wasn't tingling from her touch, I would have questioned if we'd even been holding hands.

"Dane? What are you doing over there, creeping in the dark?"

He stood up off a chair on his porch and came forward to lean on the rail. "Was about to ask you two the same thing. Heard a gunshot and got up to see what was going on. Was halfway there, but Gage sent a text that everything was fine. But now I'm sitting here on my porch, wondering why my new neighbors, who claim to be brother and sister, are holding hands and kissing in the moonlight."

Well, fuck. I groaned. Couldn't the guy just cut me a freaking break? Did he have to be so perceptive all the damn time? Though Whitney and I had been careless tonight. That part really was my fault. But I was so attracted to the woman, I didn't know how I was supposed to be around her and not give away our secret. "We're not brother and sister," I said to Dane.

Whitney elbowed me sharply.

I turned to her in exasperation. "Would you rather him think I'm fucking my sister?"

Whitney's mouth dropped open. "We aren't fucking at all!" She glared at Dane. "Seriously, we're not."

Dane's gaze flitted between the two of us like we'd both just grown an extra head. "So you aren't brother and sister? Or you are, but you aren't fucking? Just making out?"

"Not related. Not getting naked," I said. "That's about the gist of it."

Dane just looked more confused, his eyebrows pulling into a deep frown.

Whitney groaned. "We'll be out of here first thing in the morning, okay? If you could please just do me a favor and not alert the masses until then, that'd be great."

"What?" Dane and I both said in unison.

Panic coursed through me. If she told her boss our cover had been blown, we'd get sent back to the city. Which might be bearable if she was there, too, but what if she got removed from the case entirely and I didn't get to see her again? I wasn't going to let that happen.

"You can't go," Dane said. "Rem promised to help with the roundup."

"I agree with him," I said to Whitney. "We stay."

"Can't. Protocol."

"Already broke that, multiple times."

She put her hands on her hips and glared at me. "He knows we aren't who we say we are, Rem. That's dangerous."

I glanced over at Dane. He was studying us both silently.

"He's known since day one."

Whitney pinched the bridge of her nose as if I'd suddenly given her a headache. "What do you mean he's known since day one? Known what exactly?"

"That I'm Remington James. He saw my arrest. Put two and two together."

"And you didn't say anything to me? Jesus, Rem, he could have told the entire town we were here! I know this place is remote, but it just takes one person to mention it to the press, and then it becomes a scandal and we've got your old buddies storming this place with guns!"

"I didn't tell anyone," Dane said quietly. "I made a deal with Rem, and as long as he sticks to his end of the bargain, I'll stick to mine."

Whitney narrowed her eyes in Dane's direction. "And I'm just supposed to trust you? I don't even know you."

Dane shook his head. "You don't have to. Rem already did."

I stepped in closer to Whitney and squeezed her arm. "He's known for two weeks, babe. We can trust him."

She shook my hand off and glared at me. "Maybe I

can trust him, *babe*. But I obviously can't trust you, can I?" With that, she stormed off into our cabin.

Dane chuckled in the darkness. It was the first time I'd ever seen him so much as smile. "Shame she's not your sister, huh? Probably would have made your life less complicated right now."

He wasn't wrong.

16

WHITNEY

I stormed up the stairs of our cabin and stared at the open door for a moment. We'd turned out the light and shut the door behind us when we'd left. Hadn't we?

I reached for my gun and cursed when it wasn't in its usual spot. Damn Rem for pulling me out of bed in the middle of the night. And damn this ranch for lulling me into a false sense of security. What was I thinking, going anywhere without my gun? What was I thinking, kissing Rem out in the open, even if it was in the darkness? I'd become too careless.

Rem came up the stairs behind me.

I held up a hand in a stop motion. "Did you shut the door and turn out the lights?"

"I was wondering that myself. I thought we did."

"Me, too."

Rem's strong fingers wrapped around my arm and squeezed it gently. "Get behind me," he said quietly. "I'll go first."

I shook my head. "Uh, no. Cop. Civilian," I said, gesturing between the two of us. "I go first."

Rem grumbled something beneath his breath, then, "We go together."

"Fine, whatever," I snapped at him, still cranky he'd been keeping secrets from me the entire time we'd been here.

"On the count of three. One, two—"

I didn't wait for three. I darted around the doorframe.

To a completely empty room.

"Dammit, Whit! We said three!"

"No, *you* said three," I whispered back, grabbing my gun from my open top drawer. I stalked toward the bathroom, while Rem went for the closet. They were the only two doors in the small cabin, and really, the only two places anyone could hide. We both jerked open our doors in unison, though neither of us uttered a word to coordinate it.

"Clear," Rem said.

I rolled my eyes. The bathroom was also 'clear,' as Rem put it. I shoved my gun into the waistband of my jeans and came back into the main room, casting an eye around. "Anything look out of place to you?"

"No. You?"

"Nope."

Rem went over and peered out the window. "Might have been Dane. Maybe he came to get us when he heard the gunshot. We can ask him tomorrow."

"No point. We'll be leaving once I report that our cover has been blown."

Rem sighed and leaned back on the wall. He crossed

his arms over his chest, but he didn't look angry. Just sad. "I don't want to leave."

I softened a little. "Look, I'll ask for another country location, okay?"

He cocked his head to the side. "Do you come with the new location as well?"

My heart pounded. "I don't know," I said truthfully, "but I doubt it. I'll be pulled from the case most likely."

"That's what I thought." He pushed off the wall and crossed the room, stopping right in front of me. I had to tilt my head back to keep my gaze trained on him.

"Don't try to convince me otherwise," I said stubbornly. "I have to report this."

"I wasn't going to. I'm sorry I didn't tell you about Dane."

"You should be. That was stupid."

"I know." He tucked a stray lock of hair behind my ear. His fingers trailed down the side of my neck.

Despite myself, I shivered beneath his touch.

"Let me make it up to you."

I rolled my eyes. "You didn't even try to make that sound platonic."

"So it sounded sexual? Good. That's how I meant it."

I sighed. "Haven't you heard anything I've been saying?"

He grasped my chin and lowered his head until his lips hovered over mine. "I heard. But if this is our last night here, I want to make it count. If you aren't going to be my guard any longer, then we aren't hurting anyone if we're together tonight. Right?"

I wavered, even though my gaze kept involuntarily

dropping to his lips. Heat tingled my skin at the very thought of spending the rest of the night with him.

"Don't say no," he whispered, leaning in, his lips brushing the side of my neck. He gathered up my hair and moved it out of his way, and dammit if I didn't tilt my head, giving him better access. "Please, Whit," he whispered between slow kisses to my neck. "This ends as soon as you pick up that phone. We both know it. And I don't want to walk away not knowing what you feel like. What you taste like."

My resolve cracked. A shiver rolled down my spine, pushing me off the wall and into his arms. I linked mine around his neck and fused my mouth to his. It was a silent yes, but it was somehow still so very loud. It echoed around me as if I'd screamed it.

Rem kissed me back hard, snatching my breath, his fingers digging into my hips as he lifted me into his arms.

I wrapped my legs around him, and his erection rubbed against my core. I moaned into his mouth, eager to get him out of his jeans and feel all that he had beneath them. He walked us to the bed with my fingers spearing into his hair, tugging him closer, scratching at his scalp. He laid me out on the bed, and I yelped, his big body coming down on top of me.

"Shit, you okay?" he asked, rearing back.

I laughed. "Fine. I just have a gun pressing into my kidney."

He grasped my hand and heaved me into a sitting position. "Do you trust me?" he asked again.

"You're beginning to sound like Aladdin, you know."

He raised one eyebrow in question.

"Do you trust me? That's what Aladdin says to Jasmine. It's what gives away his true identity."

A smile lifted the corners of his mouth. "I'll take that as a compliment. I always thought Aladdin was a handsome dude."

"He was my favorite," I admitted.

"I'm going to be your favorite by the time this night is through. But you didn't answer my question. Do you trust me?"

Despite his earlier lie, I nodded. He might have lied, but I trusted him not to physically hurt me. And to prove it, I let him take the gun from the back of my jeans. He looked it over for the briefest of moments before putting it on the bedside table.

"Like it?" I asked.

He pushed me back on the bed and covered me with his big body once more. "Not as much as I like you. Let me show you."

He hesitated, waiting for my permission, and when I nodded, he kissed me again. The weight of him on top of me was delicious, and we kissed like we were sixteen-year-olds, completely hot for each other but not quite ready to get naked yet. I wrapped my jean-clad legs around his waist, and we ground against each other until I was hot and needy. Only then, when I was frantically ripping at Rem's clothes to no avail, did he grab my wrists. He gathered them up above my head and locked my fingers around the wooden post of the headboard.

"Don't let go," he warned.

My hips jerked as if they had a mind of their own, but he'd moved to straddle them, so my core was left wanting, missing the feel of him. His erection strained at his jeans, and I longed to reach out, undo his zipper, and take him into my eager hands. But I'd been told not to let go. And that was fucking hot. As much as I wanted to touch and taste him, I ached to have him touch me first. So I held tight to the spindle and tried not to squirm when his fingertips ran the hem of my long-sleeved shirt, floating over the skin of my belly. He pushed the material up, taking all the layers I had on with him, until my stomach and my bra were exposed. I lifted my shoulders so he could get the shirt over my head, but he didn't even bother removing it all the way. It gathered up around my wrists. His mouth, hands, and eyes all drew back to my bare skin and white cotton bra.

I suddenly wished I'd put on the lacy black set, but Rem didn't seem to care that my underwear was practical, rather than sexy. His big hands cupped my breasts, his thumb rubbing over my already hard nipples, and I wriggled beneath him, wanting more.

His fingers snuck beneath my back, undoing my bra clasp before it followed the rest of my clothes, landing up by my head. I let go of the spindle to move them aside, but Rem caught my fingers. "I said, don't let go."

"But—"

He kissed me hard, bruising my lips. "You're not the boss right now."

His hand locked around mine as he slid down my body, leaving a trail of hot, open-mouthed kisses in his wake. When he finally let go of my wrists, I didn't dare move. I didn't want him to stop.

I arched my back up off the bed, needing more, and his hot mouth landed on one nipple. Sensation sparked through me, agony and exhilaration all at once. His tongue swirled around me, then moved to the other side while his fingers glided to my belly and straight into my jeans.

"Oh!" I moaned, his finger reaching my clit.

Fuck, that felt good. So much better than if I'd been doing it myself, thinking about his face. Having him here, touching me, kissing me, his face hovering over mine—it was all a thousand times better than how I'd imagined it would be. I'd always been the dominant one in every-thing I did. And that included sex. I liked being on top. Being in control. When was the last time I'd surrendered to just being purely pleased by a partner?

I couldn't remember.

Rem's fingers left my sex, and I whimpered.

"You better believe I'm going back there," he promised. "I got impatient. I need to get these jeans off you."

"Hell, yes. Get them off."

He grinned and shifted to the edge of the bed. He yanked off my shoes and socks and made quick work of my jeans, taking my cotton panties with him. Cool air washed over my skin and between my slightly parted thighs. Goosebumps rose, but I wasn't cold. Not in the least. I was more turned on than I'd ever been, and that kept me warm. Being fully naked in front of a man who was still fully clothed was somehow so erotic. I liked it. But I wanted to see him naked more.

"Take your clothes off," I whispered, making my words soft, even though there was a demand in my state-ment. "I want to see you."

For a moment, I wasn't sure Rem had even heard me. His gaze raked over my flesh, taking me higher and higher in my need for him, until I thought I might self-combust if he didn't quit looking and start touching. But then he toed off his boots and socks. His shirt was next, gone in a flash of fabric and dropped on the floor.

I sucked in a breath. Smooth, tanned skin covered tight, taut muscles that rippled across his abdomen. His pecs were defined, his chest covered with a smattering of dark hair that turned into a happy trail that led beneath the denim of his jeans.

Fuck hanging on to the bedpost any longer. I sat up and prowled across the bed. I flicked the button of his jeans, and he let me yank them down his legs, taking simple blue boxer briefs with me. His erection sprang free. He was long, hard, and thick. And so damn suckable I couldn't resist. With my hands and knees pressing into the lumpy springs of the mattress, I took the head of him in my mouth.

He hissed, swearing low under his breath, and as my lips slid down his cock, he gathered my hair up, pulling it back off my face. Then he tugged it sharply. It didn't hurt, in fact, if he'd done it again, I would have welcomed it. Except for the fact it moved me away from where I wanted to be.

"This isn't how this was supposed to go, but your mouth is amazing. I don't want to stop you."

I grinned, and let my tongue dart out to lick at the tip of him. "Then don't."

I took his dick in my mouth once more, sucking and blowing and using my tongue to massage the thick vein that ran up the underside of him.

"Eyes on me," he said, voice low.

Wetness seeped between my legs at the command,

and his hand came to rest on the back of my head. I stared up at him while I took him deeper and deeper into my mouth, loving the way his gaze burned me. There was no pressure on the back of my head, he let me set the pace and the speed, but his fingers clenched and relaxed in my hair as I built his pleasure.

Pushing up so I was balanced only on my knees, I wrapped one hand around the base of his cock and the other around his balls. The salty taste of his arousal urged me on, until he pulled away sharply.

"Fuck, Whit," he panted, abs contracting. "You're going to make me embarrass myself if you keep doing that. It's too good."

I didn't even have time to feel good about that before he was tilting my chin up to kiss me again. Our kiss tasted of him, but he didn't seem to mind. His tongue plunged inside my mouth, and I groaned at how deep and hot this was. It ricocheted all the way down to my core.

He dropped his knees to the floor. "Sit on the edge of the mattress," he said hoarsely.

I did as I was told, scooting into a sitting position. He kissed me again, then spread my legs wide, baring all of me to his view, and fitted himself in between. "Lie back."

The mattress squeaked beneath me, but I barely heard it over my gasp. Rem's mouth covered my sex. He was unforgiving, wasting no time in getting to where I wanted him most. He parted my lower lips with his tongue, pushing inside me and retreating, flicking up over my clit, then doing it all again. Like they had a mind of their own, my legs spread wider, and I brought my feet up to rest on his shoulders. I was so naked, so vulnerable, and yet I didn't feel it. I trusted him. Trusted him with my pleasure. With my body.

When his fingers delved deep inside me, the world around me spun. My thighs shook, and I suddenly realized my moans of pleasure were filling the room. The sounds shocked me. I'd never been one to make a lot of noise during sex, but the moans and cries fell from my lips with no chance of stopping them. They grew louder and louder as Rem's magic fingers and tongue worked in unison, and I writhed on the bed, desperate for relief.

"Rem!" I yelled, knowing it was too loud and just not giving a fuck. I needed to release the pent-up tension inside me somehow, and since he wasn't letting me finish, yelling was the only way it was going to happen. "I need to come," I groaned.

"I got you," he said, his voice deep and husky. For the briefest of moments, everything stopped, and then there was the crinkle of a condom wrapper.

I blinked open one eye, ready to make a joke about how quickly he'd got that on, but then he was dipping the head of him inside me, and all coherent thought went straight out the window.

"Hold on," he said gruffly. "I can't be gentle with you screaming my name like that. You're so hot. Just need to be inside you."

I pressed my fingernails into the skin of his back, and his muscles rippled beneath my palms.

"Gonna fuck you now, Whit. Hard and fast. Because I got to. And then I'm gonna do it soft and slow, I promise. Just hold on."

"I will." The words were little more than a breathy

agreement. I was already so high I couldn't get down without him. I'd take him any way he wanted to have me.

Rem's hips slammed home. His cock filled me, stretched me, and every inch was perfect. That was all it took to send me over the edge. My orgasm roared through my body, my internal walls spasming and clenching down on his thick length. I yelled his name again while stars danced across my vision. He withdrew almost the entire way, and I cried out at the loss of him before he soothed the ache once more. His thrusts were fast and strong, each one filling me completely. Our hips met, our skin slapping around the noise of my cries and his groans. I closed my eyes and just let pleasure fill every cell of my body. He was right. It was all I could do to just hold on. My legs flopped out, too exhausted to wrap around him any longer, and I held him while he slid in and out of my body. My hips lifted with each thrust, his movements growing faster until his big frame shook over me.

He cried out his release, my name on his lips. His mouth caressed my neck, and I held him as he rode it out, my own orgasm still pulsing around him. His weight pressed down on me, his body stilling, and I raked my nails down his back, while we both fought in vain to catch our breath.

He felt good. He felt...right. There was no room in this space for regrets. I had none. I'd slept with a man who was off-limits, but I couldn't bring myself to regret it. I'd never had sex like that in my life, and I doubted I ever would again. There was no possible way I could regret what we'd just done.

Rem rolled off me, and I was still lying splayed out,

completely boneless on top of the covers, when he returned from disposing of the condom in the bathroom.

With one lazy eye, I watched him walk naked, back toward the bed. He frowned at me. "You're going to get cold like that. Do you want to have a shower?"

I shook my head. "I don't think I can move."

"Because it was good?"

I laughed, because for once, he hadn't sounded cocky and self-assured. It had sounded like an honest-to-God question. "Are you serious right now, Rem? That wasn't good. That was mind-blowing."

Relief filled his expression, and he climbed back onto the bed beside me, trailing fingertips all over my bare skin. I shivered as he traced a nipple.

"You're cold," he said, pulling back the blankets.

"I'm horny," I replied with a laugh. "Or sensitive, rather. I don't know. But you touch me, and my body trembles in response."

He chuckled and gathered me up, tucking himself in behind me, then lifted the covers over the both of us. "Then get in here and let me make you tremble some more."

I shifted my hips back, expecting to find him limp after the workout we'd just given his cock. But he was already getting hard again. His semi nudged my backside.

"Are you freaking kidding me? Already?"

He kissed my shoulder. "If I only get one night, I'm going all night, Whit. And I mean, all night."

I trembled again. But this time it was in anticipation.

17

REM

I didn't want the dawn to come. But inevitably it did, and when the first rays of the new morning roused me from sleep, I opened my eyes and found Whitney's naked body still in my arms.

She breathed slowly and softly, letting me know the sun hadn't roused her yet. My dick was hard again, though I had no idea how. We'd screwed like rabbits all night. Four, maybe five times. I'd lost count. But I couldn't get enough of her. Her body was pure heaven, and the way she responded to my every touch only made me want to touch her more. She tasted of sweet honey, and I could have set up camp between her thighs and died there a happy man. Fuck, her screaming my name when she came...I'd never heard anything sexier. Even now, I just wanted to wake her up and spread her legs and just devour her until she held me to her sensitive flesh and begged me not to stop.

But she'd be sore this morning. In a good way, I hoped, but she'd liked it when I was rough and had begged for it whenever I'd tried to slow things down. Fuck, if that wasn't the hottest thing ever.

There was one thing I knew for certain after last night. Whitney had ruined me for all other women. I'd never had a night like that, and I instinctively knew I never would again. People didn't just connect so easily. One-night stands were normally quick and awkward and messy. But Whit and I had been coordinated and instinctive and just...right. Mind-blowing. In more ways than one.

I didn't want it to be a one-night thing. I wanted sex like that for the rest of my life. But with Whitney and I being separated today, I'd be back to relationships that fizzled out, or single nights with women I didn't care about.

That thought left me feeling hollower than I'd ever felt in my life.

I shifted closer to Whitney and tried to memorize the feel of her body and the smell of her skin.

"What time is it?" she mumbled. Her fingers laced through mine, and with relief, I pressed my lips to her skin again. I'd hold her until the very last moment, when she'd push me away.

"Time to not call your boss?" I asked hopefully.

Whitney rolled over in my arms. She looked tired, but considering how little sleep we'd had, I wasn't surprised.

"I have to," she said softly. "You know that."

I nodded. I knew. I'd known the entire time that she would do the right thing and call it in.

"At least we had one night," she said.

"Not enough," I mumbled.

"What was that?" she asked, a frown creasing her forehead.

I smoothed it away with my thumb. "Nothing. Go back to sleep. It's too early to call anyone."

To my dismay, she got out of bed anyway, pulling the sheet around her. Something inside me deflated. She was self-conscious with me already, and I hated that. I wanted her strutting around naked, knowing my eyes were on her and that I thought she was the hottest, most beautiful, most desirable woman in the world. Because she fucking was. That body shouldn't ever be covered up in front of me.

But I bit my lip, knowing that it wouldn't make a difference. I could already feel the space between us in that one movement.

When she paused in the bathroom doorway, the gap widened into a chasm. "Thanks for last night, Rem. It was amazing."

I studied her for the briefest moment, and then nodded. "You're welcome." *You're welcome? What the actual fuck, Rem?* I waited until the sound of running water started up in the bathroom and then I rolled over and groaned into the pillow.

I was fucking pathetic. And I needed to get a grip if I was going to survive leaving her today.

18

WHITNEY

ater ran in rivulets down my body, and I chased them with a sponge, loaded up with soapsuds. My body bore the proof of what Rem and I had done last night. My skin still hummed, and small love bites covered my cleavage. Water ran between my legs, over the still swollen and sensitive flesh of my well-worked sex.

I leaned against the shower wall, barely noticing how cold it was, when the memories of last night burned so hot through my mind. I closed my eyes, and felt all over again, Rem's body covering mine. His thick cock inside me, filling me. His fingers bringing more pleasure than I'd ever felt in my life. And something more than that. A connection that had taken me by surprise. It hadn't felt like fucking a random stranger. We barely knew each other, and yet we'd moved together as if we'd been doing it all our lives.

And I was about to end the entire thing before it had even really started.

Tears welling in the backs of my eyes took me by surprise, and I shook my head, wiping at my face before they could spill over. I was being ridiculous. I was here to do a job, and right now my job was to report that our covers had been blown. First and foremost, I had to keep Rem safe. And that meant calling my boss and organizing our way out.

The thought left me cold, and no amount of hot water or remembering what we'd done last night could warm me.

I turned off the shower and got out, shivering as I wrapped an old pale-blue towel around me. I twisted another around my hair before I realized I'd forgotten to take clothes into the bathroom with me. Sighing, I covered my eyes with one hand, and with the other, I opened the bathroom door, letting out a billow of steam into the main room. Walking blind, I felt my way around the furniture, ignoring the fact that even though I couldn't see the very naked man in my bed, I knew he was there. After last night, every cell of my body was attuned to him, drawn to him like a magnet, begging me to drop my towel and crawl back into bed with him.

"Whit?" he asked, laughter behind his words.

"Mmm?" I fumbled around the walls with one hand, searching for the bureau.

"Um, why do you have your hand over your eyes? You're the one in the towel. Shouldn't it be me who's not looking?"

I shook my head. "I trust you more than I trust me."

"Trust me to do what?" His voice was suddenly closer, and I shivered at his nearness.

"Trust you to do the right thing. We said one night. It's

not night anymore. And I've got to call my boss. But I forgot my clothes and I can't look at you when I'm naked and you're naked and...I just need my clothes."

I squeezed my eyes tighter when his lips landed on my shoulder, his tongue tracing a path up my neck. "Rem," I warned.

"You had water there. I was just helping you dry off."

Nothing about his lips and tongue on my neck was making me *dry*.

Something soft pressed against my outstretched hand, and when I peeked through my fingers, Rem was handing me my clothes with a very solemn look on his face.

Completely naked, but his face was serious.

I dropped my hand, unable to control my laughter. "You're terrible."

"That's not what you said last night."

He was right there. Dammit. "I don't want to call my boss," I admitted.

He stepped in and put an arm around me. Despite knowing I shouldn't, I let my head rest on his chest. The fuzz of hair there tickled my cheek, but he was warm and comforting, and I liked being in his arms.

"I don't want you to call her either, but I know you will. It's the right thing to do, and that's who you are."

Yeah, I was the woman who did the right thing in the morning. Not so much in the darkness. I pulled away. "I need to get dressed."

Rem sighed then kissed the top of my head. He grabbed some clothes from his own drawer and with one last lingering look, trudged into the bathroom.

Guilt coursed through me. I knew he didn't want me

to make the call. *I* didn't want to make it either. I'd already embarrassed myself in front of my work colleagues with the whole Karsten situation. Now I was going to admit that a witness under my protection had blown his cover. It might not have been directly my fault, but it still didn't look good.

I put on my clothes while Rem showered, and then I sat in one of the armchairs. I tucked my feet up beneath me, and with sluggish movements, I dialed Janice's number.

It took her so long to answer I almost gave up. But right as my finger was moving toward the cancel button, her clipped voice sounded in my ear.

"Whitney? Anything wrong?"

The urge to say 'no' was overwhelming. "My witness' cover has been compromised. I need to organize to have him moved. And to have someone else assigned to the case."

Janice sighed. "Compromised, how?"

"One of the ranch hands here recognized him two weeks ago. I'm sorry, Sergeant. I only found out last night, too late to call." Too late to do anything but have wild monkey sex with the witness anyway. Shit. I was a terrible fucking detective. I should be fired.

I scrubbed my hands over my face, waiting for Janice to tell me off.

"Two weeks ago? And nothing has happened in that time that makes you think your witness is in danger?"

I sat up a little straighter. "Uh, no."

The open door to our cabin flashed through my mind, but I quickly dismissed the thought. If Dane had been in our room, he hadn't done anything. Nothing had moved. Nothing had been taken. More likely than not, the old door hadn't latched properly, and the wind had blown it open. And we'd probably just left the light on ourselves.

"Then I have all faith that you can handle the situation. Threaten the guy with jail time. Have him sign a non-disclosure agreement. I don't care. I've got a case that's blowing up and the press on my ass, and I don't have time to rehome a criminal who's decided to tattle on his friends."

"He's not a—" *Criminal.* That was what I had been going to say. The man who I'd gotten to know in the last two weeks—who made me laugh and made me scream his name in bed—he wasn't any more a bad guy than I was.

"You broke up there, Whitney. He's not a what?" Janice questioned.

I could practically hear her tapping her foot, impatient to get off the phone. From the buzz in the background, I could tell she was already at work, despite the early hour. Or perhaps she hadn't been to sleep yet, and that was part of why she was so short and uncaring about the situation. Either way, I didn't question her. That wasn't my place, and I knew it. If she'd told me to handle it, I'd handle it.

"He's not a problem," I said. "The witness or the ranch hand. I'll deal with both."

"Good," Janice said. "You've only got a few more weeks, and then you'll be back for the trial anyway. Just keep your head down. You'll do fine."

"Of course. Just one other thing. How is Mia?"

I bit my lip waiting for an answer. It had been two

weeks since Mia had been attacked, and a full week since I'd had any news on her.

Janice's voice was softer when she answered. "Better, last I heard. They'd brought her out of the induced coma, but she's still on very heavy painkillers and hasn't been able to be questioned yet."

"No leads on her attacker then?"

"Nothing yet. Once she can talk, I'll send our best team over to see her, though."

I knew Janice would. She might have had little sympathy for Rem, but she cared for the team she ran. I knew that. It was why she'd sent me here. It was why I believed her when she said she was doing everything she could for Mia.

"Okay, thank you. For everything. I'll let you go."

"Take care, Detective."

"You, too," I said quietly, but she'd already hung up.

It was only after I sat there looking at the phone, with the sound of Rem's shower still running in the background, that I considered the fact I hadn't even thought to ask about Karsten, and whether he'd made bail or had a trial date set. With pleasure, I realized it was because I really didn't care.

I paced the room, waiting for Rem to get out of the shower, completely unsure how to feel about the fact we weren't going anywhere. My stomach flip-flopped in excitement and anticipation of telling him we weren't leaving earlier than planned. But as quickly as excitement surfaced, so did doubt. We'd agreed this thing would only be one night. It had only happened because it was supposed to be one night. But I already knew I wouldn't be able to stay away from him. I'd had a taste, and like a junkie, I already wanted more. More of the way he looked at me. More of the way his hands on my body made me feel. But we hadn't discussed any of that before we'd fallen into bed last night. We'd made no promises. No commitments. I couldn't expect anything just because we'd had one night of hot sex.

I shoved my hands in my pockets and contemplated banging on the bathroom door to hurry him up, but I still didn't exactly know what I was going to say, so that didn't seem like a wise plan either.

Banging on the front door of the cabin startled me out of my whirlwind thoughts, and I rushed to open it.

Dane stood on the other side. His cowboy hat was pulled low on his forehead, a red-and-blue-checked shirt poking out beneath a sheepskin-lined jacket. "Rem in?"

I eyed him critically. I needed to do a background search on him, though how I could do that from all the way out here in the middle of nowhere I didn't exactly know. I wondered if the house had Wi-Fi I could tap into. Reception in the cabin was dodgy at best, and though I could receive the odd email, I didn't fancy my chances doing any real detective work from a phone that dropped internet connection every few minutes. I opened the door wider. "In the shower. But come in. I wanted to talk to you."

Dane cocked his head to the side but didn't step through the doorway. "'Bout what?"

"What's your story?" If he had nefarious plans, it wasn't as if he'd tell me, but hey, didn't hurt to ask.

"Thirty-six. Single. Worked here on the ranch for twelve years. Virgo. Eldest son of three—"

"I said your story, not your dating profile."

Dane's gaze swept my body, but it wasn't in the same sexual way that heated my blood like when Rem did it. Dane's gaze was sharp and calculating. Like he was sizing me up, determining whether I was a worthy competitor.

"What's yours?"

"I'm a detective."

"I said your story, not what's on your badge."

I didn't say anything.

A smile spread across Dane's face. "That's what I thought. How 'bout we make a deal? You tell me yours, I'll tell you mine."

Yeah, that wasn't going to happen. I wasn't making deals with a man I knew nothing about. "Rem and I are staying," I said, choosing my words carefully. "I'm going to need you to sign an agreement that says you won't reveal our identities. I'll throw every charge I can think of at you if you put him in danger. And I can be *real* creative."

Dane chuckled. "And if I do, you'll help with the roundup? Both of you?"

What the hell was it about this roundup? But I nodded.

"Just show me where to sign, then."

Relief settled over me. I'd looked the man in the eye, and he'd given his word. I was still wary, but the back of my neck hadn't prickled the way it did when I knew someone was feeding me bullshit. That didn't mean I'd take my eye off him. I'd have one eye on Rem, the other on Dane. Just in very different ways.

19

REM

With my ear plastered to the bathroom door, I caught the end of Whitney's conversation with Dane. Dane's heavy footsteps clumped down the porch steps, and I did a little on-the-spot dance, gyrating my hips until my towel slipped off. But who cared? I cock-pumped the air like a lunatic.

I froze when the door opened, mid hip thrust, with my arms in the air.

Whitney raised one eyebrow. "I guess you heard that then, huh?"

I dropped my arms and rushed her, not caring I was naked and still dripping water from the ends of my hair. "Hell yes, I heard! We're staying?" I pulled her tight to my chest and squeezed her, picking her up off her feet and swinging her around.

She batted at my chest.

I released her, frowning when her expression wasn't one of riotous joy. "What's wrong?"

"Nothing, I just don't know where this leaves us. Are

we a thing now? Are we roommates? Just because Dane knows the truth, doesn't mean we can go blabbing it to everyone. Scout, Gage, and Ollie still don't know, and we need to keep it that way. We can't be doing what we did last night, all over the ranch."

I groaned.

"What?" she asked, shoving her hands on her hips.

"I'm just thinking about fucking you on every available surface of this ranch. Out on the porch. Up against the wall of the barn. On the grass beside Mr. Lolly Golly…"

She cracked a smile. "You want to do the nasty with that creepy gnome watching?"

"Ha!" I yelled. "See! You think they're creepy, too!"

She shook her head and reached around me to grab a towel from the bathroom. She thrust it into my chest. "For Christ's sake, Rem, we need to actually have a serious conversation, and I can't do that when you're getting hard over garden gnomes."

I grudgingly took the towel, muttering it wasn't the garden gnome I was getting hard over, no matter how much that little creep gave me the eye.

But she was right. She sat on the bed, watching as I put my clothes on, and then I sat beside her, twisting so we faced each other. I picked up her hand from her lap, and slowly, giving her time to pull away if she wanted, I laced my fingers between hers and brought them to my lips. Her knuckles were probably the one place on her body I hadn't kissed last night, and so I brushed my lips over each one while I watched her face, trying to gauge her expression.

"Rem, I—"

I leaned in and kissed her, silencing the protest I knew was coming. "Let me speak first? Please?"

She nodded, pressing her lips together into a line.

Shit. Tougher audience than I'd been expecting. But I'd win her over. Not with jokes this time. "I want to be with you," I said earnestly. "I know it's only been weeks, but I've never wanted anyone more than I want you right now. Last night was amazing, but it wasn't enough. I want to hold your hand and wake up with you in the mornings and make love to you at night. I know this is all too much too fast, but I'm putting it out there anyway because we're on borrowed time. And until just a few minutes ago, I thought this was all going to end."

She let out a long sigh. "That's...nice."

My heart sank. "But? I sense a but."

"But there's so many reasons why we can't just jump into a relationship."

"Name one."

"I'm a cop. You're a witness."

"We already crossed that line. What else you got?"

She frowned. "Fine, fair enough. How about the fact my relationship of two years just ended the day we met."

My lip curled at the very mention of her ex. "Do you still love him?"

I knew it was unfair to ask, but I did want to know.

She shrugged. "No. I don't think so, but how can that even be? You don't just fall out of love with someone in two weeks. I should still be in the wearing sweatpants and eating ice cream straight from the tub stage."

"Yet, it was my name you were moaning last night. I didn't hear a single murmur about ice cream."

She rolled her eyes, but her smile was widening. "You're so fucking cocky."

"I think you like it."

"I think I like you," she said softly. "But I'm not ready for a relationship. Sex is one thing. But what you're asking for is more than that. Isn't it?"

I shook my head quickly. "Forget what I said. If what you want is just sex, then that's what I want, too."

"Don't be a guy."

"I'm not trying to be. I'm just trying to give you what you want, Whit. Don't you realize I'll be whatever you need me to be? If that's a relationship, then I'm in. If that's just sex, then you already know I'm really good at that, and if you've forgotten, get naked, and I'll show you again. Please say you've forgotten?"

She shook her head, her eyes twinkling. "I haven't forgotten."

"Damn," I swore with a laugh. "I was really hoping you had memory problems." I sobered again and rubbed her palm with my thumb. "In all seriousness, if we can only be friends, I'll accept that, too. Just tell me what you want. I'll give it to you."

She pressed one hand to the side of my face. "Who are you?" she whispered. "And why are you still single?"

I shrugged.

She brushed her lips over mine. "I can't stay away from you," she said against my mouth. "I already know that. I crossed a line I never would have crossed for anyone else, but something about you is damn near irresistible, Remington James. But this can only be sex. I'm not ready for more. And the others can't know."

I forced my expression to hold. I'd meant it when I'd

said I'd be whatever she wanted me to be. I just wanted the chance to get to know her better. It didn't matter that the flickering light inside me died when she said that all we were was sex. Sex was a whole lot better than never seeing her again, which was exactly where I'd thought we were going to be by the end of this day. Instead, I'd get to go to bed with her tonight, and hold her close and kiss her until our bodies melded together. That was so much better than being alone.

"Just sex, and just in this cabin. Got it." I gave her a mock salute.

She caught my wrist, her small fingers wrapping around it, not even meeting on the other side. I let her tug me toward her. She winked before our mouths met. "Just sex, but perhaps not *just* in this cabin. The idea of you going down on me while Mr. Lolly Golly watches is actually kinda hot."

Have mercy. She was going to bring me to my knees. And I was going to love every minute of it.

20

WHITNEY

"What are you smiling about?" Scout asked the minute I walked into the barn.

The smile fell right off my face, morphing into a frown. "What? I'm not smiling?"

Scout grabbed my arm and towed me to the other side of the horse stalls, away from the men who were sorting through the storage room. Tents and poles and sleeping bags were being tossed out, ready to be inspected before we packed to leave for the roundup tomorrow.

"Rem, the tent with the green stripe is yours," Gage called, directing traffic. "Red one is for Whit."

Scout didn't seem interested in making sure she got a bedroll or the sleeping bag with the extra-high star rating, since it was going to be near freezing camping outside at this time of year. She pushed me into a space hidden from view of the guys, though they hardly seemed interested in what we were doing anyway.

"You had sex!" she hissed. "That smile on your face is universal girl code for 'I just got laid'!"

I pulled my arm from hers. "Sssh! What are you talking about? I did not!"

"Then why did you shush me?"

"Because you're crazy, and I don't want the guys sending in the men in white coats to get you. Who the hell would I have been having sex with? Your grandpa?"

She recoiled and wrinkled her nose. "Ew, Whit. Why? Why would you say that?"

I giggled. "Sorry. I know."

"Was it Ollie? It was Ollie, wasn't it?"

I shook my head. Ollie was handsome, but he was barely twenty-one. Way too young for me.

"Dane then? Oh God." She screwed up her face, and for a moment I thought she was going to dry heave. "It was Gage, wasn't it? Oh, that's just gross. Don't tell me anymore. I don't want to hear about my brother in bed."

I laughed and linked my arm through hers, steering her back toward the guys. "It was totally Gage." I nodded as enthusiastically as possible while trying not to laugh.

"What was Gage?" Gage asked, poking his head out from the storeroom. His cheek was streaked with dirt, and his gaze darted between his sister and me.

"Scout was just asking about the night of wild monkey sex we had."

Gage's eyebrows shot sky-high at the same time Scout moaned about throwing up in her mouth.

"What?" Rem growled, his gaze staring me down.

Tingles darted across my skin at the intensity of his stare.

"See!" Scout shouted. She sidled up to Rem. "Siblings should not discuss these things in front of each other!"

Gage just watched the entire scene unfold with a confused furrow on his brow. "How much did I drink last night?" he muttered to Ollie, and I laughed under my breath.

Scout patted Rem on the arm and gazed up at him. "It sucks you're gay, Rem. If you weren't, we could pay them back with some fun of our own."

"Oh, come on!" Gage yelled. "Don't talk like that in front of me!"

Ollie shook his head. "Too much sibling rivalry going on here. Let's get a beer." He shoved Dane toward the door.

Dane didn't need asking twice. He hightailed it out of the barn.

But at the last minute, Ollie stuck his head back in. "You're gay?" he asked Rem.

"No, I'm not," Rem said through gritted teeth.

"You're not?" Scout asked, hope lighting up her eyes. She turned to me. "But you said—"

"My *sister* over there says a lot of things, apparently. We need to have a talk about that." While everyone else had been playing around, Rem's expression was serious.

Scout's eyes went wide. Gage wiped his hands on the back of his jeans and grabbed his sister by the elbow. "Come on, leave them be."

"But, I—"

"But nothing, quit being nosy. Let them talk. See you up at the house, okay?"

Rem watched their backs until they disappeared out of the barn. The moment they rounded the corner, he stalked over to me, his eyes dark. A little thrill rushed through me as I let him walk me back until I hit the barn wall.

"You slept with Gage, huh?"

I grinned and shrugged, his arms caging me in. "Would that bother you?"

"Yes."

The word was a full-blown, possessive alpha growl, and it curled my toes in the most delicious way. I loved the Rem who goofed around and made me laugh, but this side of him was something else. Hot. Powerful. *Mine.*

"What ya going to do about it, then?" I was goading him deliberately, wanting to see where this went.

He leaned in so close the outdoorsy scent of him filled my nose. He smelled of dirt and sweat, and beneath that, a soap scent clung to his skin from his shower that morning. It was an intoxicating mixture, one I never would have thought I'd like just a few weeks ago. But Rem's scent drove me mad. He ran his nose up my neck, and his fingers came to the button on my jeans. He popped it open and slid down the zip.

"Is this what you wanted me to do?" he murmured. "Claim you? Make you remember that nobody else gets to touch you here?" He slipped his fingers beneath my panties and cupped me. A gasp escaped me. Anyone could come back at any minute and we'd be caught red-handed. But fuck. The thought of getting caught. His hands down my underwear. His words... Hot.

"We said this was just casual," I murmured back between gasps, as his fingers searched for my clit. "I'm not yours."

"No?" Rem questioned. In one strong movement, he

yanked my jeans and panties down my thighs, baring my sex and ass to the cool afternoon air. "Turn around."

I didn't hesitate. Twisting, I faced the wooden barn wall, using my hands to support myself. My breaths came in short, sharp pants, and moisture beaded between my legs. I'd never been one for public sex. I was a cop, for fuck's sake, and it was illegal. But when Rem bent me over a little and pushed my shirts up so my ass was on full display, I didn't stop him. In fact, a small moan slipped from my mouth.

His palms skated over the cheeks of my ass, and then a stinging slap sounded in my ears. I flinched and jerked my head back, twisting to look over my shoulder at him. "Did you just spank me?"

He raised one eyebrow. "Did you like it?"

I bit my lip but couldn't keep the grin off my face. Because did I like it? Oh God, yes. My ass tingled, and my clit throbbed.

A grin spread across Rem's face. "Turn back around."

I did as I was told, anticipation roaring through me. Rem's palm glanced off my other cheek, and my internal muscles clenched down.

"Oh damn," I whispered. I was on the verge of orgasm and the man had barely touched me. He was bringing out something in me I hadn't even known I wanted. Public nudity? Spankings? Who was I right now? All I knew was I wanted to find out.

His hand traced over my tingling skin, and then he bent over me. "I just wanted to remind you, even if we're not in a relationship, this"—he dipped his hand between my thighs—"is still mine. Only mine. That's how I roll,

Whitney. I'll give you anything you want, but I don't want you sleeping with other men."

"I didn't sleep with Gage," I whispered. "You know I was just playing, right?"

Rem fumbled with his jeans, and then there was a crinkle of a condom wrapped. My core clenched in eager anticipation.

"I know," he said. His cock pushed between my thighs, brushing over my clit. "But I couldn't resist the chance to slap your perfect fucking ass. I've been wanting to do that from the first moment I saw you. Now hold on."

There was nothing to hold on to, but I braced myself against the wall and spread my legs farther. The head of him pushed inside, and then inch by inch, the rest of his thick cock filled me. He stretched me, just like he had the first time we'd been together. He rolled his hips, pumping himself in and out of me, while I drove back to meet him.

"What if someone comes in?" I said as he picked up speed.

He laughed. "Then they better take a seat and enjoy the show, because I'm not stopping."

I moaned at the very thought.

"You like that?" Rem asked, his hips to my ass. "You like the idea of a show?"

My face blushed hot, and I didn't answer.

"Touch yourself," he commanded. "Rub your clit."

Yes. I reached between my legs and pinched my sensitive nub while Rem's fingers dug into the padding of my hips. The sounds of flesh against flesh and my moans and his breathing, all mingled, taking me higher and higher. I rubbed my clit faster, harder, until sparks of pure pleasure built low inside me.

"Rem," I moaned.

Another stinging slap to my ass sent me spiraling over the edge. "Oh!" I cried out before turning my head and muffling the sounds of my bliss with my shoulder. "Oomgfg."

Rem rode me hard while I lost myself to a mind-altering orgasm. My legs trembled, and my hand dropped away from my clit, too sensitive to touch it any longer. Rem wasn't having any of that, though. He took over the job, working me until I bucked and writhed, prolonging the orgasm until I totally blissed out. He groaned into the back of my neck, his lips pressing to my skin. He found his own release finally, his grip tightening on me until he'd finished.

When he withdrew, it took me too long to move. I was completely spent, even though I'd done little but just hang on for the ride. Rem dragged my panties back up, and I gasped because they touched my clit. I groaned as my jeans did the same. They were tight and rubbed in all the wrong—or rather, right—places. I finally turned around, and Rem devoured my mouth in a kiss.

"No more talk of other men, deal?"

I nodded dumbly. But then I thought of something. My face heated again. "But..."

As if he could read my mind, Rem pulled me to him and slid his hands down over my ass. It still tingled from his slaps. "I'll spank you anytime you want, Whit. You don't have to make me jealous first."

I smiled into his shirt. Good to know.

21

REMI

*A*fter our rather public screw session in the barn, I didn't push my luck again with Whitney that night. Instead, we climbed into bed in our cabin, and I folded her into my arms. We snuggled in together until we both fell asleep.

But nightmares plagued my dreams. Memories from my old days with the club—the people I'd known, the things I'd done—played over and over again in my head. Shooter's twisted smile featured heavily. He pointed crosshairs at me, his target aimed straight at my head. I didn't flinch, just stood there, knowing that once Shooter had you in his sights, your days were numbered. He never missed. Then the image of me morphed into an image of Whitney. Her huge, terrified eyes stared out at me through the dream haze, and I fought to get to her. I thrashed my arms and legs, lunging, tugging, yanking anything I could get a grip on. But strong arms and evil, grinning faces held me back. Men in leather cuts bearing the Kings of Chaos logo. Pyro and his constantly flicking lighter. Raven and his dead black eyes. My father, cruel and calculating, his stare cutting right through me until screams ripped from my body.

The cabin door slammed open, cracking off the wooden walls.

"Rem!" someone yelled through the fog.

I fought to get to the surface. The room was dark and disorienting, and it took a moment for the image to fade away into tendrils of fog. A light came on, and I blinked at the sudden harshness.

Whitney's small hands stroked over my biceps, making me realize there was someone else in the room. Gage watched us, his head cocked to one side.

"What?" I huffed.

"Nothin'. I was coming to make sure you two were awake when I heard you screamin'. We leave in ten."

He didn't ask what was wrong, or if I was okay. And I was grateful for it. Sweat dotted my skin, partly from fear, partly from embarrassment.

"Fine. See you then."

Gage turned and walked away, closing the door behind him. It was only then I realized he'd seen Whitney and me in the same bed together.

"Well, fuck. How are we going to explain that one?" I asked Whitney.

Whitney shrugged. "I'm less worried about that and more worried about you. Were you having a nightmare? I woke up with you flailing around the bed."

"Shit, did I hurt you?" I cupped her cheek and ran my gaze all over her. Her long-sleeved pajamas had little avocados on them. They were rumpled, and her blonde hair was a mess, sticking up at weird angles, but she didn't appear hurt.

"I'm fine. Are you, though?"

"Yes," I answered, even though I really wasn't. The dream had set me on edge, and my heart still pounded, the images too clear, too fresh in my head to be forgotten so easily. I pulled away from her. "We need to get ready."

She nodded, but there was a reluctance in it that I chose not to comment on. I pulled on layers of clothes and grabbed the backpack I'd filled last night. It held a few changes of clothes, along with some food and camping supplies Scout had divided up between the six of us. We were all going on the roundup, leaving only Gramps at the house, holding down the fort. We should only be gone two nights, and the old man, despite being a cranky old bugger, still had his wits about him and would be just fine alone for a few days. Besides, somebody had to stay behind to take care of the chickens and milk the cows.

When Whitney was ready, we trudged up to the barn in silence. The fear I'd felt in the nightmare clung to my skin. It was so thick I could practically taste it, and I was grateful when we reached the others. They were all there, saddling up their horses in the dark. This is what I needed. Distraction. More people. Whitney was fine, and if I hovered over her constantly, projecting my fear onto her, she'd know something was up. I didn't want to smother her. She'd said this thing was casual, and even though I'd pushed the point that casual to me still meant no sex with other people, I didn't want to be too full-on with her. We were safe out here, thousands of miles away from anyone who might want to hurt her to get at me.

There was no need to stick to her side like glue and send her running for the hills. She was strong and independent. I instinctively knew she'd be turned off if I became a stage five clinger.

Even still, I saddled her horse for her, because she had so little experience and I needed to be sure she was safe. She thanked me, taking my help graciously, and, making sure no one else was looking, I copped a feel of her ass as I hoisted her up into the saddle. She rolled her eyes at me, and I gave her a cocky wink, trying to force myself back into a jovial mood.

I had three days out in the open air on the back of a horse. I had a beautiful woman who let me worship her body. And I had some amazing, hardworking people around me. All good things.

Yet I couldn't shake the feeling of foreboding that the dream had left me with.

Dane, the most experienced horseman of the six of us, led the way, the rest of us falling into single file behind him. There was a ripple of excitement among us that I recognized from other roundups I'd been on. The break in the usual routine was welcome by all, even if we were cutting it awfully close to when the snows would inevitably come. My breath frosted in the air, and I was glad for the multiple layers of clothes beneath my jacket.

The sun rose over the mountains, and I breathed in deep lungfuls of fresh air, trying to clear my head. It was undeniably beautiful out here, and for a good hour, nobody spoke much. I wasn't sure if it was because everyone was low on caffeine and still hadn't woken up properly, or if they were just enjoying the early morning peace and their own silent thoughts. Eventually, Gage let his horse drop back, even with mine. I glanced over at him, watching him chew something over.

"What's on your mind, Gage? I can hear you thinking from over here."

"Your sister..."

I stiffened. "Yeah?"

"You share a bed with her?"

I snorted on a laugh, glad I'd already thought up an answer. I'd instinctively known he wasn't going to let it go so easily. "The air mattress was packed for today. So, yeah."

He nodded. "Right. Of course. That makes sense. Sorry."

He fell silent for a moment, but I could tell there was more. "Spit it out."

The younger man's cheeks went pink. "Well, it's just I've been thinking about what she said yesterday. You know, about her and I having sex? And I—"

I held a hand up. "You don't want to go there."

"Pretty sure I do." Gage laughed.

Remembering how Whitney had thrown me in it with Scout, I couldn't resist having a little fun of my own. "You aren't her type, bro."

Gage pulled a face. "Why not? Nobody has ever complained before."

Yeah, I bet they hadn't. Gage was a good-looking man, I'd give him that. I'd bet he had women throwing themselves at him when he went into town. Which was exactly why I didn't want him anywhere near Whitney. "She doesn't go for the tall, dark, handsome thing you've got going on. She likes 'em shorter. Fatter. If I'm being honest, she's got a thing for gnomes."

Gage's eyebrows shot up into his hairline. "Gnomes? Is that some city slang I don't understand or are you talking about gnomes like Mr. Lolly Golly?"

I just gave him a look as if to say, *it's weird, I know*, and let him make his own mind up.

"Wow. That's a thing?"

"Yep." I had to cough to cover my laughter.

"Gage, get up here," Dane called sharply from the head of the line.

Gage and I both snapped to attention at the odd tone in Dane's voice, and when Gage urged his horse into a trot, I did the same thing. We skirted around Scout and Whitney who were chatting as they rode, and Ollie who had his earphones in. Dane had brought his horse to a complete stop and was staring at something on the ground.

"What's wrong?" Gage asked.

"You been camping out here lately?" Dane pointed to the remains of a campfire. A charred can of baked beans and some tin foil lay amongst the ashes. It appeared to be fresh. Not more than a day or two old.

"Not me. I wouldn't leave rubbish out here like that."

Dane's mouth pulled into a tight line, and he gazed around the countryside as if he might see someone wandering back, ready to claim their illegal campfire.

A prickle of worry gnawed at me.

But Gage shrugged. "No big deal. Probably just some kids from the high school blowing off steam out here where their parents can't hear or see what they're doing."

"That happen a lot?" Whitney asked.

I hadn't noticed her approach, but now she shot me a glance. I knew we were having similar thoughts.

Scout nodded, seeming completely unconcerned. "Oh yeah. Happens a lot during the summers. There's a dirt road they can use to get almost this far in. Normally they just stay near their cars, but I guess they wandered farther. We've never made a big deal of it in the past, but if they're going to be leaving rubbish out here, that's a different story." She slid down off her horse and picked up the charred remains of the trash that had been left behind. "I'll call the high school and ask them to put a message out that it won't be tolerated. That worked for a while last time."

"I'll put some extra *no trespassing* signs up," Gage said. "And check the lock on the gate. I thought it was padlocked, but not like it's all that hard to cut a padlock." He steered his horse around Whitney's and then laughed. "Quit worrying," he said to her. "It's just a bunch of kids. Not the boogeyman."

I shot her a glance. She did seem worried. She was gazing around, biting her bottom lip in much the same fashion Dane was. Her gaze met mine, and I gave her what I hoped was a reassuring smile.

Gage nudged his horse again, and the other four trotted after him, leaving Whitney and me behind.

I waited until they were out of earshot. "You concerned?"

She shook her head. "Not really. No reason to think this is anything other than what Gage and Scout think it is."

"Right. So why is your hand hovering over your gun like you're about to whip it out at any moment and start shooting?"

She looked down and, realizing I was right, she put

both hands firmly on the reins. "We should catch up to the others. Just keep an eye out, okay?"

"Deal. One more thing, though."

"What's that?"

"Kiss me."

The tension in her expression seeped away, which had been my sole intention.

"I'm not kissing you out here."

"Then I'm not going to do all the things I have planned for you tonight."

She raised one eyebrow. "In a tent? With the others around?"

I wiggled my eyebrows at her. "Who said anything about a tent? I like the idea that we might get caught. And I know you do, too. Now kiss me, or I swear, my tongue will stay in my mouth the entire camping trip. And we both know that's a waste of pure God-given talent."

"Might be worth it if it means I don't have to listen to your smartass comments the entire trip."

I nudged my horse into a walk. "Well, if that's how you feel..."

I counted down the seconds in my head. *Three...two...one...*

"Rem!"

I pulled my horse to a stop and waited for hers to catch up. With a quick look to make sure the others weren't in sight, she leaned across her horse and pressed her lips to mine. I grasped the back of her head and kissed her hard, until our horses grew restless and we were forced apart.

Her kiss stole my breath, and my dick hardened uncomfortably beneath my jeans. "I don't think I can wait until tonight," I admitted. "We should have stayed home. I could have been making love to you all over our cabin right now. Having a boner while riding all day isn't exactly comfortable."

Whitney peered over into my lap. "That hurts, huh?"

"Uncomfortable. Yes. Want to help me out?"

A wicked grin spread across her face. "As tempting as that sounds, I kind of like the idea that you're out here, having to wait. I want you picturing me naked, taking your cock in my mouth and—"

"Oh fuck, Whit. Stop," I groaned, doubling over trying to readjust myself so the saddle and my jeans didn't completely strangle my junk.

She spurred her horse into a canter, the sounds of her laughter trailing back to me. I let her go. There was nothing else I could do with an erection harder than a rock. Instead, I waited for the blood in my dick to go back to where it was supposed to be, and planned every wicked thing I'd do to get Whitney back. I hoped she enjoyed delayed orgasms. Because I was going to torture her and love every minute of it.

Just as soon as I got this boner under control. Dammit.

22

WHITNEY

*W*e found the beginnings of the herd of cattle right as the sun was beginning to set. Dane called it good for the day, and I followed suit, swinging my leg off my horse and then detangling my other foot from the stirrups. I still hadn't quite mastered this whole horse-riding thing, but I'd managed not to embarrass myself today. I hadn't fallen off, and the horse hadn't run away with me clinging onto its mane for dear life. So that was something.

But oh my God. The minute I tried to put one foot in front of the other, my legs buckled.

Rem caught me by the arm, steadying me. "You okay?" he asked, concern etched into his features.

"Not used to spending all day in a saddle."

Rem leaned in closer. "Rest up then, because there's more riding to do tonight."

Heat flushed my body even as I shoved him away. Cocky asshole. Admittedly, I hadn't really made it hard on him. Ever since that first night together, every look, every whispered, dirty word, had me wanting him all that little bit more. He was fun, and flirty, and did things to my body that no other man ever had. I couldn't help but want to be around him. I couldn't deny for a second, that no matter how sore I was right now, when he came for me tonight, I'd be ready. My thighs clenched in anticipation.

"Quit standing around, you two. Get your tents up or you'll be doing it in the dark. Sun goes down quick this time of year."

Rem saluted Dane, which clearly annoyed the older man further, but he didn't comment. Dane already had his traveling tent halfway up, and I hadn't even pulled mine from my bag. Deciding to take Dane's advice, I found my tent and snapped the few poles together, while I searched the ground for a flat spot. We all had tiny one-man travelling tents that would fit little more than our self-inflating air mattresses and sleeping bags. They weren't even tall enough to stand in, and I eyed Gage's tent, wondering how his six-foot-four frame would even fit inside. I'd bet his feet would hang out the ends.

I wandered away from the horseshoe shape the others were making, kicked a few rocks out of the way, then spread out the base piece.

"What are you doing all the way over there?" Scout called.

"She snores," Rem answered before I could even open my mouth. "And not that nice, gentle sort of snore either. Sounds like some sort of bear being choked in his sleep."

Scout winced.

"Really, Rem?" I asked, shaking my head.

"Well, why else would you set your tent up away from everyone else's?" He asked the question with so much sugar in his voice it practically dripped honey down his chin.

He had a point, though. We both knew why I wanted a little privacy, but I wasn't about to tell the others that. Scout already looked like she suspected the two of us were completely insane. Which perhaps we were.

Thankfully, Dane asking for help with the fire and dinner saved me from further interrogation. Rem quit his smartass remarks and not-so-subtle attempts to rile me up, and we ate a simple meal, cooked over the campfire. The night air grew chilly and damp, and we huddled close to the fire as the hours wore on. Scout made hot tea, and it warmed me from the inside. I sat as close to Rem as I dared, with the firelight flickering over us, wishing he would put his arm around me. I was warm and cozy and verging on sleepy. The skies above us were wide open and so bright and full of stars. I breathed deep and tried to imprint the moment in my memory. Living in the city, I'd never thought about what it would be like to sit out by a bonfire after riding a horse all day. I'd never thought I'd enjoy the gentle mooing sounds that came from the nearby cattle. And I never thought about having a man by my side. A man I slept with but wouldn't let myself feel anything for. My heart squeezed. Most likely, I wouldn't get this chance again. I'd told him I wasn't ready for a relationship, because I shouldn't be. My relationship with Karsten had barely ended. A swirl of unease rose in my belly at the thought of leaving Rem at the end of all of this. Even though Janice had allowed us to stay on, that didn't mean we didn't have an expiration date. And it was little more than two weeks away.

"You okay?" he whispered.

I forced a smile. "Great. It's just really something else, being out here. Thank you."

"For what?"

"For this place."

We both knew it wasn't entirely him who had brought us here. But his single demand to be placed in a country location was what had started this. So he deserved at least a little of the credit.

Ollie stood, stretching, and declared he was going to bed. Not long after Gage did the same thing. Within minutes, their snores echoed around the campfire. I smiled. One thing I'd learned about country boys, in the time I'd been here, was that they had no shame in going to bed early and crashing hard. Considering how early they started the day, I couldn't blame them. I stifled a yawn but didn't want to leave Rem's side. And we could hardly just sneak off to bed together when Dane and Scout were still awake.

Dane eyed the two of us, and I realized we were probably sitting too close, but I couldn't bring myself to move away. Dane rolled his eyes then turned to Scout. "Come get some more wood with me?"

She seemed pleased to be asked, bounding up from her spot on the grass to follow him. Dane looked over his shoulder at us before they disappeared into the darkness, and jerked his head toward my tent.

Rem grabbed my hand, and we both ran, stifling laughs as we went.

"Hurry, hurry," I murmured, hopping around from one foot to the other impatiently while he undid the zipper.

He stopped and turned around. "It's been one day

since we last had sex. Are you seriously that desperate for it?"

"Oh, shut up," I whispered, and shoved him out of the way. He landed on his ass in the dirt, and I took over the zipper work. I squeezed inside and started to do the zipper back up.

"Hey!" He struggled to his feet. "You aren't going to let me in?"

We both knew I was, but I had to play the game.

"I can hear their footsteps," he taunted, as if he didn't have a care in the world.

My lady parts were screaming they had *every* care in the world, and that each one depended on him being inside that tent tonight. Game over. I reached out and grabbed a handful of his jacket and pulled him inside. We fell onto the air mattress in a tangle of arms and legs, both shushing each other as we fought to get the zipper up.

Scout's voice filtered back, right as we got it closed. We both froze, too scared to move in case the air mattress squeaked.

"Do you think she saw?" he breathed more than said.

I was lying on top of him, his gorgeous face just inches from mine. And I suddenly didn't care. Didn't care whether the whole world knew about the two of us. All of that faded away.

"I like you." I whispered the thought, straight from my heart.

His gaze locked with mine in the muted light from the fire outside. There was meaning behind those three little words. I'd meant them as more than they appeared at face value. My head still screamed this was too much too soon after Karsten, but my heart told her to shut the fuck up and get on board. I wasn't in love with Rem. But there were feelings there, no doubt. I *liked* him. A lot. Probably a lot more than people who were supposedly having casual sex should.

"I like you, too," he whispered. Then he strained up and kissed me softly.

My heart soared at the featherlight kiss. It spoke words he hadn't said, but I felt them and returned the unspoken sentiment. His tongue stroked the seam of my lips, and I opened for him. His fingers snaked into my hair, clamping down on the back of my neck as we kissed.

With one deft move, Rem flipped our positions, and I found myself on my back, the air mattress protesting the weight of two fully grown humans with a loud squeak. Rem reared over me, and I fumbled to find the button on his jeans through the layers of clothes. He didn't make it any easier by lowering his mouth to my neck and sucking gently on the sensitive place below my ear. Despite the cool air around us, heat pooled low in my belly.

"I want you," I whispered, trying again for his fly.

"I need you," he whispered back.

I froze. I sought out his eyes once more and was shocked by the depth of emotion I found there. I wrapped my legs around his waist and dug my fingers into the fabric of his jacket, pulling him down on top of me so our bodies were flush. I pressed my mouth to his again, no softness left this time. I kissed him hard, telling him exactly how much I needed him, too. He groaned into my mouth.

"What on earth is Whitney doing in that tent?" Scout asked. "Sounds like she's wrestling a bear."

"Or choking one," Dane deadpanned, using Rem's earlier smartass remark.

I fought back a laugh, and Rem put a finger to my lips. I sucked it into my mouth, watching for his reaction.

"Fuck, that's hot." His gaze was trained on the place his finger and my mouth met. Then suddenly we were both struggling to get our clothes off in the cramped space. Somewhere between his jeans going down and my bra falling off my shoulders, Scout and Dane went quiet, but all I could think about was getting Rem where I wanted him. On me. In me. Everywhere.

"Get into the sleeping bag," he urged when we were both naked. "You'll freeze to death otherwise."

I wasn't even feeling the cold. Rem's big body was like a space heater, and the tent was doing a surprisingly good job of keeping in our body warmth. Or perhaps I was just so turned on my blood had actually risen a few degrees.

"Too small for both of us."

"Good point. Open it and put it over you at least."

I shook my head. "I don't need it." Our entire conversation was hushed, but I hoped Dane and Scout had gone to bed and weren't just sitting around the fire trying to enjoy the peace and quiet that Rem and I were probably ruining.

"Good. Because no restrictions means I can do this." He flipped us again so I sat straddled over his abs. Behind me, his hard dick bobbed, straining toward me.

I couldn't resist reaching back and circling my fingers around the base. I gave him a few quick pumps of my hand.

"Ride me, Whit," he whispered. His palms skated over my thighs and up my sides before cupping my breasts. He pinched my nipples in the darkness, and I was surprised when sparks didn't light up the tent. Instead, they shot through my body all the way to my core. I wanted to ride him. I wanted him filling me. I ached to have him inside.

I scrabbled in my bag for the condoms I'd packed, but he caught my wrist. "Not the sort of ride I meant. Move forward."

Frowning, I shifted forward until I was sitting on his chest.

"Farther," he coaxed, his fingers never letting up their kneading on my breasts.

If I moved any farther I'd be sitting on his...oh. "Sexy and dirty, huh, Cowboy?"

His hands dropped to my thighs, and he pulled me the rest of the way, sliding beneath me. With no headboard or wall to hang on, and the tent fabric inches from my nose, I leaned back on my arms, digging my fingers into the air mattress either side of his chest. I braced some of my weight on my knees, fearing I'd smother the man in my pussy before he even had a chance to go down on me. Though I had a feeling he might not have minded.

His tongue licked through my folds like it had a mission of its own, and I fought back a cry of pleasure. My head dropped back, and my naked breasts pointed toward the sky beyond the tent. Rem's fingers dug into my thighs, and he licked my pussy until my hips rolled. I couldn't help it. I needed more. More of his tongue plunging inside me. More of his nails scratching my skin. More of the way he made me want to do things I'd never done before, like sit on a man's face and gyrate like I was in a porno.

"Want to touch you," I breathed, fumbling behind me for his cock. But with the relentless way he tongued my sensitive flesh, I couldn't focus or find a rhythm. My orgasm was building, but I was determined I wouldn't come before him. We'd come together.

Lifting my hips away from his wickedly talented tongue, I turned and maneuvered us into a sixty-nine position, delighting at the hiss from the back of his throat as I lowered myself over his mouth once more. His tongue drove straight back inside me, pushing and prodding, spearing me as deep as possible while his fingers gripped my thighs, guiding them apart.

Fighting to keep my cool, I concentrated on his long, thick shaft. I took the head of him inside my mouth, swirling my tongue around him, and then bobbed my head, taking him deeper. I circled my fingers around the base and found a rhythm, using my hand and my lips in unison. Tiny beads of moisture leaked from his tip, and I lapped my tongue over them.

With no conscious thought from me, my hips rolled in time with Rem's movements, leaving me free to concentrate on working him hard and fast to catch up to the level of bliss I was floating on. I sucked him deep, enjoying his dick in my mouth as much as I enjoyed his tongue on my clit. When his fingers thrust deep inside me, it was lucky my mouth was otherwise occupied because it muffled the moan that threatened to rip through me.

"Come, baby. Come," he urged from between my thighs. But I stubbornly held out, not letting my mind go there, even though my body fought desperately to fall over the edge.

"Together," I gasped. I cupped his balls, and the first spurts of his ejaculation burst across the back of my throat. Only then did I surrender to my own orgasm. I sank down onto him, unable to support myself on legs that trembled violently as my orgasm barreled through me. I squeezed the base of Rem's cock, needing something to hold on to, but he didn't seem to mind. His hips jerked, thrusting deeper into my mouth, and I worked my tongue and my lips until he was groaning against my inner thigh.

"Fuck, Whit. Fuck."

I could relate. I wanted to scream out his name so loud it echoed off the mountains around us. But instead I rode his mouth and fingers and sucked him until we were both panting, breathless, and sated.

When the last ripples of pleasure subsided, I slumped to the side, resting my head on his muscled thigh while I caught my breath. I suddenly became aware of the cold and wriggled around, pulling the open sleeping bag over us and nestling into his arms.

"We need to put clothes on," I murmured, stroking through the smattering of dark hair on his chest.

He shifted so I was beneath him, his legs spreading mine wide. "Soon. But I didn't get to do this..." His cock nudged at my entrance.

I raised an eyebrow, even though it was so dark he wouldn't have seen it. "How are you hard again already? It's been minutes."

He chuckled, swiping through the wetness between my legs. "Doesn't seem to be a problem when you're around. And naked." The head of him nudged just inside me, and we both froze.

"Condom," I said, groping around in the dark for the box I'd pulled out earlier. It was so hard not to lift my hips and get him inside me. I'd thought I was sated, but now, with his cockhead nudging toward my G-spot, I wanted him all over again. Slow. Soft. I wanted to make love. Not just get off.

"I'm clean," he said gently, a question in his voice.

I paused. I wanted to do this bare. I wanted it to be just him and me. Skin to skin. No barriers. I'd never done that before. Karsten had always insisted on condoms. I only understood why once his dirty laundry was aired, but now I was grateful. I wanted my first time to be with Rem.

"Me, too," I confirmed. "And I'm on the pill."

"So...? This is okay?"

I strained up to kiss him, lifting my hips at the same time. "It's okay," I confirmed. "I want to. I trust you."

That seemed to be the permission he needed. With a single, long, slow thrust, he filled me. For a moment, Rem stilled, his muscles tight as if he was stifling a loud groan of pleasure. He withdrew just as gradually, and the emptiness he left behind had me aching. He slid back in. He braced himself on his forearms, the sleeping bag slipping off his broad back as he rolled his hips, filling me, and then retreating, over and over again. His gaze locked with mine, and I didn't look away. For once, I didn't fight for control. I just went with him. Molded to him. Moved with him. Took him into my body like he was the only one who'd ever mattered.

His lips pressed against mine, in the sweetest, most heartbreaking touch that made me want to keep him.

This wasn't fucking. This was making love. And it was everything.

"Rem!" a guttural yell broke through the bubble Rem and I had created.

I jerked, hearing the panic in Dane's voice.

"What the fuck?" Rem swore. He pulled out of me and sat back on his knees. His cock gleamed in the low light of the tent, covered in the effects of our arousal.

I twisted beneath Rem, reaching for the zipper of the tent before I remembered exactly how naked I was. Outside the tent, Dane's heavy footsteps fell, hard and pounding. I groped around for my clothes. I spotted Rem's jacket in the orange glow and then shot a panicked glance toward Rem. There was suddenly so much more light in the tent than there had been moments earlier. "Where is that orange light coming from?"

Scout's bloodcurdling scream ripped through my confusion. "Rem!"

I had no idea why they were all screaming his name, but the time for hiding what we were doing was over. "He's in here!" I shouted, yanking the zipper of the tent, even though I wasn't dressed. "What's wron—"

I blinked in the sudden brightness.

Rem moved quicker than I did. He pushed past me, through the small opening wearing nothing but his boxers.

Rem's tent was engulfed in flames.

"There's no one in there," Rem yelled, running toward Dane and Scout, who were frantically trying to smother the fire with their jackets.

I watched wide eyed as Scout spun around, her

confused gaze darting between Rem, his tent, and then finally me.

Dane's shoulders slumped, and he paused, breathing hard. He didn't say anything, just went back to putting out the fire.

Rem took the jacket from Scout's trembling hands. Her eyes were wide.

"I'm fine. Wake Gage and Ollie, just in case it spreads."

She nodded and ran to do as he said. I had no idea how Ollie and Gage were still asleep through all the yelling and carrying on. Dane and Rem went back to attacking the fire. I found my panties and with Rem's jacket dwarfing me, I scrambled out of the tent, gun in hand.

Gage and Ollie stumbled from their tents, rubbing their eyes, and stood with Scout, watching the other two extinguish the flames. I joined them, gun pointed at the ground but ready. I turned in slow circles, surveying our surroundings, looking for anything out of place. But it was so damn dark, that beyond the light of the bonfire, it was impossible to see anything.

A whole forest full of men wearing Kings of Chaos cuts could be out there, planning their attack, and I wouldn't have been able to see them.

"Fuck," I cursed. We were sitting ducks.

"Um, Whit?" Gage asked calmly.

I spared him a glance but went straight back to scouring the darkness.

"Why do you have a gun? Do you know how to use that?"

I would have laughed if I hadn't been so concerned

about how the hell Rem's tent had mysteriously caught fire. "I'm a cop. If you brought a gun, get it."

Scout made a choking noise behind me. "Why does he need a gun?"

I didn't answer.

Dane stomped on the last of the flames, and then he and Rem joined our little posse. Frown lines pulled at his forehead when he noticed the way Scout was shaking. He looked like he wanted to comfort her, but instead, he shoved his hands into his pockets. "They're not who you think they are," he said to her, like that was supposed to make her feel better.

Ugh. Men. So fucking useless when a woman was upset.

A warm hand pressed between my shoulder blades. I flinched, but in the next second, my body recognized Rem's and relaxed.

"You want to put the gun down? You're scaring people," he suggested quietly.

Gage came back from his tent with a shotgun and pointed it into the darkness in the same direction I was.

"Can somebody please tell me what the hell is going on?" Ollie asked. "It's still dark, and I haven't had coffee so I can't think. You two are pointing guns at cows, Rem should have been a roasted marshmallow, and why the hell does Whitney have no pants on?"

Scout snorted on a laugh, and Rem chuckled softly.

"There's no one out there, Whit," he said gently, running his arm down mine toward my fingers strangling the gun. "Relax."

I spun around, fixing a steely gaze on him. "Don't you

see your tent in ashes? If you'd been inside, you'd probably be well on your way to dead right now!"

I suddenly realized my fingers trembled. "Shit," I swore softly and loosened my grip on the gun. I cast an eye around the group, all staring at me, and let out a breath I hadn't realized I'd been holding.

"I think it was just the wind," Dane piped up. "Must have picked up a spark from the fire. Rem's tent is old and canvas. Probably super brittle and dry. I was sitting right here the whole time, but I didn't see anything. One minute everything was fine, the next, there's flames coming out of tent. I had an inkling you two were together, but I wasn't one-hundred-percent sure. I didn't want to risk it."

Rem held a hand out to Dane.

The older man went to shake it but pulled his hand back at the last minute. "I'm sorry, I'm glad you're fine, but I can't shake your hand when you're as good as naked. Seriously, dude, that underwear leaves nothing to the imagination."

Scout's eyes dipped down Rem's body.

A wave of annoyance rose and broke over me. "Okay, we all need to have a talk."

"It's the middle of the night," Rem said. "Maybe this can wait?"

"Actually, I really want to hear the story now," Scout said.

"Same," Gage piped up.

Ollie rubbed his eyes. "You've all lost me. I have no idea what's going on."

I sighed. "Someone make Ollie some coffee, because this might take a while."

23

REM

"So, just to be clear, she's a cop. You're in witness protection. And you've been screwing the entire time you've been here?"

"Ollie, how many times are you going to make them say it before you believe it?" Scout called from the back of her horse. "Get over it already."

"I can't!" he yelled. "It's like *Days of Our Lives*, and I'm so here for it!"

"Dude, shut up." I sighed. "Whitney has a gun. I'm not going to stop her if she tries to shoot you. Just sayin'."

Ollie shook his head, his glee still evident in his goofy smile.

"You do realize they were never actually brother and sister, right?" Gage laughed before taking off to round up a cow that had gone off course.

Their banter carried on, but I urged my horse on to catch up with Whitney. Her face was a mask of stony silence. "You okay?" I asked, wishing I could wrap my arms around her. "Sorry about Ollie. Just ignore him."

"I'm fine," she said in a tone that conveyed exactly how *not* fine she was.

"You still thinking someone was out there last night?"

Her gaze pierced mine. "You don't? You saw the squatter's campsite. You put out the tent fire with your own hands. You honestly don't think any of that is connected?"

I shrugged. "It just doesn't make any sense to me. The Kings of Chaos are well-trained, smart men. There's a reason my father recruited each and every one of them. We were the strongest club around. They don't go camping illegally and setting old tents on fire."

"Not just any old tent. *Your* tent."

"Which I wasn't in."

She didn't say anything, just continually scanned our surroundings, despite the fact that for miles, all you could see was the rear ends of hundreds of cows. I hated she was so worried about this. But the more I thought about it, the more I was convinced the fire had just been a freak accident. If the Kings had been out there, they would have just walked right into the middle of camp and started shooting. We all would have been dead before we even knew they were there. Not that I said that out loud. I knew Whitney could handle it, but I didn't want to worry the others.

A loud whistle pierced the air, and a few hundred yards to the right, Dane waved me over. With a final look at Whitney's frosted features, I spurred my horse into a canter, bringing him up beside Dane's chestnut mare. He ran his reins through his hands, pulling and tugging at the leather straps and fiddling with them in a very un-Dane-like manner. I eyed the reins he'd wrapped around his fingers so tight his fingertips were turning purple.

"You're worried, too?" I asked, squinting at him.

The sun was starting to get low, but we were only an hour out of home and we'd all decided that pushing through to avoid camping again was the smarter option. The wind from last night had picked up and brought with it a small amount of sleet. It wasn't pleasant to ride in, even though it had been over in less than an hour. But none of us wanted to spend a night trying to sleep in it. We'd make it back if we didn't stop unnecessarily.

"That obvious?"

"You didn't see anything, though, right? There's no reason to think—"

Dane held a hand up in a stop motion. "I'm not talking about last night."

"Oh. What then?"

"I need your help."

"With...?" I prompted. The man was as unresponsive as a stone sometimes. But I was intrigued, nonetheless. Dane was a competent guy. He prided himself in being in control. It obviously pained him to be asking for my help.

A particularly cold gust of wind rushed by, and Dane hunched into his jacket. "How did you and Whitney start...you know."

I frowned. "You know?"

Dane sighed. "Hooking up. How did you start hooking up?"

I blinked. Of all the things in the world, that was the last thing I thought he'd ask me about. Unlike Ollie's ribbing, Dane looked like he honest to God wanted to know how Whitney and I had gotten together. From the intensity of his gaze, I half-expected him to whip out a notebook and start taking notes.

"Uh, I don't really know. A lot of flirty back and forth, I guess. And then I kissed her."

Dane's shoulders slumped.

"Was that not the answer you were hoping for?"

"Not really. I don't do banter well. Or flirty."

That didn't surprise me. We'd been here weeks, and I think he'd smiled once in that time.

"Who do you want to flirt with?"

Dane's gaze diverted over my shoulder. It was too far back to be aimed at Whitney, and anyway, he didn't strike me as the type to move in on another man's woman. Not that Whitney was officially my woman, but I still didn't think he'd go there. "Ah, Scout."

If Dane's cheeks weren't already pink from the cold, I thought that might have done the job.

"Does she know you've got a thing for her?" I asked. "You've worked here a long time. You must have had a drunken hookup or something, surely?"

Dane shot me a hard look. "No, dickhead. It's not like that."

"Oh," I said, understanding his quick reaction. "You really like her then?"

Dane ground his teeth. I was obviously getting under his skin. "Just ask her out."

"Can't. What if she says no?"

"Then you go into town and get so drunk you forget your own name." I grinned at him. "I'll come."

"You're no fucking help," he grumbled. "You're worse than Gage and Ollie at this. I thought they gave some shit advice, but you're in the running to take the trophy."

"Okay, okay." I laughed. "But what if she says yes?"

His face paled. "That might be worse," he admitted.

Poor asshole had it bad.

"I'm too old for her."

"She's not a kid. Maybe you should let her decide that."

A glimmer of hope sparked in his eyes. "You think?"

"I don't pretend to know what women are thinking. In my experience, it'll save you a whole lotta heartache if you use your words like a big boy and just ask."

Dane's mouth lifted at the corners.

"Oh, holy shit, did I just get a smile out of you?"

The smile fell. "We're done here. Keep this to yourself or next time your tent is on fire, it'll be with you in it."

He trotted off. I sat back in the saddle completely and utterly amused with myself.

We hit the home pastures about thirty minutes after darkness completely overtook the land. Unlike other nights where the skies were lit by fat full moons and more stars than a man could ever count, when night came, it came dark and smothering. The temperature dropped, and my mind drifted away from the task of penning the massive herd of cattle, to thoughts of hot meals, scalding showers, and a warm body in bed beside me.

But the job wasn't done until every last cow was accounted for. Ollie jumped off his horse, opening the pasture gate while the rest of us worked to get the herd through the opening. Calls of "Go on, get," and "Push 'em, up," rang out, and I worked my tired horse to move the last few stragglers in. Ollie closed the gate behind the last one and let out a whoop of glee as it latched.

"Good work," Gage called, riding past Scout and Dane. He high-fived them, then stopped in front of Whitney and me. "Go take a shower, then come on up to the main house. Gramps will have made something hot."

I slapped his hand. "Sounds like heaven. It's too frigging cold out here."

The others led their horses to the stables, and I nudged mine in the same direction.

"I'm just going to go check the perimeter."

I pulled my horse up and turned him back around. Whitney had hers walking in the opposite direction to everyone else, heading for the dirt road that led to the front of the property. Her shoulders bunched around her ears, and she sat stiff as a board, eyes searching the dark night.

"It's near freezing," I said, careful not to just say she couldn't go. If I'd learned anything about Whitney, it was that she liked to be in control. Me telling her she couldn't do something was as good as sending her out to do it. "There's a storm coming, and that horse is tired. He needs a break."

Whitney leaned down and patted the horse's neck before straightening. "You're right."

I heaved a sigh of relief. There was no way in hell I wanted her out in that approaching storm. I followed her back to the stables, then we went in different directions, her horse's stall at the opposite end of the large stable to mine.

I lifted the saddle from my horse and ran my hands over his back and sides, and then down his legs, checking for injuries. He was sweaty and tired, but he was young and strong, and well used to the rigors of ranch life. "You're a good boy," I murmured when he nuzzled at my shirt. "I'll bring you all the treats tomorrow, okay? But tonight, you get fresh straw and a healthy dinner." I checked that he had clean water and filled his feedbag extra high. He'd worked hard, and he'd need the extra calories.

Once he was settled, I grabbed the tack that would need cleaning tomorrow, and wandered down to where Whitney was. The big light-colored quarter horse munched on his dinner, but his rider was nowhere to be seen. I wandered back to the storeroom and found Scout, worrying her bottom lip. Setting my saddle down on a bale of hay, I glanced over at her. "You okay?"

She shook her head. "I was just coming to find you. Whitney's gone out again. Took a fresh horse."

Outside the barn doors, the wind whipped through the trees. "How long ago did she leave?"

"A few minutes."

"Dammit."

"You going after her? I tried to stop her, but she was having none of it."

I raked a hand through my hair. Every part of me screamed to get on a horse or a bike and go and find her. Being out there alone and in the dark wasn't a good idea. "She's stubborn. I doubt she'd listen to me even if I did go after her." I edged toward the doors and peered out into the night, but I couldn't see anything. "She'll come in once the storm hits. Until then, I think she probably needs the space. Let's let her have it."

Scout looked like she wanted to argue, and I couldn't

blame her. Hell, I wanted to argue with my own logic. The alpha male in me wanted to storm into the night, throw her over my shoulder, and drag her back to our cabin. But the logical side of me knew she needed some space to sort through the events of last night. I'd made my mind up about what had happened, but if Whitney hadn't, then I couldn't rush her. This is who she was. She was a cop. A protector. I didn't want to change that, and so instead of following her, I went up to the main house with Scout and hoped she'd come back soon.

24

WHITNEY

*E*xhaustion seeped into my bones, my muscles, my everything. With each step of the horse beneath me, my joints cracked, and I wanted nothing more than to just get off and join the others at the main house. The yellow lights shone behind the curtains, looking homey and inviting each time I passed by the building, but I couldn't shake the feeling of foreboding. The images of flames engulfing the tent where Rem should have been sleeping kept me going.

He could have been inside. Trapped. Burning. Fear churned my gut. Someone had been out there last night. My gut screamed it. But Rem's explanations made sense, too, and my logical mind agreed with him. But I still couldn't shake the sense that something wasn't right. I was missing something.

So I rode because I couldn't just sit there, waiting for something worse to happen. The shadows moving in the softly glowing windows urged me on. There were people I cared about in that house, and it was my job to protect them. *Them.* Not just Rem. We'd brought this to their doorstep. I wouldn't leave them vulnerable.

Slowly, I circled the house in the dark, trusting my horse had better eyesight than I did. We rode right to the edge of the woods, skirting the home pastures, the barns, and then rode down the row of cabins that had been my home for the past few weeks, before doing it over again. The wind became a howl, and I blinked in surprise when softly floating snowflakes became biting icy shards. Beneath me, my horse whinnied, but fear drove me on. There was someone out here. Someone who wanted to hurt Rem, and I'd taken an oath. An oath to serve and protect. It was my one job. I wouldn't let him down.

The storm swirled, and my horse danced around, startled by something I couldn't see. "Whoa, whoa," I said in a calm voice, but my heart rate picked up. Was she reacting to the storm? Or could she see something I couldn't? A sudden crack of thunder echoed off the mountains. Lightning lit the sky. The plains.

The shadowed figure coming toward me.

"Who's there?" I yelled into the howling storm, but my words were masked by another crack of thunder so loud my eardrums rang. My horse reared up, and I reached for my gun. With only one hand on the reins, I didn't have a hope in hell of staying on her back. Her frantic hooves pawed the air, and I hit the dirt with a bone-crunching thump. Pain ricocheted through me, but I scurried out of the way, crawling across the uneven ground, avoiding the horse's hooves before she took off into the storm.

"Whitney!"

Rem ran the last few steps to kneel at my side. My

hand fell away from my gun holster. I breathed hard, through the pain radiating from my tailbone, and the fear churning in my gut. Shock engulfed my system, numbing me.

Rem grasped me by the shoulders. "Are you all right?" he yelled, panic lacing every syllable. I must have nodded, or maybe he saw for himself that I wasn't badly injured, because then he was pulling back and shaking me.

My head bobbled. It took me a minute for my head to clear, but when it did, I brushed his hands away. "Why are you out here?"

"Why am I out here?" His face was a mask of frustration. "Why are you out here?" he demanded. "I swear, Whit. I'm trying to be what you need. But when that storm picked up, I had to come find you. Why didn't you come in?"

"There's someone out here. I'm a cop. This is my job. This is what I'm supposed to do. I'm here to protect you."

"And who's protecting you? Huh? While you're trying to get yourself killed. There's no one out here! Nobody but you!" He pushed to his feet, and for a moment, I thought he might leave me there. I couldn't blame him. He was angry. I was, too. At myself, mostly. Because he was right. What the hell was I doing? I wasn't helping anyone like this.

But then he held out a hand and helped me get to my feet. He looked me over, then with a sigh, he gathered me to his chest. His lips pressed to my hair in a kiss that squeezed my heart. I turned into his jacket, suddenly overwhelmed with the urge to cry. I sniffed hard, not wanting to let that show. This wasn't what we were. We were banter and sex and teasing. We weren't emotion and feeling. I kept blurring the lines between us. But when I lifted my head to tell him that, he kissed me so softly my heart exploded into a million pieces.

"I can't stop thinking about the fire," I whispered. "You could have been trapped inside..."

"Hey, stop. I wasn't. It was just a freak accident."

I buried my face in his jacket and my legs buckled. But somehow that was okay, because he was there to catch me. He held me up, and I surrendered to the feeling of letting him in.

"This won't seem so bad once you're warm and your belly is full," he promised. "Tomorrow, I'll do whatever it takes to make you feel safe again. We'll ride perimeters. Or we can go back to the city. Whatever you need, Whit. I'll do it."

"What if I just need you?" I breathed, sure the wind would snatch the secret words before he could hear them.

His mouth hovered over mine. "Don't you know you already have me? You've had me since the very first moment I saw you, walking past my prison cell." He kissed me soft and slow, and I clung to him, drawing in his strength, and the promise in his words.

Then, in typical Rem fashion, he stepped away, chuckling. "But one day, when we're telling our grandkids how we met, we're really going to have to come up with a better story. I don't want them calling me Grandpa Jailbird."

*W*e tramped our way through the falling snow, clinging tightly to each other. I let my head replay Rem's sweet words and let my heart beat with the knowledge something had shifted between us. It didn't need to be said. There didn't need to be a "Will you be my girlfriend?" moment. Or an awkward, "So hey, we're not just fucking now?" conversation. He'd been holding back because I was. It had been me keeping him at arm's length, using my job and my breakup with Karsten as reasons why this thing between us couldn't be more than just physical. I'd let the wall down and realized Rem had always been there on the other side, just waiting for me.

It had been under a month since Karsten had smashed my world into pieces. And Rem had put it back together in the shortest amount of time possible.

We found my horse, pawing around the barn, and stopped to let her inside. Rem checked her over carefully, while I prepared her stall with fresh food and water, guilt eating away at me for having her out in this sort of weather. Relief rushed me when Rem pronounced her uninjured. We left the horse to her dinner and made our way up to the main house, shaking the snow off on the porch before letting ourselves inside. Heat blasted our faces, and everyone looked up from the dinner table, cheering when they spotted us.

Well, everyone except Gramps. "You're late for dinner," he snapped.

Scout and Gage muffled smiles while Rem and I hung up our coats. My mouth watered at the delicious aroma of thick stew and fresh-baked bread. After profusely apologizing to the grumpy, yet surprisingly good cook, Rem and I ladled food into our mouths like we'd not eaten for a month.

"Weather is bad," Scout said, drifting from the table to the living room after we'd all eaten our fill.

Rem and Gage went to clean up, but when I'd offered to help, they'd refused. So instead, Scout and I sat on a window seat watching the wind whip snow around. I had to admit, it was a lot nicer to be watching than in it.

"It'll be white as far as the eye can see when we get out there tomorrow. Good thing we pushed on tonight." Scout squeezed my hand. "Thank you for being here. For helping. It's been tough the last few years, since our parents died. It's hard to get everything done in time when we're always two people down."

"Oh, I'm sorry. I didn't know." I felt like a jerk. I hadn't even considered where Scout and Gage's parents were.

"It was a car accident. They both died on impact. Better that way, I think. At least no one suffered. And they're together."

"But you and Gage…"

"We had each other. And Grandpa. We're blessed."

It was the sort of comment you could only make years after losing someone, when that initial sting had passed and you'd realized life went on, even when you missed someone every moment of every day.

"Sorry to interrupt," Dane said.

I peered up at him. A fine layer of sweat dotted his forehead.

Scout frowned and pushed to her feet. She reached

up and put the back of her hand to his forehead. "Are you okay? You seem ill."

Dane did appear a sickly sort of green. "I don't do vomit," I said, shifting out of the upchuck zone, and backed toward the kitchen, leaving Scout to tend to Dane.

I jumped when Rem hissed, "Hey, get out of the way." I spun around to find him peeking out from behind the living room doorframe.

"Where did you come from? And what are you—"

He grabbed my arm and shushed me, then pointed back to where Dane was awkwardly shoving his hands in his pockets. He glanced over his shoulder at Rem, who made an encouraging shooing motion with his hands. Dane appeared to be in physical pain, and Scout kept right on fussing over him, like a mother hen.

"What's going on?" I whispered, leaning back against the wall.

"Dane is asking Scout out."

My eyes widened. "Oh wow, good for him. I can't wait to see how this goes down."

Ollie, who was just coming out of the bathroom down the hall, yelped and sprinted over to us. "What was that? Dane is asking Scout out?"

"Apparently."

Scout had just insisted that Dane lie down on the window seat and was fanning him with an old newspaper. Dane kept shooting us helpless looks.

Rem chuckled behind me. "It's like a car wreck, but I can't look away. What the hell is he doing?"

"No idea." I laughed. I nudged Ollie, but he was stiff and silent beside me, his gaze locked on the admittedly strange scene going on in front of us.

Dane batted Scout's fussing fingers away and struggled to sit up. "Stop, Scout, I'm not sick. I just wanted to ask you something."

He swallowed hard. I had to bite my lip to keep from stepping in and helping the poor guy out.

"I can't watch," Rem whispered. "I mean, I can, but God, it hurts. This is not what I meant when I said he should just go for it and ask her."

Ollie shot him a glare that had both Rem and I stepping back.

"You told him to ask her out? He's old enough to be her father!" Ollie's comment was well above a whisper. In fact, it was more like a shout, with barely disguised anger. Both Scout and Dane turned around to stare at him.

"Whoa with the hostility!" Rem said, giving up any pretense of hushed conversation.

Scout's gaze bounced between Ollie and Rem and then back up at Dane. Her eyes went squinty as if she were staring into the sun...or as if she couldn't quite believe Dane was trying to ask her out right now. "Is that true?" she asked. "Is that what this is?"

Dane shoved his hands in his pockets and looked at his feet. "Uh, well..." His cheeks were bright pink.

'Oh, hell no." Ollie stepped closer and took Scout's arm. "If he's breaking the bro code and asking out Gage's sister, then I am, too. Go out with me. There's karaoke at the West End on Saturday night."

"No, wait. That's where I was going to take her," Dane interrupted.

Scout stood blinking rapidly at them both.

Rem let out a low whistle. "Damn. Did not see that one coming. This is awkward."

I elbowed him hard, not sure who I felt sorrier for in this situation. Dane for getting cut off at the pass, Scout for being put on the spot, or Ollie for...well, no, I didn't feel sorry for Ollie, because he was totally cutting in on Dane's territory right now.

"This is all your fault," I said to Rem. "You gave Dane terrible advice."

"I did?"

"Yes! Don't you remember Scout had a crush on *you* like, five minutes ago?"

A wide smile spread across Rem's face. "Oh yeah. She did, huh?'

I kicked him.

"Um, excuse me, you two, but you're kind of killing me right now." Dane shot death looks in our direction.

"Sorry," Rem and I both muttered.

We all turned back to Scout, whose mouth flapped open and closed like a floundering fish. She turned to me with big eyes that yelled, "Help me!"

The part of me that had to always be in control took over. I clapped my hands together, like I was doing crowd control at a scene. "Okay, here's what's going to happen. Scout thinks you're both very nice, right, Scout?"

She nodded.

"And Scout is a young, modern woman, with choices. There's absolutely no reason she can't go out with both of you."

Scout's eyes went big, and she mouthed, "I can?" at me.

I gave her a stern look.

She nodded. "Right, yes. Of course, I can. We'll all go

on Saturday night. A group date. Rem and Whitney will go, too."

Dane scowled. Ollie didn't seem very impressed either, but Scout had found her feet. "Like it or lump it, fellas. I've got other options, you know?"

At that, without waiting for them to agree, she strutted past them, toward her bedroom. I winked at her as she passed.

Ollie and Dane both stared at me. I shrugged. "What?"

Rem slung his arm around me. "You don't get country boys, do you, babe? You've no idea what you just started."

25

REMI

"Get up."

"No. Get in." Without even opening an eye, I lifted the covers, inviting Whitney to get back into bed. I already knew she'd be dressed to go out, just like she had been the last four mornings in a row.

When no tight warm body slid into bed with me, I forced my eyes open. Whitney scowled at me, hands on her hips.

"What good is having a girlfriend if she isn't here to spoon me in the mornings?"

The corner of her mouth twitched. "What good is a boyfriend who wastes the entire day in bed?"

I raised one eyebrow. "A whole day in bed with me is never a waste, babe. Which you'd know, if you ever slept past dawn."

"You're a poor excuse for a country boy, you know? I bet Dane and Gage have been awake for hours."

"Grew up in the city, remember? And come on, I know I said I'd do whatever you needed to feel safe again, but we've been searching this property high and low for four days now and we've found nothing. No sign of anyone still camping illegally. No sign of anyone wanting to light another tent on fire. I thought you agreed yesterday that we could ease up?"

She worried her bottom lip between her teeth. "Something still feels off."

I grasped her hand and tugged her down. She plonked her butt on the mattress, the springs squeaking beneath her. That damn bottom lip was still being mangled by her teeth. I reached up and popped it free. "I hate that you're still worried about this. You need a break. The stress is going to make you gray."

"What, like you?"

"Excuse me, what? I am not going gray!"

She shrugged, all innocence. "If you say so."

I pushed past her and hurried to the bathroom mirror to inspect my hair. I poked and prodded at my scalp but couldn't see anything out of the normal.

A towel landed at my feet. "Good, now that you're up, have a shower and get dressed. We leave in ten."

She shut the door.

Dammit. That was not how this morning was supposed to go. I had plans. Plans that did not involve wandering all over the property, looking for something that wasn't there. I'd been completely serious when I'd said I would do whatever it took to make Whitney feel safe again. But this constant need of hers to always be moving, always be searching, always waiting for the next thing to go wrong wasn't helping. We'd done it her way for the best part of a week. Now it was time to do it my way.

I had a quick shower and when I emerged, Whitney was eating a bowl of steaming oatmeal while reading a paper that had to be a few days old, because that was the only way they seemed to come around here. They were delivered to the main house, where Gramps had first dibs. Then sometime over the next few days it would make its way through Scout, Dane, and then eventually into Whitney's hands. Why they didn't just get their news from their email accounts or Facebook like regular people, I didn't know. The Wi-Fi signal wasn't that bad, if you stood at the top of the tallest hill on one foot and jumped every now and then. But Whitney had seemed to pick up the habit, and she was cute with her reading glasses, sipping orange juice and flipping pages.

I slid into the seat opposite and watched her read. Eventually, she looked up over the top of her glasses. "You're staring."

"Because you're beautiful."

She put the paper down on the table. "Why are you sucking up? We're together, you don't have to do that anymore."

My mouth dropped open. "Seriously? It's been four days. You think I'm not supposed to pay you compliments anymore? That's it." I reached across the table and took the glass of juice from her fingers.

"Hey! I—"

"Hey nothing. Whatever you had planned for today, cancel it. It's Rem day."

She snorted. "It is not Rem day. Your birthday isn't until June."

"You know when my birthday is?" I asked with a pleased smile.

She shrugged. "I pay attention to details. Detective, remember?"

"Right. But not the point. It's 'Rem decides what we're doing' day, and you're too uptight and stressed. You need to lighten up."

Her gaze narrowed. "Wow," she deadpanned. "Nothing makes me feel all free and bubbly like being told to lighten up."

I ignored her. "Quit scowling and just say you'll come with me. It'll be fun. I'm going to make you forget all your troubles."

She paused. "That so?"

She might not have wanted to admit it, but I could tell the idea was appealing to her. It had to be tiring, carrying the weight and responsibility she did. Not to mention the worry over me, us breaking the rules by dating, and her friend still being in hospital. They were all heavy burdens and they made her seem much older than she really was. The woman needed some fun, and if I knew anything, I knew fun.

I linked my fingers through hers, leading her toward the door. Her slim hand fit so perfectly between my bigger fingers, and my palm tingled at her touch.

We walked in companionable silence up to the main house, and I stuck my head in the door without knocking. "Yo! Gage! You home?"

Nobody answered, but the whole reason we were here was hanging from a hook by the door. I grabbed the keys to Gage's truck and pocketed them.

Whitney frowned. "What are you doing? Stealing Gage's truck?"

"Borrowing."

"Did you ask?"

I shrugged, giving her a boyish grin. "He won't mind."

I should have known that wouldn't fly with Whitney.

"We are not stealing his truck!"

"Fine, we'll leave a note." I strode across the main room and into the kitchen with Whitney trailing me. After some rummaging, I found a pad of paper and a pen. "Dear Gage," I said out loud as I scribbled the words on the page. "Stole your truck. Hope you don't mind. Love, Whitney."

I couldn't hold my laughter in when Whitney stormed over and snatched the pen from my hand. She crossed out Whitney and changed the ending of my note so it read, Love, Rem the Dickhead.

Then she threw the pen at my head, gave me a smug smile, and flounced past me to the door. I only laughed harder. God, I loved teasing her.

I caught up with her on the path that led to the road where Gage's dirty blue truck sat waiting, ready to be 'stolen.' As I passed the fat little gnome, I had a flash of inspiration. I grabbed Whitney's hand. "Wait. Let's make this interesting."

She shook her head and backed away a step. "Oh no. Hell no, Remington James. You've got that look in your eye. Whatever you're going to say, no."

I played innocent. "What look? I don't know what you mean." I inched closer to her, wrapping one arm around her waist. I lowered my head so my lips brushed her earlobe. "Do you trust me?"

"You know that line only worked once for Aladdin. It ain't gonna work more than that for you either. Get on with it."

"Fine. Then steal the gnome."

She snorted. "What? Why would I do that?"

"Because you always do the right thing."

"And you never do?"

I shrugged. "I mostly do. But sometimes, being bad is fun, too. You should try it. I bet you've never done a single bad thing in your entire life."

"I junk-punched Karsten."

"Hardly bad. The man deserved it."

"I cheated on a test once."

I raised an eyebrow. "Seriously?"

She sighed. "Well, no. Not really. I just accidentally caught a glimpse of Sally Jenkins' math paper in fourth grade. She had the same answer as me. I'd already worked it out. But, I did go back and check that my answer was the same as hers. So it counts."

I snorted on my laughter. "So doesn't count."

Whitney pulled a face. "Fine. I like rules. I follow them. Does that make me a bad person?"

I leaned in and kissed her. "No. It makes you the best sort of person. The sort of person I wish I'd had in my life when I was younger." I paused for dramatic effect, letting her think we were done with this conversation. Then I pounced. "But we're still stealing Mr. Lolly Golly."

I scooped the creepy gnome up from his place of pride in the garden and ran for the truck. Whitney squealed and ran after me, diving into the passenger seat. "Oh my God. Drive quick. If Gramps saw us take that thing, he's going to kick us out."

I pushed the gnome onto Whitney's lap, then shoved the keys in the ignition and gunned the engine. "Is this what it's like to be sixteen and sneaking around behind your parents' backs?" I gave her a wolfish grin.

The truck kicked up mud as we peeled out of the driveway, and it wasn't until we were almost at the main road that Whitney straightened in her seat. She peered into the side mirrors, as if she were worried Gramps was chasing us with his shotgun. "Well, I didn't really do much sneaking. My parents were very forward-thinking. Always treated my brother and me like we were adults. So I came and went as I pleased."

"But you were always home by midnight, weren't you?"

Her cheeks went pink. "Ten actually."

I snorted on my laughter. Classic Whitney. She hadn't changed a bit.

She slapped my arm. "Shut up. What were you doing? Partying 'til dawn? Getting kicked out of school?"

"Something like that." I reached across the center console and took her hand. "You were lucky. My dad was in prison by the time I was sixteen. My mom didn't really care what I did. She spent most of her time at the club-house, so I did, too."

"What was that like?"

A tightness spread across my chest. Memories bombarded me. Smoky rooms. The men playing pool. Whiskey flowing. Women dancing. The fact I was sixteen hadn't stopped any of them. I'd been getting drunk since I was twelve. Fucking the club women since I was fourteen. And nobody batted an eyelid whether I went to school or not. I squeezed Whitney's hand and stared out at the bright-blue sky and the huge expanse of wide-open space. "It's not worth talking about. It's not pretty. And it's not my life anymore."

Whitney looked down at Mr. Lolly Golly on her lap and ran her hand over his faded red cap. "That bad huh?"

I nodded. "I'm not proud of it. But it was all I knew."

"You should be proud of yourself, though. You got out. You changed your life. How many guys who grew up the way you did can say the same? You're a fighter. I like that."

Warmth invaded the edges of the vise around my chest. "You mean it?"

Her fingers found the back of my neck, and she rubbed the skin there, unknowingly chasing away the prickliness I'd felt just moments before. "I mean it. You're a good guy, Remington James. I'm glad I got to meet you."

"Right back at you," I said softly, leaning into her touch. We went silent again, and I drove aimlessly, hoping I was heading toward the town. We'd been on the ranch the best part of a month and hadn't left once. The only time I'd been through the town had been the night we'd arrived.

Eventually, buildings dotted the sides of the road, and the distances between them became less and less until we entered what I guessed was a town, though it was little more than a single street of stores.

"We should keep driving." Whitney gazed out the window. "You shouldn't be seen out in public. Someone could recognize you."

I frowned. "I'm tired of hiding at the ranch. I want to just do normal couple things with you. Just for one day, okay? No one will recognize me. I'll keep my hat on and my head down."

Whitney frowned, but I smoothed over the back of

her hand with my thumb. "Please?" I asked. "One day. That's all I'm asking for. Then we can go back to the ranch and ride the perimeter for the rest of our stay. Deal?"

Whitney wrinkled her nose. "I really hate that perimeter," she mumbled.

I grinned. "I'll take that as your agreement then." I pulled the truck over and parked it on the side of the road. "Wait there," I instructed.

Whitney did as she was told while I got out and trotted around to the passenger side to hold the door for her.

"How gentlemanly of you," she said, taking my outstretched hand and hopping down from the cab.

I shut the door then trapped her against it, stealing her breath.

"Whoa, that's less gentlemanly." She laughed. "Settle down. We're in public and supposed to be keeping a low profile."

I backed off. "Fine, fine. I'll behave." I opened the door once more and grabbed Mr. Lolly Golly from Whitney's seat.

"Why are you bringing that?"

"Because he's our little friend for the day, and we're taking him on an adventure. First stop, right here." I thrust the gnome into Whitney's hands. "Go put him in the middle of the road. I want to get a pic of him on the main strip."

"What? Why?"

"We're gnoming."

"That's not a word."

"It is! You know, where you steal a gnome, take him

on adventures, then send the photos back to the gnome's owner?"

Whitney's mouth dropped open. "You want to do that to a sweet old man? You're evil."

"That sweet old man nearly shot us for being cattle thieves just a few weeks ago. And he yells at you all the time. Have you forgotten that?"

"Huh," Whitney said.

I could practically see her mind warring over whether to do it and have some harmless fun, or whether to tell me off again for technically breaking a few teeny tiny laws.

"Come on, Whit. Live a little."

"This is peer pressure, you know. I won't fall for it."

I waited.

A grin spread across her face. Her hand sneaked around to the ass pocket of her jeans, and she pulled out the cell phone she used to contact her boss. She tossed it to me. "Get the camera app open. I'm running him into the street, but if a car comes and smashes him to smithereens, you're doing the time for murder."

She darted into the street then raced back to my side. "Quick! Before someone sees us!"

It was barely eight on a Tuesday morning, and there wasn't a car, human, or animal to be seen. But I indulged her and snapped a few shots of Mr. Lolly Golly on his first adventure before strolling out to pick him up.

Whitney took the phone from my hand and grinned as she flicked through the photos. "Where will we take him next?" she asked, her eyes shining.

"Careful," I warned. "Living a life of crime is addictive. And you look like you might be enjoying it."

She slapped my arm. But when I put it around her shoulders and kissed the top of her hat-covered head, she molded into my side.

We drove around some more, taking our time, and exploring all the little streets that really held nothing of interest. But it was a thrill to just be together, like any other normal couple. Our next stop was a trip to the movies, which was like stepping back in time. For one, there was only one screen, playing one movie. And it was a movie I'd seen six months earlier, but Whit hadn't. So I bought her popcorn, and she picked out a range of candies, and we sat in the back of the dark empty theatre. We pretended to watch the movie for all of five minutes, then went to second base like we were sixteen. Mr. Lolly Golly sat on the seat beside me, getting his voyeuristic perv on. We snapped a pic of him with the popcorn then moved to our next destination.

We stopped at a café that doubled as a gas station. It was the only thing around that seemed like it served lunch-type food. We picked up a couple of sandwiches and soup in carryout containers, and I asked the young guy behind the counter where the best spot for a picnic was. We found the creek the town was named after, but it was so cold by that point that a picnic seemed a crazy idea.

"Car feast instead?" I asked Whitney.

She nodded. "It might snow again."

Clouds were coming over thick and heavy, so I left the engine running, keeping the cab warm enough that we didn't need our jackets.

"Want half my sandwich?" I asked her.

She nodded, trading for half of hers, and we both

spooned up mouthfuls of rich soup that made the cab smell delicious and warmed me from the inside.

"You nervous about the trial?" Whitney asked between mouthfuls of food. "It's only two weeks away."

I put my Styrofoam cup of soup into a holder and leaned back, watching her eat. She took delicate nibbles of her sandwich but slurped down her soup like someone was going to take it away from her.

"No, I'm not nervous," I said, answering her question. "I've barely thought about it to be honest."

"You haven't?"

"Been too busy thinking about you." It was the truth, too, not just a line. She occupied all my thoughts in a way no woman had for a very long time. Or ever, really.

She smiled, but it was almost a grimace, and I twisted in my seat so I was facing her. "Hey, what's wrong?"

"I'm nervous for you. What happens after the trial?"

"Well, hopefully they put Miles Mitchell in prison, and that's the last I hear about it."

"You think it's going to be that easy? That he won't want some sort of revenge? What about the other guys in the club?"

I sighed. These were all the questions I hadn't wanted to think about. "I don't know, Whit."

"I don't think you're going to be able to walk back into your own life the way Hank promised you."

"I have to. I've got a brother. Friends. A job."

"If you go back, all of those people could be put at risk if the club comes after you, looking for retaliation."

I shook my head. "It won't be like that." It couldn't. I refused to give up everything I'd worked for.

Whitney didn't say anything, but the silence hung

over us, as ominous as the building storm. I picked up Mr. Lolly Golly and eyed the abandoned play equipment that sat lonely on the bank because kids weren't crazy enough to be out in this weather. "Come on, let's get a shot of him on the swings. Or down on that dock. If we wait a little longer, it might start snowing. Mr. Lolly Golly could make a snowman friend." I was babbling to fill the space, and to change the topic. I didn't want to think about what would happen in two weeks when we had to leave this place. I liked it here. I didn't want to think about real life and what that meant for me.

Or worse. What that meant for Whitney and me. If she went back to being a detective and I went back to bullfighting on the pro circuit, where the hell did that leave us? My insides hollowed at the thought. We'd built a bubble, where she and I worked perfectly.

But bubbles popped. And so would ours. It was inevitable.

No bubble lasted forever.

26

WHITNEY

Fearing for our lives, I talked Rem out of sharing Mr. Lolly Golly's adventures with Gramps. We just quietly returned the gnome to his rightful spot, no harm done. Rem caught me looking through the photos later that night, though, and gave me a soft smile. He'd been right to push me out of my comfort zone a little bit. I'd needed it.

It was with that thought in mind that I let myself be dragged to a small-town karaoke bar. On Saturday night, the five of us—Ollie, Rem, Scout, Dane, and I—drove into town together and joined the line of people waiting to get inside.

The middle-aged couple in front of us shuffled forward, and we followed suit, taking a few steps to close the gap that had opened up. I eyed the woman's thick coat enviously. Mine was really not cutting it. Winter had really hit, and it was no joke. But in my defense, I hadn't been expecting a lineup. I thought we'd just walk straight inside, where presumably, they had heaters. But Scout had explained that there was little else in the way of a nightlife, so if anyone was going out, this was where they went.

The not-so-melodic wailing of a butchered Mariah Carey song wafted out, and I winced when an attempted high note went way off course. "Is someone strangling a cat in there?" I asked Rem. "Should we call animal protection?"

"I'm sure they have a no strangling policy." He slung his arm around my shoulders, and I gratefully sank into his body warmth. The line moved a few more steps. Just another five or six people, and we'd be inside, out of the biting chill. And inside where the singing was like nails down a chalkboard, but hey, who needed eardrums anyway?

Scout elbowed me. "This is supposed to be fun. Remember?"

"What exactly about chaperoning your weird three-some date is fun for me?"

Scout grinned. "It's fun for me, though."

I laughed. "Yeah, I bet it is."

We both glanced back at Dane and Ollie who were being distinctly weird. I couldn't blame them. I didn't think this was what either of them had been expecting when they'd asked Scout out.

When we finally made it inside, I made a beeline for the bar, ordering whiskey shots for all of us. Rem raised an eyebrow.

"What?"

"Nothing. I just didn't think you were a drinker."

"I'm not!"

"The shots say otherwise. Not that I'm judging. I am

down for whiskey." He reached past me and grabbed one of the little glasses, downing it without bothering to wait for the rest of us.

I wrinkled my nose. He was probably right. I shouldn't be drinking while I was undercover. But I just wanted to be warm. Hard liquor seemed a good way to get there quickly.

Rem pushed a shot glass into my hand. "I can practically see your thoughts. Drink. You can take one night off and have some fun. You haven't had a break in over a month."

I hesitated, running my gaze over him. He'd let his stubble grow out into a full-fledged beard, and he had a ball cap pulled low on his brow. Unless people got right up in his face, nobody was going to recognize him.

The lure of drinks with my friends was too much. I downed my shot, loving the way it burned into my chest. "Another," I told the bartender.

Rem grinned. "Make it two. We're drinking tonight!"

Scout and Ollie cheered. Dane appeared as uncomfortable as I was, so I passed him a shot, which he threw back quicker than I'd thought possible.

"Dutch courage?" I asked him quietly. We followed Rem, leading the way to a small table.

Dane nodded. "I don't know what's wrong with me. I haven't even said anything to her yet."

Ollie wasn't having any such problems. He was telling Scout some story about the last time he'd come to this bar. The conversation flowed easily between the two of them, and Scout's smile was wide.

I patted Dane's arm. "You got this. You just gotta get in

there and show her there's another side to you. One she hasn't seen before."

"What if she thinks I'm too old? Or too much like her brother?"

Rem poked his head into our conversation. "I'd be more worried she thinks of you as a father figure."

"Rem!"

Dane glared. "I'm not old enough to be her father," he huffed.

"Who's a father?" Scout asked, only catching the end of the conversation.

"No one," Dane said quickly.

Scout's brow wrinkled, but she shrugged, following Ollie when he nabbed a table. It was too small for the five of us, but we were lucky to get a table at all with the number of people in the room. Rem sank onto one of the chairs, pulling me onto his lap. Ollie took inspiration and did the same with Scout. Dane scowled as he took the last seat. He crossed his arms over his chest and shot Ollie a dirty look.

"Well, this is enough awkward for me." I twisted so I could see Rem's face. "Come dance?"

He nodded, and I got to my feet, pulling him up with me. Dane seemed distressed by us leaving, but hey, sink or swim. I was pretty sure he'd find his feet once the alcohol loosened him up a little.

The man hosting the karaoke called up a new singer, a young woman with flaming-red hair that fell down her back in waves. A country song started up, and when she opened her mouth, whoa. She belted out the first line, and the crowd around us all stopped and cheered. Like the ultimate pro, though, she just kept right on singing. I snaked my arms around Rem's waist but found him standing stiff and rigid. He stared off toward the bathrooms.

"You okay?" I asked.

As if I'd interrupted his daydream, he shook himself and focused back on me. "Yeah, sorry. That was weird. I thought I saw somebody I knew."

Warning alarms went off in my head. I reached for the purse that hung over my shoulder on a delicate strap. My gun was tucked away inside. "Who? Where? Show me."

He gathered me flush against his chest and grabbed the back of my head, leaning down and kissing me hard.

I shoved him away. "No, wait. We need to—"

"Kiss. There's a million blond men in the world. It's no big deal. I don't even know why his face was familiar. Might have been the guy who served us at the movie theatre the other day. No biggie. It wasn't anyone from the club. So just kiss me, Whit. That's all I've wanted to do today. Just hold you in my arms and dance and kiss you. Can't we just do that? I just want to forget who we really are for a moment."

I sighed and let Rem lift my arms and drape them around his neck. I stared up into his dark-brown eyes and my insides softened. "How do you do that?"

"What?"

"Always get your own way. I keep trying to do the right thing, and you keep making it impossible to resist you."

"It's my boyish charm."

"It's something." We swayed in time to the music. "You make me reckless. Careless."

"I make you live in the moment."

He was right. He did.

A shadow crossed his face.

I snaked my hand into his hair and tugged the ends gently. "Hey. What's that about?"

"Nothing."

"You've gone all quiet and broody."

"I just wish things were different. I wish we'd met in this bar tonight."

"What would you do if we had?"

"Buy you a drink. Bore you stupid with my rodeo stories. Then take you home."

I stifled a laugh. "You aren't going to do all those things tonight? We've already had a drink. It's only a matter of time before the rodeo stories start. And we live together, so I'm pretty sure you're taking me home."

"Only temporarily, though."

I went quiet and laid my head on his chest. "I know."

He stopped dancing, and I lifted my gaze again.

"What do you want, Whit?" he asked. "When this is all over, I mean. Is this it for us? Less than two weeks and then we're done?"

A lump rose in my throat at the very thought. "No," I said without missing a beat. "We're not done. At least not from where I'm standing."

"Not done from over here either."

My heart swelled. "I don't know how to make this work," I whispered. "All I know is that I want to."

"This isn't a rebound, then?" His gaze burned through mine, hope written all over his features.

I shook my head hard and pressed up onto my toes so our mouths were only a few inches apart, our gazes closer to level. "You were never a rebound," I whispered. "You couldn't have been. Not when you're you, and I'm me. We're too good together."

"I agree. That night of my arrest should have been the worst moment of my life. And then I met you, and now it seems like it was only the beginning. I want to keep this going. Once we go home, and the trial is over, and all of this is behind me. I'm going to claim you. I'm going to tell the world that you're my girl. I'm going to tell them I love you."

My heart stopped.

A goofy grin spread across Rem's face. "Yeah, I said it. I'm in love with you, Whitney. Don't freak out, okay? Don't even say anything. Just kiss me."

So I did. I kissed him as the songs changed, and the world around us disappeared. I kissed him as my head spun, and minutes turned into hours.

I kissed him until three little words fell from my lips.

"Take me home."

27

REMI

*L*aughing like a couple of schoolkids, who had just been caught making out on the doorstep, we raced back to the table the others were still occupying. I trailed my fingers up and down Whitney's spine, and she tucked herself beneath my arm, her lips close to my neck.

I hadn't meant to tell her I loved her. I wasn't even one-hundred-percent sure, until in that moment, it all suddenly became clear. I'd blurted it out before my rational mind had even had a chance to process. I pulled her tighter to my chest. I meant it. I meant every syllable of those words. I knew she wasn't ready to say them back and I didn't want her to feel pressured in any way. But there was no stopping them once I realized they were there. Now I was going to take her home and show her exactly how much I loved her body as well as her heart, her mind, and every other thing that made her special.

Right after I kissed her stupid. Again. We stopped just a foot away from the table, and I covered her mouth with mine. She responded immediately, tilting her head back and fisting the front of my shirt. Her lips parted, her tongue sought out mine, and we moved together until we were both panting, desperate for more.

"I don't know if I can wait until we get home. You up for a quickie in the bathroom?" I said quietly.

Scout groaned loudly. "Heard that! I think I liked it better when you two were siblings."

A couple at the table next to us shot us an alarmed look, and Scout clapped a hand over her mouth, stifling her laughter. I didn't bother explaining to the eavesdroppers. What did it matter? In less than two weeks we'd be out of here. We'd go back to our real lives. Together. I didn't know yet exactly what that would be like, but it was something I'd fight to make happen.

"We're out of here," I said, clapping hands with Dane. My gaze fell on a parcel wrapped in brown paper and twine that hogged half the table space. "What's that?"

"Oh!" Scout said. She jumped out of the chair I'd vacated earlier. She shoved the parcel toward me. "The bartender gave it to me when I went to get another round of drinks. Said someone left it for you."

I frowned at the parcel, picking it up. It was soft beneath the wrapping, and lighter than I'd been expecting. "You sure it was for me?" I asked Scout. "I don't know anyone here."

Whitney's mouth pulled tight. The smile fell from Scout's lips as she realized the weight of my words.

"Shit," Dane muttered. "Sorry, bro. I should have thought about it. I wasn't paying attention..."

I shook my head. Whitney's gaze roamed the bar, bouncing from one table to another. She clutched her purse, and I knew she was itching to pull her gun out. But with no immediate threat, we both knew that would do nothing but cause a panic.

"Just open it," she gritted out.

I slipped the hastily tied string from one corner and then the other, and balled it up, tucking it in my pocket. With rising dread, I peeled away the brown paper wrapping and then blinked at the contents.

"What is it?" Scout asked, craning in.

It was a mess of black leather and blood-red paint. Ripped shreds of fabric, that had once been a jacket. Piece by piece, my brain put together the letters and symbols. A K here. A skull there. Half a C.

A Kings of Chaos logo in shreds. Huge slashes, where the material had once been whole.

I fingered it gingerly and flipped it over. Something smaller clattered to the table.

Whitney sucked in a breath. Ollie swore.

A small name tag with a single word embroidered with black thread.

Viper.

And through it, the serrated blade of a hunting knife.

The room around me spun while I tried to scan our surroundings. They were here. The club. Whitney had been right all along, and now I'd put her and everyone in this bar in danger.

Whitney covered the knife back up with the tattered remains of the jacket I'd worn for half my adult life.

"Where did they get this from?" Whitney asked, slipping straight into detective mode.

But I couldn't think. All I wanted to do was get her out of here. Away from this bar. Away from this town. If the

Kings had come for me, she couldn't be anywhere near me when shit went down.

"Rem! Was this at the ranch?"

I refocused on Whitney. "No. I haven't touched that jacket since before I went to prison. It's been in the back of my closet in my apartment. Somebody has been in my home."

Her mouth pulled into a tight line. "We're leaving."

"We'll come," Dane said.

But Whitney held up her hand. "Don't. You're safer here in a crowd of people. The three of you need to stay in town tonight, okay? Call Gage and tell him to get Gramps out, too."

"You think they're going to be looking for you at the ranch?"

"I don't know, but it's not worth finding out. Dane, can we take your car? There won't be a flight tonight, but we'll go back to the ranch, get our things, and drop it back to you on our way out of town."

Scout's eyes went wide. "You're leaving?"

"We have to," I said, this time fully on Whitney's side. "I can't be here anymore. These aren't men you want to underestimate." Though I already had. All the little things I'd ignored and written off as coincidence, playing them off as no big deal because they hadn't been hard proof, now seemed like blaring warning signs.

And I'd ignored them all.

My brain still screamed this wasn't the King's style. It was too sloppy. Since when had they ever bothered to scare people? That wasn't them. They went in, guns blazing, taking no prisoners.

But what did I know? I wasn't one of them anymore.

Years had passed. Times had changed. The evidence was right there in front of me, in pieces. A warning that couldn't be ignored.

Dane tossed his keys to me and then clapped me on the back. "Be careful."

I nodded.

With my hand on the small of Whitney's back, we weaved through the crowd and back outside into the cold night. Snow fell in our hair, and gusts of icy wind sent needles of pain through my skin. It was only a short run to Dane's pickup, but Whitney held her hand up as we approached. In the darkness of the gravel lot, she pulled her gun from her bag.

"Got a spare one of those in your boots?" I asked, but the joke was halfhearted and fell on deaf ears.

"Check the cab. I'm going to check the bed."

Every muscle in my body wanted to stop her. I wanted to tell her to stop and wait and let me do it. This was my mess. I'd been the one who had pushed her to ignore her instincts, distracted her with kisses and sexual innuendo. It should be me who got us out of it.

But I respected her too much. And I knew her. I knew she was more than capable of handling this situation, and so I took my cues from her. If she said check the cab, then that was what I'd do, even if my heart was in my mouth the entire time.

We moved in unison down either side of the truck, Whit with her gun out, pointed low to the ground, her movements quick and sharp. I jerked open the driver's side door.

Nothing.

Before I could even look to the back of the truck,

Whitney was doing the same on the passenger side.

"Nothing here. Let's go."

Whitney called the local sheriff's department, identifying herself and asking for backup, then her boss to organize our way out of town. I declared I needed to warn my brother when we got back to the cabin, and Whitney agreed. But after that, we drove in silence, both of us lost to our own thoughts. With each passing mile, the weather outside the truck grew worse. The gentle snowflakes turned into ice pellets, pinging off the windshield and away into the darkness of the night beyond. The road that led to the ranch was like driving into the unknown. Visibility dropped, and I slowed the vehicle to little more than a crawl. Eventually, the main house came into view. No lights burned behind the curtains, and Gage's rusted blue truck was gone from its usual spot by the garden. Nothing else had changed. The cows still huddled in their pens. The rocking chairs still sat on the porch. But the ranch felt different. Darker. Colder. In the space of the two hours we'd been gone, it had changed from a place where I could breathe freely, to a place where demons lurked in the shadows. Demons in the form of men who didn't belong. Men who weren't from this life and tainted everything they touched.

I was one of those men. I'd brought the Kings of Chaos here and tainted this beautiful spot with the ugliness inside me that I'd tried to bury. Tried and failed.

I pulled the truck to a stop outside the cabin I shared with Whitney.

In the morning, I'd be on the first flight out of Wyoming.

If we made it through the night.

28

WHITNEY

*M*y eyelids drooped, and I blinked hard, refusing to let them close. I jumped up and down on the spot a few times, shaking some energy into my tired limbs.

The porch boards creaked behind me, and I spun on my heel, gun raised.

"Whoa, Whit. It's me. I brought coffee." Rem's voice was low and calm. Two coffee mugs were clutched in his fingers. A tiny splash of brown liquid sloshed over the side, dripping off his hand. It was the only sign that me pointing a gun at his head might have worried him.

I lowered my weapon. "You should be in the cabin."

"So should you. It's freezing, and you've been out in the darkness for hours." He passed me a mug of coffee. "There's no one here. Come inside and get some sleep. Let the locals do their thing.""

"Can't." I was too tired to elaborate. I did need sleep, and the sheriff had sent over a couple of men, who were standing guard with me. But I was too wired. Every instinct in me screamed to get the hell out of this place. But the storm had made that impossible. By the time we'd made it back to the cabin, the visibility had been atrocious. The locals had arrived not long after we had, and we'd been told to sit tight and wait out the bad weather, at least until the morning light made driving to the airport safer. I could have overruled them. But the frightening winds and whipping snow had me heeding their warnings. I didn't know this area. I had little experience even driving a regular road in the snow. I didn't want to end up crashing Dane's truck into a freezing ditch.

Watching that knife fall out onto the table kept playing out in my head. Rem's tent on fire. Our open cabin door. I couldn't shake the feeling someone had been watching us almost the entire time we'd been here. My blood ran cold. Despite the fact my body begged for sleep, my brain constantly screamed danger, danger, danger.

Danger meant protect. Protect the people I loved. The *person* I loved.

I bit my lip to stop the words from tumbling out. I'd wanted to say them back to him earlier in the bar. I should have. I wished I had. Because now I wouldn't get the chance. And he'd never know the way I felt about him.

I'd made a mistake here. I'd let myself fall for a man, and look what had happened. Just like when I'd fallen for Karsten. No good came from me letting my guard down and letting men into my life. Either I got hurt. Or in this case, I hurt someone else.

"I'm sorry," he said quietly. He held his mug an inch away from his lips, and steam misted over his face.

"It's not your fault."

"It's not yours either."

I didn't say anything. There was no point arguing. He was a witness. I was a cop. When I said it wasn't his fault, it was true. When he said it, it was just an attempt to make me feel better. And I didn't need it.

"Did you call Abel? Is he okay?"

Rem nodded. "He's fine. Nothing out of the ordinary happening at his place, but he's on alert. I'll check in with him again tomorrow."

"Good." I took another swallow of my coffee before pushing the half-empty mug back into his hand. "I need to keep moving. Stay in the house."

I could practically see the war inside him playing out. He wanted to argue. He wanted to yell at me, tell me to go inside and rest, to let him take over. But he was smart enough to realize I wasn't going to listen.

"What can I do to help?"

My insides turned mushy. He was such a good man. I knew he wanted nothing more than to go all alpha male on me, sling me over my shoulder, and lock me up somewhere safe. I knew because I felt it in every look he gave me. Every touch. The man loved me. I felt it, as much as heard it. And when Rem loved, he loved hard. I'd seen that in the way he talked about his brother. And the way he spoke about his friends, and even his job.

But he respected me, too. Something Karsten had never done. For that, I was grateful, but I also hated it. Because it made it so damn hard to walk away from him right now. I couldn't even imagine saying goodbye to him once the sun came up.

"Could you pack our things? I want to be on the road at dawn."

He gave me a soft, sad smile. Then he nodded and walked away.

My heart clenched. But I searched the darkness once more, praying it stayed empty.

---

*A*t the first sign of light creeping over the horizon, Rem appeared on the porch, our bags clutched in his hands. He threw them in the back of Dane's truck, then leaned on it, waiting for me.

He was the ultimate cowboy, standing there like that: boots, jeans, jacket, and hat. His hands shoved deep in his pockets. Denim clinging to muscled thighs. His beard neatly trimmed and so damn sexy. His eyes tracked my every movement, concern etched into the crinkles at the corners. "You okay?" he asked.

I wasn't. I was tired. Confused. Scared. I wanted to run across the yard and throw myself into his arms and let him hold me. But I didn't. The wall I'd built up around my heart in the early hours of the morning wouldn't let me. I'd thought we'd get more time. More time here on the ranch, and more time back at home.

But hope had died inside me during the night. It might only be two weeks until the trial. But a threat had been made on Rem's life last night. That couldn't be taken lightly. He needed to go into witness protection. Not just now. After the trial as well. I wasn't even sure he realized yet. And I couldn't bring myself to tell him. I didn't know how.

I let him drive. I was too tired to safely be behind the wheel, and I must have nodded off the minute we were on the road. I didn't wake until we pulled to a stop in front of the only motel in town. Rem checked his phone. "Dane sent me a message last night with his room number. He's in number twenty-three. Wait here, I'll go get him. He said he'd drive us into the airport."

"I'll come." I rubbed my eyes. "I want to say goodbye to Scout and the others."

"There won't be anyone at reception this early, but Dane should know which rooms they're in."

I nodded and got out of the car, catching myself on the door when my legs buckled under me. Apparently, the quick nap hadn't done much to replenish my energy stores.

We wandered along the row of doors. It was so quiet our footsteps seemed louder than normal. Or perhaps that was the fact my feet were dragging so heavily. I didn't have it in me to step lightly.

Rem stopped in front of a door with flaking white paint. A silver twenty-three was nailed to the middle of it. Rem knocked quietly.

A loud groan came from inside, and I frowned, looking up at Rem. He checked the number again.

"You sure this is the right room?" I asked. "That didn't sound like Dane."

"I was just thinking that."

Rem knocked again, and a flurry of action seemed to happen behind the closed door. After another long moment, it opened a crack and one bloodshot eye peered out.

"Dane?" Rem asked.

The door opened an inch farther, and Dane blinked rapidly in the bright light. He was shirtless, in only a pair of boxer shorts. They were inside out.

"Since when do you wear boxers?" Rem asked. "I thought you were a commando guy?"

"What?" Dane asked, looking confused.

I ignored that line of questioning. I didn't even want to know how Rem knew about Dane's underwear preferences. "Big night?" I asked. "You look like shit."

He straightened a little and ran a hand through his hair. "I don't even know. My brain hurts." His voice was coarse, as if he'd been talking a lot. Or singing a lot, maybe?

"Can you drive?" Rem asked, a frown creasing the space between his eyebrows.

Dane clutched the door tighter. "Not without vomiting. Just take my truck. Leave the keys inside. I'll get Gage to take me to the airport later to pick it up."

Country people were so unbelievably trusting. The cop in me blanched at the idea, but we had to get there somehow. It wasn't like there was an airport shuttle that ran back and forth on the hour. "Do you know which room Scout is in?" I asked. "I want to say goodbye."

Dane winced. "Yeah. I know." He opened the door a little wider.

Scout's blonde head poked out sheepishly from behind him. "Hi." The T-shirt Dane had worn last night hung from her smaller shoulders.

I raised one eyebrow, a smile pulling at the corners of my mouth for the first time since before everything had happened last night. Scout's cheeks went pink.

Rem chuckled. "Poor Ollie. Which room is he in?"

"Actually, I'm in here, too," Ollie's voice called from somewhere in the depths of the room.

Dane groaned and pressed two fingers to his temples.

My eyes widened, and I grabbed Scout's arm, yanking her out into the early morning sun. She squealed and tugged the bottom of Dane's shirt farther down her legs. I wondered if she even had panties on.

I grabbed her for a hug, turning my face so my mouth was near her ear. "The minute I get home, I'm calling you and you are going to tell me every little detail of whatever the hell went on here last night."

She stepped back an inch, her grin so wide it had to hurt. She winked.

Rem gave Dane a man hug that looked awkward as hell, but I knew the two held genuine affection for each other. "Thanks for everything," Rem said. "I'm real glad I got to meet you, and I want you to come out and watch a rodeo sometime, yeah?" Rem pulled back an inch, his nose wrinkling. "I'm gonna quit hugging you now, though, because you smell like sex."

Dane went bright red, and Ollie laughed from inside the room.

Scout hugged Rem, and he kissed her on the cheek. "Good for you, girl," he whispered, making her laugh.

I gave Dane a wave, because he looked too green to hug. I elbowed Rem. "Let's go before Dane vomits on one of us."

"I'm fine," he gritted out. Clearly a lie.

"Bye, Ollie!" I called, who yelled back but still didn't come to the door. I didn't even want to know why. If Scout had him tied up in there somewhere, I didn't need to know about it. She was clearly way kinkier than I'd given the country girl credit for.

Rem and I got back into Dane's truck, and he started the engine before glancing over at me. We both burst into laughter. Mine was fueled by exhaustion and worry, but it felt good, nonetheless.

"Fuck," Rem swore, wiping tears of amusement from the corners of his eyes. "That was not what I was expecting."

I tried to control myself, but I'd reached that point where I couldn't stop. I laughed until my stomach hurt.

Rem got us back on the road, and I eventually settled down. Though every few minutes, I'd remember the look on Scout's face, and I'd burst into a whole new round of laughter.

Rem kept darting little glances at me, between concentrating on the road stretching ahead of us. "You're seriously stunning when you laugh, you know that?"

The comment sobered me. I stared at his profile. So handsome. So strong. He was everything I'd wanted in a man. And I'd had it for such a short amount of time. A sob rose up my throat so quickly and unexpectedly that I had no chance of stopping it. "I love you," I whispered. I brushed my tears away with the back of my hand, embarrassed. "I'm sorry. I'm exhausted."

Rem pulled the car over on the side of the road and got out, slamming the door. I watched through blurry eyes as he rounded the hood of the truck to come to my door. He yanked it open, unclipped my seat belt, and then I was in his arms.

My head dropped back, and his lips found mine. I clung to him, desperately trying to get closer, our tongues tangling, needing more, trying to devour each other. I put everything I had into that kiss on the side of the road. I pretended this was just the beginning, when really, I think we both knew it was a goodbye.

"I love you," he said fiercely, cupping my face between his palms. "This isn't it. I know it feels like it. I know what last night meant. But this isn't it, you hear me? I will come for you. The minute it's safe. I'll come. And we'll be together."

I blinked up, not daring to believe his words, but not brave enough to deny them either. "I love you, too."

His mouth caught my sobs, and his kisses fought to hold me together. We stood there, as the sun rose, kissing and whispering words of love, promising each other a future that might never happen.

Then we got back in the car. This time, I drove us to the airport, where we got on a plane that would take him out of my life.

And there wasn't a damn thing I could do about it.

29

WHITNEY

*S*ergeant Minor glanced up when I rapped the back of my knuckles across the glass pane of her office door. "Whitney. Good to have you back. How are you?" She motioned for me to come inside.

I closed the door behind me and sank into the seat across from her. I didn't bother answering her question about how I was. What was I supposed to say? I was heartbroken over leaving Rem? Scared about everything that had happened? Worried about where he was right now and who was keeping him safe? Were they doing a good job?

Couldn't have done a worse job than me, I supposed. I'd let myself get distracted. No. Worse, I'd let myself get so far past distracted that I'd fallen in love with him. It was my own fault I wasn't with him now.

"I made a full statement with Hank. Explained everything that happened. Though you already know that CliffsNotes version."

"That's not why I asked you to come see me before you went home. We weren't expecting you back for another two weeks."

I opened my mouth to protest, but Janice silenced me with a look. I closed my mouth and waited.

"If you need something to do in that time, you can check in on Mia. And her husband, too. I don't think he's handling it too well."

My shoulders slumped. "She's still no better?" I had come straight from the airport. I hadn't even stopped by my place to get my personal phone.

"The last report I had was exactly what I relayed to you while you were on assignment. There was no change, but no reason she shouldn't wake up. She just has to do it in her own time. Lucas could use your support, I'm sure."

I straightened in my chair. "Of course."

Janice nodded, and I made my way to the door again. My hand was on the knob when she spoke.

"Oh, Whitney?"

I glanced back over my shoulder. "Yes?"

"You didn't ask about Karsten. Do you want to know where his case is at?"

I tried to keep my expression neutral. Fact was, I didn't really care. I hoped he'd had his trial and was enjoying a stint in prison. It was where he belonged. But Janice seemed to want to tell me, so I nodded.

"His charges were dropped. Insufficient evidence."

My mouth dropped open. "You're kidding me? So he's out?"

"He was never in. I thought you knew? He was just waiting for his trial."

"They gave him bail?"

She nodded.

Irritation prickled at me. "So, he's gone back to his family. Like nothing ever happened."

Janice's voice softened. "I don't know. I'm sorry. I know how you feel about him."

"Felt." Past tense. I didn't feel shit for Karsten. A laugh bubbled up inside me. It was ridiculous how little his name had come to mean in such a short amount of time. I wanted him in prison, because he'd broken the law. I thought we'd had more than enough evidence to bury him, but money talked. He could afford the expensive lawyers, who'd obviously been worth their money since he was walking around a free man.

I did hope his wife hadn't taken him back, though. I hoped she had enough respect for herself to kick his lying, cheating ass to the curb.

Ugh. I felt dirty even thinking about him. When I got home, I'd take a hot shower and scrub my skin and house of all trace of him.

Janice watched me quietly. "Whit, I know I'm your boss, but I like to think we're friends, too. If you need to talk..."

"I don't want to talk about Karsten."

"You can talk to me about anything."

Shit.

Guilt washed over me. I hadn't explained to her what had happened out at the ranch with Rem. I'd given my statement but hadn't mentioned the emotional or physical connection the two of us had established.

I bit my lip. I tried to force out the words. Something else entirely came out. "I'm fine."

Janice nodded toward the door. "Dismissed then. See you in two weeks."

I filled the next few days promising a cranky Rusty I'd never leave him again, visiting Mia, and purging Karsten from my life. I took down every photo of the two of us. A lot of his clothes had disappeared from the closet we'd shared, and I frowned as I stared at them, realizing he'd been in my house while I'd been at the ranch. My skin crawled at the thought. I bagged up everything of his I could find. His suits, his shoes, ties, aftershave. All of it went into two big trash bags. I tried shoving them into the trash can, but it wasn't big enough, so I left them behind some potted plants in the entranceway. I'd take them to the dump as soon as I could, but at least they were out of sight and out of mind.

I hired a locksmith to change the locks. I went online and maxed out my credit card to buy myself all new sheets and bedding, including a new mattress. Then I rolled up my sleeves and cleaned my house from top to bottom, until the whole place reeked of eucalyptus-scented disinfectant.

I didn't care. I just wanted a clean, fresh start.

For when Rem came back.

My heart clenched. It was stupid to get my hopes up. To hope he might not have to go into witness protection once the trial was done. I was selfish for hoping he wouldn't go. There were real threats on his life. I'd seen it with my own eyes. Witness protection was the safest place for him. But witness protection meant giving him up for good. Meant him giving up the life he loved. It was hard to reconcile all those things. If I was this confused, I couldn't imagine how Rem must feel.

I just wanted to see him.

Hold him.

Tell him I loved him.

I wiped absently at the tear rolling down my cheek and eyed the suitcases still sitting on my bedroom floor. I'd done nothing but unpack my toiletries. I was too afraid my clothes would smell like Rem. Or worse, afraid they wouldn't.

It had been days, and I couldn't leave two huge suitcases on my bedroom floor forever.

"Rip the Band-Aid off, Whit," I mumbled to myself.

I pulled out a shirt and smiled when I realized it wasn't one of mine. It was one of Rem's T-shirts, with a bucking bull on the back. It was made from soft cotton and long enough to just cover my ass. I'd stolen it to use as a nightshirt. I held it to my nose and inhaled. Rem's scent filled my lungs, immediately calming my rapid heartbeat. It was the closest thing I was going to get to his arms, and I didn't care it was the ugliest shade of yellow-brown I'd ever seen. I took off my shirt and replaced it with Rem's.

The rest of the unpacking went much quicker. I unloaded a pile of underwear into my drawer, grateful I'd done laundry just the day before we'd left so I'd had nothing to wash but the clothes I'd worn home. I rifled through the mixture of plain cotton underwear, noticing the lacy set I'd brought was missing.

I'd never gotten around to wearing them for Rem, he'd seemed to prefer me without underwear anyway. But he'd packed my things while I'd been stalking the night, waiting for a group of men who had never appeared. What a waste of a last night that had been. I wished now I'd spent it curled in his arms, or beneath him, his body moving over mine. A wry grin lifted the corner of my mouth as I thought about Rem tucking my underwear into his pocket. Dirty cowboy. The thought of him taking a souvenir warmed me all over, heat shooting straight between my legs. With his scent on the shirt I was wearing, I could almost pretend he was here. I closed my eyes, picturing his face. The way his eyes crinkled slightly in the corners because he smiled so often. The cut ridges of his abs and that delicious V of muscle that ran either side of his hips. His cock, so perfect, though I'd never told him that. But he'd known, from the way I moaned.

My nipples tightened. I gripped the neck of the shirt and held it to my nose, breathing in his smell. A pulse picked up between my legs. "I wish you were here," I murmured.

I slid my hand down the front of my sweatpants and inside my underwear. Daylight streamed into my bedroom from the open window, but I was on the second story, and none of my neighbors' houses looked directly into mine. Still, it felt deliciously wicked to do this in the middle of the day. But it felt good. With my eyes closed, I pretended my hands were Rem's. In my head, my fingers became his. Stroking my outer lips. Circling the nub of nerve endings before searching lower, deeper between my legs and slipping inside me. My hips bucked as two fingers stroked in and out, pumping in time to the beat of my heart. In my head, Rem kissed me. My head dropped back, and my fingers moved faster, my free hand coming up to squeeze my nipple through my shirt.

"Come for me, baby," he whispered, the sound barely an echo in my mind of another time we'd been together, and I worked myself harder, faster. Shivers coursed through me. My legs trembled, my fingers slick with my own pleasure. "Come, baby. Yell my name."

"Rem!" I yelled, clenching down on my fingers. "Oh!" My legs buckled, and I caught myself on the poster leg of my bed. I leaned hard on it, my core pulsing and contracting as waves of pleasure slipped over me. Eventually, I pulled damp fingers from my underwear and sank onto the mattress. Aftershocks tingled through my entire body. My breath came in pants, and I finally opened my eyes.

Disappointment crushed in. Was that all I had left to look forward to? Making myself come while I dreamed of the man whose every look set me on fire? The orgasm had been good. I could give myself credit for that.

But I'd had the real thing.

I wanted it back.

With a sigh laced with defeat, I stood and dragged myself to the shower. I needed to go see Mia. I needed my best friend, even if she couldn't talk back.

I got changed into a long skirt, boots, and slipped a thin jacket over my top. For the first time since I'd been home, I added earrings, a scarf, and light day makeup. It was time to start my life again. I was in a limbo of sorts until the trial when I'd get to see Rem again, but until then, I couldn't keep dragging my ass all over the place. I need to eat regularly. Exercise. Start getting my head back in the game for when I'd go back to work next week.

I drove myself downtown through the sparse afternoon traffic and parked in the hospital lot. I didn't bother stopping at reception, already knowing the way to Mia's room from my previous visits. I followed the twists and turns of the corridors, trying not to wrinkle my nose at the unpleasant hospital smell. Some fresh air wouldn't have gone astray, but none of the windows opened.

The door to Mia's room was already ajar, and I slowed my steps as I approached. I tapped the door with my fingernails and pushed it open a little wider.

Lucas glanced up and smiled, motioning me in. "Hey, I was just about to call you."

"You were?" My stomach swirled, and I ran my gaze over Mia's still form, but everything looked the same as yesterday. She was still attached to a multitude of monitors and tubes.

"She woke up."

I snapped my head back to Lucas. "What?"

His smile turned wide. "Just for a moment. But it was her, Whit. She squeezed my hand, and I could tell she recognized me."

A sob burst from my chest. "Oh, thank God."

Lucas stood from his seat, offering it to me. I gratefully sank down before the relief threatened to take my legs out from underneath me.

Lucas put his hand on my shoulder and squeezed. "She asked for you. Your name was the only thing she said."

Tears rolled down my face. "She did?" I picked up Mia's hand. It was colder than it should have been, and I rubbed it briskly, searching her face for any signs of her waking again, but there was nothing.

"The doctor said she'll be in and out. She's been unresponsive for a long time, and her injuries were severe. We still don't know if she'll have long-lasting damage."

"But this is a good thing, right? That she woke up? That she recognized you and remembered my name?"

Lucas grinned. "It's a very good thing."

I gripped Mia's hand. "You're tough. You're going to beat this. Then we'll go back to work. Together. Partners, always."

Lucas patted my shoulder. "I need to make some calls. Her parents will want to know, and I'll call your boss. Will you stay with her?"

I nodded. "Of course. I'm not leaving until she opens her eyes again."

He gave Mia one last, lingering look and then strode out the door, producing his phone from his pocket as he went.

"You've got a good one, there," I said to Mia when he'd gone. "You're lucky. He really loves you."

She didn't respond. I put my head down on the mattress beside our joined hands and closed my eyes, suddenly exhausted. "I have a good one, too," I murmured. "Or had. I don't know if he's really still mine. But I love him, M. I don't want to lose him."

A fresh round of tears built behind my eyelids.

"Whit."

I jerked upright. Mia's dark-brown eyes blinked up at me blearily. I burst into tears, taking her hand and squeezing it. "Oh my God. You're awake. You're actually awake. I can't believe it. I mean, I did believe Lucas when he said you'd woken up, but I just had to see it with my own eyes. Should I get a nurse? Are you in pain?"

She still seemed so frail in that white bed. She'd lost weight while she'd been in here. But that didn't matter. I'd take her out for burgers and fries every day and fatten her back up if it meant I got my best friend back.

"Car..." Mia's voice was weak, barely more than a croak.

I pulled my chair forward so my ear was closer to her lips.

She swallowed, her throat bobbing, and I winced. The movement looked painful. "Ssssh," I soothed. "Don't try to speak. I'm going to get you a nurse."

I stood to find the call button, but her fingers dug into my palm with a grip I wouldn't have thought possible for a woman who'd been unconscious for weeks.

"Car..." she said again, her voice cutting off.

"Car? Your car?"

She shook her head slightly.

"Car...Lu-ca? Lucas? He's just gone to call your parents. I can find him if you want?"

Exhaustion mixed with frustration was written all over Mia's face, and I felt so guilty I couldn't understand her. "I'm so sorry." I bit my lip.

"Carst..." she tried once more.

"Carst? Cast? Karsten?"

"What about Karsten?" a voice said from the doorway.

Well, that explained what Mia had been trying to tell me. I would have known that voice anywhere. I'd lived with that voice until about a month ago. It was the voice

I'd thought I'd spend the rest of my life listening to. How stupid I'd been.

I ground my teeth together and willed myself to remain calm before I turned around. This wasn't the time or place to castrate a man, no matter how much I might want to. "What are you doing here?" I asked Karsten. "You shouldn't be here."

His jaw ticked. "She's my friend, too. You don't own her just because we broke up."

"We didn't break up. You have a family. A wife and a child, and I dumped your ass for being a lying, cheating, filthy piece of scum." The words fell from my mouth with a fake smile, every syllable laced with artificial sugar. Fuck him.

Karsten held up his hands in mock surrender. "I didn't come here to fight. I just came to see Mia."

Mia pressed my hand again, and when I looked at her face, her eyes were more alert than I'd seen them yet. They darted between me and Karsten, seeming panicked. Shit. I shot Karsten a dirty look and then smoothed Mia's hair back from her face. "I'm sorry about that. I'm going to get your nurse, okay? Just hang tight."

I strode to the doorway, grabbing Karsten by the arm and dragging him out with me. As soon as we were out of Mia's earshot, I shoved him away from me. "What the fuck was that? Don't come into her room starting shit when she'd been unconscious for weeks. What the hell is wrong with you?"

He shook his head and took a step toward me. "I didn't. I know I screwed up. And I kept hoping to bump into you. Can we talk?"

"We're talking."

"I mean properly talk. Please, Whit. You don't know the full story. There's so much you don't know."

"I think I know enough."

He sighed. "Just give me one hour. Please."

Lucas came around the corner and stopped when he saw the two of us arguing in the hall. "Everything okay here?"

I nodded. "Fine."

"I was just asking Whitney to come have a chat with me."

Lucas turned to me, an unspoken question in the way his eyebrow rose.

Karsten took another step closer. "I need to apologize. Please, just hear me out."

Lucas grabbed my hand and pulled me a few steps away. "I know it's not my business, and you know I'm Team Whitney, always. But he came by yesterday, and we had a good chat. He knows he can't win you back, but he does seem to want to honestly talk things out with you. He just wants a chance to explain. But if you don't want to hear it, I'll have the nurses call security right now."

I sighed and glanced back at Karsten. He had his wounded puppy dog face on. "Fine. Whatever. I've got some bags of your stuff anyway. Come back to the house, and if you're quick enough, I might not have set them on fire."

Karsten blanched, which amused me. I strode back to Mia's door and stuck my head around the corner. Her eyes were closed, her deep, even breathing telling me she was asleep again. I turned back to Lucas. "She woke up for a few minutes, but she's asleep again. Get the nurse to see her, okay? She seemed a bit distressed."

Lucas kissed me on the cheek quickly.

"Tell her I'll be back after I've dealt with the douche canoe."

"I'm right here," Karsten mumbled.

I smiled sweetly. "I know. Now let's go before I change my mind."

30

REMI

*E*ven hours later, as I stared at the blank walls of my new safe house back in Las Vegas, I didn't know how I'd managed to let her go. We'd held hands the entire flight, and eventually, I'd put my arm around her shoulders, and she'd leaned into my chest and fallen asleep.

I was tired, too, but I didn't want to miss a minute with her. My entire future suddenly felt so up in the air. When we'd stood on the side of the road, it had been on the tip of my tongue to promise her forever. I didn't know how this woman had gotten so fully under my skin so quickly, but it had never felt so right.

It wasn't supposed to be all taken from me so quickly. Anger burned, hot and fast, and hadn't let up since we'd landed. I'd had to pry her from my arms, and my heart felt like someone had put it through a meat grinder, watching her walk in the opposite direction with the driver who had been sent for her.

We didn't get to leave together. My own driver waited

for me, a plainclothes police officer. He'd escorted me to a nondescript car and driven me to this house just outside the city. Another officer had waited inside, but I'd barely murmured a greeting. I'd found a bedroom, flopped down on the bed, and stared at the blank walls, thinking about everything I'd gained at the ranch. And then lost in the space of one night. No, not lost. It had been taken from me.

The anger built gradually while I replayed each memory with Whitney. Moments I should have treasured more. The anger snuck up on me, slowly, quietly, until before I realized it, days had turned into nights. The feelings threatened to consume me. They bubbled through my veins like lava, spreading hate. It burned away the man I'd become. The man I wanted to be. And left me with the man I'd tried to bury. The one who had forgotten his own name, because his club only knew him as Viper.

I hated my father. That was what I realized as I lay there, seething. He'd taken everything from me. I'd been a kid. And he'd pushed me into this life. One where the club was everything, and nothing else mattered. He'd never shown me anything else. Especially after Abel had left. I'd been his heir. Heir to his motherfucking motorcycle club crown. What a fucking piece of shit inheritance that was.

Amongst all the anger at my father was a keen sense of loss. A Whitney-shaped hole. We'd been joined at the hip, my feelings growing deeper every day, and now suddenly, she was gone, and I had no idea when or if I was ever going to see her again.

Darkness fell, and the sun rose. How many times, I

didn't know. I lost track of the days, each one blurring into another. The officers assigned to guard me came and went. Some nicer than others. Some brought me food, with worried looks etched across their faces, insisting I eat. Others sat in the living room watching *Law and Order* reruns, content to let me mope.

It was one of those officers on duty when I finally dragged myself out of my head. I staggered to the bathroom and stared at myself hard in the reflection of the mirror. My beard had grown and become straggly. I hadn't showered in days, and the stench of despair hung on me, as much as my own body odor did. My eyes were shot through with red.

"Too much like him," I murmured to myself. "Too fucking much like him." The thought shook me out of my funk. Too much like the old me I'd worked so hard to bury. The man who stared back at me was the image of my father.

I got in the shower and scrubbed my skin raw. I washed my hair twice and even put in conditioner, though that turned out to be a mistake. It was the same scent as Whitney's, and the smell sent a pang of regret and loneliness through my chest. I fucking missed her.

I wrapped a towel around my waist and dug through the bathroom vanity for a pair of scissors but came up with my electric razor. Then I spotted my toothbrush and toothpaste in the holder. Huh. I hadn't unpacked. One of the officers must have taken the task upon themselves when I'd been the guest of honor at my own little pity party.

I plugged it in and got to work, tidying up my beard. Then I brushed my teeth, three times for good measure, because I couldn't remember the last time I had, and my breath could have killed a skunk.

I found clean jeans and a shirt, then pulled on a hoodie. Winter in Las Vegas was nothing compared to winter in Wyoming. I paused in the doorway, wondering how I was going to explain where I was going to my guard.

I needn't have worried. The single guard assigned to me was fast asleep on the couch. If he was one who'd been my babysitter over the past few days, I didn't recognize him. He had a spare tire around his middle that stretched the buttons on his shirt. His mouth hung slack, and quiet snores rumbled from his chest. The man was past middle age and looked like he hadn't stepped foot in a gym in the past fifteen years. If the Kings of Chaos stormed the house right now, we would both be dead in minutes. This guy couldn't protect me from a fly, let alone a gang of men, who apparently wanted my blood.

I shook my head and slipped out the door, closing it quietly behind me. I wandered the unfamiliar streets until I found a bus that took me into the city, where the streets were burned into my memory from growing up here. From there, a taxi drove me the rest of the way. Along a road that was also familiar. One I had never wanted to travel again.

"Thank you," I said to the man who dropped me off.

He gazed up at the imposing building and the high fencing surrounding it. Razor wire along the tops gleamed in the midday sun. "Visiting someone?"

I nodded.

"Want me to wait? Not too many taxis come by here."

I handed him a ten-dollar bill. "Thank you. I won't be long."

I approached the prison, willing my heart rate to remain calm. But my skin crawled. I'd spent five years in this hellhole. Just breathing the same air I had all those years ago made me want to hightail it straight back to the cab and get the hell out of there. There were too many bad memories here. And on the day I'd left, I'd sworn I'd never come back.

This time, I checked in through the visitor's doors, but it did nothing to settle the insidious feeling creeping over me. I took a badge from the woman who signed me in, and was buzzed through several security doors before a guard led me to a visiting room.

I waited. My mother had visited me a few times here, then mostly bitched about my father.

I drummed my fingers on the wooden table, chained to the floor. The security doors buzzed once more, and I looked up into the eyes of the man who shared my DNA. A smile I hadn't been expecting replaced the quick flash of surprise when he recognized me. He sat on the opposite side of the table. A guard hovered close by. Neither the guard, nor my father's odd grin did anything to make me feel safer. He wasn't the type to launch himself across the table, fists flying. He was the type who played games. Messed with your head until you didn't know up from down. Too smart for his own damn good. He wouldn't risk adding time to his sentence. If he wanted to get at me, he'd do it in other ways. Just because he was behind bars, didn't mean he couldn't get things done. He had enough guys on the inside as well as outside, who would handle whatever needed handling. I knew. Because once upon a time, I'd been one of them.

"You came," he said finally.

I rested my elbows on the table, contemplating his choice of words. "Why do you say that like you invited me?"

"Because I did. Didn't you get my messages?"

"Messages? Is that what setting my tent on fire was? Or how about the knife through my patch? You couldn't have sent a card, like a normal dad?" I sat back in my chair and gripped the sides of it so tight my knuckles turned white. The anger that had been building the last few days threatened to erupt. I couldn't think of anything better than letting it loose via my fists. Fuck him and his messages.

His eyes turned squinty. "What are you talking about?"

I held a hand up in a stop motion. "Don't. Don't do that. It might work with your lackeys, but I know you. I know when you're full of shit."

He sat back and folded his arms across his broad chest. For a man who'd passed his fiftieth birthday, he looked to be in surprisingly good shape. Though I knew from experience there was little else to do but work out when you spent all your time in a prison cell.

"Fine. How 'bout you tell me why you're here then?"

It was a fair question. One I hadn't even really thought about. Why the hell had I come here?

"Call them off. The club."

He sighed and ran a hand through his graying hair. "Whatever you think the club has done, Son. You're wrong."

I ground my molars together. "I'm testifying against Miles Mitchell. I'm not going down for something I didn't do."

The older man tilted his head to one side. "What do they want him for?"

I studied him. Once, when I'd been four, my dad had stumbled into the living room of the clubhouse. I'd been playing with a Matchbox car, running it along the ripped green felt of the pool table. I'd glanced up as his big shadow had fallen over me, and grinned when he'd hefted me into his arms. "Goin' away, kid," he'd said.

"For how long?"

"Not long. Be back soon. And when I do, I'll take you to the movies and we'll get ice cream, too. Promise." His nostrils had flared.

"Yes!" I'd cheered, throwing my arms around his neck. "Chocolate, okay? I don't like the white one."

He'd put me down, patted my head, and I'd scampered off to my mother's side. She was lying on the stained couch. The smell of her had wrinkled my nose. My dad lifted a hand in a wave and then disappeared through the club doors.

"He's lyin'," my mother had slurred.

I'd jumped, not even realizing she was conscious. Anger had raced through my little body. "He's not! He promised!"

She'd laughed. The sound cruel, coming from her twisted lips. "His nostrils flared. Didn't you see? That's his tell. Whenever he lies, his nostrils flare. Seen it more times than I can count. Get used to it, kid. Your old man lies a lot."

She'd been right. I wasn't sure if anyone else had ever noticed the giveaway, but my mother's words had proven true. It had been six months before my father had returned. And he'd never taken me to a movie in my life. That nostril flare had become my own personal bullshit meter.

I looked for it now. But there was nothing. "You don't know?"

He shook his head. Still no nostril flare.

"Murder. Said they'd pin it on me if I didn't testify."

Dad frowned. "That's not going to happen. I'll take care of it."

I raised an eyebrow. "What does that even mean?"

"It means you aren't coming back in here. And you aren't testifying either. So as I said, I'll take care of it." He barely blinked at my silence. "You don't believe me."

It wasn't a question. It was an observation.

"Why would I?"

He leaned in closer. "Nothing happens in that club that I don't control. You know that. It's why you got to walk away when you left prison. Didn't you ever question why that was so easy for you? It was because I commanded it. I own that club. I own those men. What-ever has been going on with you, it wasn't us. Now get your ass out of that chair and go live your life."

I blinked in surprise. "I don't understand."

That genuine smile he'd given me when I'd arrived returned. He appeared younger. More carefree. "Things change, Son. I've turned over a new leaf."

I snorted.

Dad narrowed his eyes. "I tell you I'm fixing all your problems and you fucking snort at me?"

I shook my head. "I was snorting at the fact you said you'd changed. Snakes don't change, *Pop*."

His lips pulled into a frown. "I suppose I deserve that. But I'm trying to be genuine here, okay? It's why I wanted to see you. And Abel, too. I'm getting out. In three months. And I want things to be different this time. I've found Jesus."

I burst into laughter. "Oh, that's fucking rich."

"Laugh all you want. But it's true. It's changed me, and the parole board saw it, too. I'm getting out. And I'd like to be a part of your life again. "

He held up a hand before I could tell him exactly how that was never going to happen. "I know what you're going to say. But let me prove it to you."

"You swear you didn't know about the club stuff?"

He held up two fingers. "Scout's honor."

I shook my head. "Scout salute is three fingers."

A sheepish grin spread across his face, and his eyes crinkled at the corners. I struggled to reconcile this man with the one I'd known on the inside. The one I'd known as a boy. I didn't believe for a second he could change so dramatically.

But I'd changed.

Fuck. I didn't know what to think.

Dad pushed to his feet. "It wasn't the club. I promise you that. If someone is threatening you, you've got more enemies than you realize."

31

WHITNEY

*M*y rearview mirror was so full of Karsten's obnoxious-looking Tesla I couldn't see anything else.

"Want to get off my ass, dipshit?" I muttered. There couldn't be more than a foot of space between our cars, and I was tempted to slam the brakes on and let him destroy his bumper by crashing right into the back of me. If I could guarantee I wouldn't end up with a case of whiplash, I would have done it. Instead, I settled for flipping him the bird, though I doubted he would have seen it through the tint on my windows.

I pulled into my driveway and got out of my car, slamming the door behind me. I didn't bother waiting for Karsten to catch up. This had been a mistake. I didn't want to hear Karsten grovel. I didn't want him in the house that I'd just disinfected of his presence. Everything about him just made me angry. He wasn't the same man I'd fallen in love with. It was as if they were two different people. The Karsten I'd known had died that night when

I'd unknowingly walked into his family's home. The one who stalked along the path to wait behind me now was a stranger. Someone I didn't know and didn't want in my house.

I twisted the key in the shiny new lock I'd had installed and pushed it open an inch, but then I spun around. "You can wait here. I'll get your things, and then you can leave."

"What? No. You said we could talk."

I ground my molars. "Well, I changed my mind. I don't want you in my home."

"It's my home, too."

My eyes went wide. "I sincerely hope you're kidding."

"I lived here for two years!"

"I'm sure your wife would disagree!"

Karsten's eyes narrowed. "You need to stop throwing that in my face. You said we could talk. We're going to talk."

He reached over me and pushed the door wider, his bigger body forcing mine inside.

"Hey!" I stumbled back a few steps but caught myself. Anger coursed through me. "Get out."

He slammed the door behind him. "No. I said we're going to talk. And you're going to listen." His voice was suddenly cold. Distant. Gone was the Karsten from the hospital who had begged for me to give him a chance.

A shiver ran down my spine, but I pulled my shoulders back and stood my ground. "I said, get out."

He moved quicker than I'd realized he could. In two quick steps he'd closed the gap between us, forcing me back to the wall. My body collided with the drywall, a gasp of air rushing from my lungs in surprise.

"What the fuck, Karsten!" I yelled, bringing my hands up to his chest and shoving him hard.

He didn't budge. His eyes narrowed, the spark of life I'd always seen there in the past, now suddenly dull. He caught my wrists and pinned them to the wall, his fingers cruel and uncaring, strangling my skin. His body pushed against mine, and I cringed away from his touch. His chest squashed my breasts. His leg came between mine, his thigh pressing on my sex.

"Is this how it has to be?" His mouth twisted in a sneer. "Don't be a fucking bitch, Whitney."

The beginnings of fear stirred in my belly. I didn't know this man in front of me. He might look and smell like Karsten. Might speak with the same voice. But this was not the man I'd known.

"Stop," I tried again, but he didn't listen. He pushed harder, pinning me, to the point where I struggled to breathe from the force on my chest. I suddenly realized exactly how much danger I was in. My gun was locked in the safe upstairs. Nobody knew he was here with me, except Lucas, who would have no reason to come check on me anytime soon. I'd always loved how much bigger Karsten was, but now it terrified me. I was fit and strong. But I was still a woman, and he was a big man. I tried to suck in a deep breath to calm myself, but it was stifled by Karsten's weight.

"Karsten, please," I choked out. "I can't breathe."

His head dipped, and I flinched in disgust as his nose ran up the length of my neck. His tongue shot out, licking just below my ear before he bit down on my earlobe. Hard.

I yelped. Tears sprang to my eyes.

He reared back, and I sucked in a breath while the pressure was off my chest.

"Are you crying?" he sneered. Quick as a flash, his hand flew at my face.

Pain sparked across my cheek from the backhand. The metallic taste of blood filled my mouth. His body trapped me once more, and he gripped my chin, jerking my face so I was forced to look at him. "Don't you fucking cry. You like this. You liked it when he did it."

"What?" I choked out.

"Don't fucking play dumb." He pulled something black from his pocket and rubbed the lacy fabric beneath my nose. "I know all about you and him. Did you wear these for him, Whit? These sexy panties?"

Shock shot through me like a lightning bolt. The panties that had gone missing from my suitcase. I'd thought Rem had taken them as a souvenir. How the hell had Karsten gotten them? Confusion scrambled my brain as I tried to make sense of it.

I couldn't. I opened my mouth to scream, but he was quicker. He shoved the panties inside my mouth, muffling the sound. "Uh, uh, uh. Sssh. Nobody wants to hear you scream, baby. No one except me, when I'm fucking you. I've *so* missed fucking you. You always were a wildcat. *My* fucking wildcat. Not his. Fuck. You think I liked watching you whore yourself to him?"

My heart hammered out of my chest. How could he know that?

Karsten laughed, watching my face. "You look so confused! It's adorable. I can just see your detective mind trying to work it all out. But here's the thing, Whit. You aren't that smart. But I am. You know how long it took me to find you after you left me all alone in that fucking hell-hole of a jail? Days. Three, from memory. All I had to do was take Mia's phone, and there was the number you'd called her from. Pretty easy to find you after that. True, she put up a good fight. But we both know how that turned out. Don't we?"

My stomach rolled. Mia's tiny form, helpless in her hospital bed, flashed through my mind. Her panicked eyes when Karsten had come into her hospital room. "You fucking son of a bitch!" I screamed, though it just came out a mumbled mixture of unidentifiable sounds around the fabric in my mouth.

He laughed again. "Now, now, if you hadn't wanted me to find you, you wouldn't have called her now, would you? It's really all your fault."

I might have made a mistake, but this wasn't my fault. It was his. He'd attacked Mia in cold blood, without any idea that he'd find out clues to my whereabouts. "You're going to rot in a prison cell for the rest of your life," I yelled.

This time, he pulled the cloth from my mouth. "What was that? You said you loved me and you want me to come home?"

"I said you're going to rot in a prison cell for the rest of your life. Same, same, yeah?"

Karsten scowled. "You're not playing nicely. I want you back, Whit. You're mine. Don't you know that?"

"You've lost your mind. I never was yours."

A muscle in his jaw ticked. "You his, then? The cowboy? Ha. Never mind. Not for long."

My blood ran cold. "What have you done?"

"Nothing, yet. Though it was fun messing with him in

Wyoming. This should have been all over when I set his tent on fire. But no, of course, he wasn't in his tent, was he? He was sleeping with my slut of a girlfriend!" He roared the words in my face, and for the first time, I smelled the liquor on his breath.

His thigh ground between my legs again, hard and sharp.

A whimper escaped my mouth at the intrusion. "What do you want, Karsten?"

His lips slammed down on mine. Hard enough to bruise before he jerked away. "You know my wife left me? Took my son and just up and disappeared like everything we'd had together didn't matter. And then you left, too. And shacked up with *him*. But not anymore. Things are all going to go back to the way they were." His fingers crept toward my throat. "I just want you back, Whit. I won't take no for an answer."

32

REM

*T*humping on the door of the safe house had me springing to my feet as if someone got me in the ass with a cattle prod. "Dude!" I hissed to the officer, dozing on the couch beside me. I kicked him, hard.

He rubbed his shin and shot me a dirty look, but I motioned to the door. He seemed confused until more thumping started up.

He pulled his gun.

I rolled my eyes. "If that's the Kings, they would have already started shooting. How 'bout you just ask who it is?"

The officer shot me an annoyed glance. "Why don't you?"

I grinned. "'Cause if I'm wrong, I'd prefer not to be the one shot in the face?"

The officer paled but was spared the trauma when a deep voice yelled, "Open up, would ya? It's me."

I cocked one eyebrow. "Who's me?" I asked the officer, who obviously wasn't concerned that 'Me' was going to start shooting. He'd put the safety back on his gun and tucked it into his belt. He strode to the door and unlocked it before pulling it wide.

Detective Lorrel's broad frame filled the doorway. He ignored the officer, walked right in like he owned the place, and thrust a bunch of papers into my chest.

I glanced down at them, immediately suspicious. "Hello to you, too. What's all this?"

"Your free pass outta here," Detective Lorrel answered.

My heart stopped. I waited for the, "just joking." It didn't come. "Okay," I said slowly, taking the papers from his hands. "Want to fill a guy in?"

"CliffsNotes version or the full length?"

"Notes. We're trying to watch *Law and Order* here. You're interrupting." It was supposed to be a joke. Though it obviously fell flat because neither the officer nor Detective Lorrel cracked a smile.

"Jesus, tough crowd," I mumbled. But it was well-deserved. I might have stopped moping in my bedroom, but I wasn't exactly back up to my regular class clown status. My father's warning played over and over in my mind. He'd firmly believed it wasn't the club who had threatened me, but it had to be. I didn't have enemies. It irked me that I couldn't work it out. The conclusion I'd come to was that my father was wrong. He'd been inside a long time. Things changed. Maybe he wasn't as in charge as he thought he was.

"Fine. I'll keep it brief. Heaven forbid I interrupt your overblown crime dramas to tell you that Miles Mitchell confessed to murder this morning."

I blinked. "Sorry, what?"

"You heard me."

"I did, I just didn't understand it. Who did he murder now?"

Lorrel chuckled. "He confessed to the murder of Leon Crawford. Gave us all the details we needed to put him away for a long time."

"Why would he do that?"

Lorrel shrugged. "Guilty conscience?"

I snorted. "Only if pigs are flying."

He passed me a pen. "Sign the papers, James. His confession gets you off the hook. Don't look a gift horse in the mouth."

"So...no trial?"

"He'll have one. But I doubt you'll be required for it. Several of the other Kings of Chaos members came forward with alibis for you."

What the fuck?

"Old footage from the clubhouse. Time-stamped. Clears you completely."

None of this made any sense. "I don't understand. Where the hell was this video five weeks ago?"

"Perhaps your visit to your pops had something to do with it?"

I stared. "How did you know about that?"

The big man gave me a steely look. "I know everything about this case, son. *Everything*."

There was something unspoken in his words. A message I wasn't quite grasping. He sighed and rolled his eyes. "Just go pack your bags. I'll give you a ride."

I wasn't going to turn him down. This apartment smelled like body odor and stale pizza. My claustrophobia didn't help.

I grinned as I hurried into my bedroom to throw my things into a bag, my mind whirling like a tornado. Dad had said he'd take care of it. I hadn't believed him for a second. But there was no other explanation for it.

My hand paused in midair, clutching a pair of socks. If Dad had somehow forced Miles to confess to get me off the hook, that meant I was wrong. He was still the king-pin. He was still firmly in the driver's seat, and if he hadn't ordered a hit on me, then who the hell had?

I shoved the last of my things into the bag and walked slowly to the door where Detective Lorrel was waiting for me. He frowned when our gazes met.

"You're green. You hurl in my car, I'm not going to be happy."

I nodded. "I'm fine. Just...confused."

He clapped me on the back. "Things will be a whole lot easier once you're outside these four walls. Nothing good comes from being cooped up in a place like this for any extended amount of time."

Didn't I know it.

I followed Lorrel to his car, parked by the curbside, and absently gave him my address. I hadn't been home in months. I hadn't even had anyone check in on the place, even though I knew someone had broken in. I'd been too busy wallowing to really even think about it. It didn't much matter. Nothing in my apartment was of value. It was more like a dumping ground, since I was on the road so often. The place was too small, and even when I had time off, I made every excuse to not be there.

I stared blankly out the window. Almost immediately, my thoughts turned to Whitney. I needed to see her. We'd left our future so up in the air, but all of this changed that. I wouldn't be going into witness protection. A heaviness lifted off my shoulders, and I sat straighter. There was nothing stopping us.

Then a little of the wind went out of my sails. I was still an ex-con. She was still a cop. What did I think was going to happen? That I'd just walk into her life and become her boyfriend? That her friends, her colleagues, would all just accept I was a convicted criminal who had served time? I raked my hand through my hair. "Shit," I mumbled.

I suddenly realized we were heading to the wrong part of town. In fact, we were heading in the exact opposite direction to my apartment. "You know my apartment is nowhere near here, right?"

"I know. Just gotta make a stop first."

I nodded. Made no difference to me. I wasn't in a rush. I went back to staring out the window. The streets were mostly unfamiliar, but I had a weird sense of déjà vu. My heart rate picked up as I recognized more and more of my surroundings. I'd only been here once. But that had been enough.

Detective Lorrel parked the car outside a familiar two-story house. I'd sat in a car, not unlike this one, looking up at this house five weeks ago. I twisted in my seat to face the detective. "What are we doing here? This is Whitney's house."

33

WHITNEY

I was going to die. The longer I stood, pinned to the wall with Karsten's liquor-tainted breath blowing over me, the more certain I became. This was how women died. They trusted someone they shouldn't. They found themselves alone, and vulnerable, with a man who had once claimed to love them. I hated the helpless feeling. It wasn't something I was at all familiar with. I hated how the fear clouded my brain, making me want to check out of reality. I longed for the familiar pressure of my gun at my hip. I imagined myself pulling it out and clocking Karsten over the head with it. Pictured his body crumpling to the floor.

Karsten released the pressure on my neck, fresh air suddenly filling my lungs. I coughed, my throat burning.

Karsten cocked his head to the side, studying me as I spluttered. He eyed my neck, where his fingers had just been, squeezing the life from me. A smile lifted the corners of his twisted mouth. "Huh. Interesting."

Despite the ache in my throat and lungs, my brain

whirled into overdrive. *Keep him talking. Stall until I can find a way out of this.*

"Tell me what you did. All of it."

He grinned. "I love that about you, Whit. You know that? Always so curious. I was almost disappointed you never realized I was out there on that ranch with you. Couldn't you feel me? I felt you. I watched. Couldn't stop watching. I left you all the signs that I was there, but you never saw them."

"You set Rem's tent on fire when we were camping?"

"Uh-huh. Couldn't stand watching his hands all over you."

"How did you get his jacket?"

He chuckled. "I had to come back home for a few days for a meeting with my lawyer. Took the opportunity to pay Mr. James' residence a visit. A home says a lot about a person, don't you think? He's not a good man."

"And you are?" I spat the words at him before I could really think them through.

Karsten's eyes darkened. "I'm your man. Your only man."

I snorted. "Oh, that's fucking rich. You're my only man, but you can have as many women as you want?" My blood boiled. Anger at Karsten. Anger at myself and the situation I'd blindly walked into. The loss of power. All of it bubbled together, swirling through my blood until common sense was lost.

Don't provoke the bear. Fuck that. The bear could go to Hell.

If I was going to die right here, at his hands, I was going out swinging. Even if my jabs could only be verbal. "You think the world owes you something, don't you? You think you're above the law, above common decency. You aren't. You're the gutter scum of this earth, Karsten. It's no wonder your wife left you. Good for her. I hope she takes your son and disappears forever. Because I sure as hell hope he doesn't end up anything like his piece-of-shit father."

When his fingers tightened around my throat again, I stared him down. I refused to blink. My gaze bored into his. Hot. Furious. Hate swirled in my veins. He'd be the last person I saw, and I was no longer scared. I was just fucking mad.

"Whitney?" a voice called from the doorway. Three sharp knocks followed.

My eyes went wide, and I opened my mouth to scream.

Karsten clapped his hand over my mouth so hard it slammed my whole head back into the wall. My vision fuzzed from the impact, a pounding immediately starting up and echoing through my skull. My head cleared, only to find a gun barrel held to my temple.

Sweat trickled down my neck.

Another three knocks. "Whit? I know you're in here. Your car's in the driveway."

I struggled with Karsten again, but his bigger body held me down, his hand preventing me from making more than a muffled mumble.

"That him? Your *lover*?" He laughed like the thought of me with a lover was ridiculous, then shrugged, clicking off the safety on his gun. "Oh well, saves me tracking him down later. Invite him in."

My eyes widened, and I shook my head as rapidly as

the grip he had on me would allow. There was no way in hell I was doing that.

Karsten pushed the gun so hard against my temple that the side of my face was forced to touch my shoulder.

"I'm going to take my hand off your mouth. And you're going to tell him to come in. Okay?"

I nodded slowly.

Karsten smiled, his lips parting to reveal shining white teeth. I'd once loved that smile. How had I never realized how savage it was?

"One," he whispered in my ear. "Two."

The gun pulled away from my temple and pointed toward the door.

The doorknob turned. "Whitney? You home?"

My struggles became frantic.

"Three."

The door pushed open.

"Run!" I screamed.

The bullet shattered the air, the explosion so close to my head my eardrums ached. Instinct took over, and I cringed away, helpless to do anything but watch horror as the bullet found its mark, ripping through skin and muscle, blood spraying across the white walls like a scene from a horror movie.

"What the fuck?" Karsten yelled, surprise clear in his voice. He turned back to me. "That's not—"

I didn't wait for him to put two and two together. I reared my head back as far as I could and then smashed my forehead into Karsten's nose.

The crunch of it breaking gave me only momentary satisfaction.

He howled, clutching at it, blood pouring from his nostrils. "You fucking bitch!"

I followed it up with a sharp knee to his groin. His yelp of pain barely registered. He doubled over, and I saw my chance. I already knew I couldn't overpower him, and wrestling him for the gun wasn't my best option when there was another one just a few feet away. I sprinted for the stairs, taking them two at a time, getting to my weapon the only thing I allowed myself to think about.

I wouldn't think about the man lying in my living room with a gunshot wound. It was too horrific to think about. My legs shook and I willed the adrenaline to get me up the stairs faster.

"Whitney!" Karsten's growl took me by surprise. He was close. Too close. Was he on the stairs, too?

I didn't dare turn around. The muscles in my thighs screamed as I scrambled upward, desperate to get out of his line of vision.

The second gunshot took me by surprise. A stinging pain burst in my calf, but it ebbed away, replaced by adrenaline. A voice in the back of my mind screamed I'd been shot, but my flight or fight instinct had been well and truly triggered. I was getting to my gun no matter what. If I had to fucking hop on one leg, I'd do it.

A crash and yowl of pain came from behind me, but I refused to stop. I skidded around the entrance of my bedroom, slamming the door and locking it behind me before racing to the little gun safe in my closet.

My breaths came in sharp, short pants, my chest aching from the lack of oxygen. The lock on the door wouldn't hold him for long. He knew I kept a gun in here.

All it would take was one well-placed shoulder barge and he'd be on top of me.

That wasn't going to happen. I wasn't going to allow myself to be the victim anymore. I never wanted to feel that fear or his fingers wrapped around my neck again.

"Whit?"

I snapped my head toward the door, not sure I'd heard properly.

"Whit? It's me. Don't shoot."

Rem.

My legs wobbled. My breath caught in my lungs. Then my training kicked back in. Get the gun. It could be a trap. Karsten could have a gun to the back of Rem's head. He could be forcing him to lure me out. And Karsten had already shown he had no qualms about shooting people. Hank Lorrel was lying on my living room floor in a pool of blood as proof.

I stabbed the combination and breathed a sigh of relief as I slipped the cool metal of the gun into my hand. Its weight was so familiar and reassuring. The control I craved rushed back in.

I ran back to the door and unlocked it. With my body protected behind the doorjamb, I pushed down the handle and let the door swing wide. Then I stepped into the hallway with my gun raised.

Right in Rem's face.

He grinned.

I darted a look down the stairs, pointing my gun in the same direction. Karsten lay in a heap. Dead or unconscious, I didn't know. And didn't care. I spun back to Rem.

"I've got a gun pointed at your head, and you're grinning at me."

He shrugged. "I figure you wouldn't shoot the man you're in love with."

A choked sound escaped my throat, and I dropped my arms. Rem closed the gap between us and pulled me against his chest. A sob bubbled up and spilled over.

"Sssh," he murmured into my hair. "It's okay."

I buried my face in his shirt, breathing in his warm, familiar smell.

"Oh my God," I yelped, pushing him away. "Hank!"

Rem caught my wrist. "He's okay. I checked after I knocked Karsten out, but before I came up here after you. Your neighbor yelled that they were calling an ambulance."

But I needed to see it with my own eyes. I hurried down the stairs, limping a little now that the adrenaline was wearing off. Fuck! My leg actually really hurt. I stepped over Karsten's lifeless body but noted that his chest rose and fell, so I guessed he'd be fine once he came to. "Where's his gun?"

Hank waved it from his spot on the floor, grimacing at the movement.

"Hank!" I limped to the older man's side. Blood dripped onto the gun from a wound near his shoulder. His free hand pressed into it, blood seeping around the edges and into his polo shirt.

My hands hovered in the air. I couldn't think straight to work out the best way to help him.

"Quit looking so worried. I've had worse."

I doubted it.

"Whit, your leg..." Rem said, pulling up my skirt. We both blanched at the blood running from a single bullet hole.

"Hold tight." He took off his jacket and held it to the wound. In the distance, sirens wailed. I hoped they were heading here.

The three of us stared at Karsten. "How did this happen?" I whispered. I was numb all over. "I thought I knew him...I never would have thought..."

My gaze darted between Rem and Hank. "How are you even both here?"

"I needed your signature on some papers. And Rem... well, he needed a lift to see his girl."

My eyes widened. Rem looked just as shocked.

"You know about us?" I spluttered. "How?"

Hank grimaced again and shifted his position. "Like I told Rem, I know everything about his case."

I raised an eyebrow.

Hank shrugged. "Fine. I know Todd. He might have filled me in."

"Who's Todd?" I asked, more confused than ever.

But Rem laughed. "Gramps."

"He was my mentor when I was younger. Was sad to see him leave, but he married a nice woman from Wyoming and took over her parents' farm when they passed on."

"No way."

"That's how his place became a safe house. Used to bring them some extra income when times were lean."

Footsteps on the path drew our attention, and two uniformed officers raced to the doorway with their guns out. They settled down quickly, though, once Hank pulled his badge.

Rem moved away when the ambulance arrived. The two women quickly assessed Hank as the more urgent

case and took him off to hospital, while a subsequent
ambulance took Karsten, and the last one was for me.
The women gave me a whistle-looking contraption to
inhale, explaining it was quick acting pain relief, while
they bandaged up my leg and loaded me onto a stretcher.
I waved to my neighbor, who was biting a nail from her
doorstep, and then peered at my leg. It felt oddly
detached from the rest of me.

Rem climbed into the back of the ambulance and
grasped my hand. "How you feeling after those pain
meds?" he asked with a grin.

"Great!" I said, then clapped a hand over my mouth.
"Oops. Too loud?"

"I think the meds have gone to your head."

"I think you've gone to my head."

Rem laughed. "Yep. Definitely on a morphine high."

I wanted to argue that I was perfectly clearheaded,
but then Rem leaned in. "I know we should have this
conversation when you aren't under the influence, but I
just need to know. Do you still want to be with me? Was
everything we said on the road that night real?"

His words sobered me. I stared into his eyes. "Nothing
has ever been as real as the way I feel about you." Then I
grinned and slapped his chest. "And I swear I'm not just
saying that because I'm high right now." I snorted on a
laugh. Shit. I really was trying to be serious, but a case of
the giggles was brewing. I clapped a hand over my mouth
to stop them falling out.

Rem pulled it away and covered my mouth with his. I
didn't feel the pain in my leg. I cupped his face and
brought him closer, letting our tongues tangle. Relief
poured through every muscle. This. This was everything.

He was my future. And I wanted nothing more than to be with him.

My head swam as he kissed me, and when he moved away, I giggled.

"What's funny?" he asked, smoothing back my hair.

"You."

"I know. I'm hilarious. I keep telling people that."

"I love you."

"I love you, too."

I eyed his tousled hair. "You're sexy."

He chuckled. "You are, too."

"And kind of dirty."

He leaned in and kissed the side of my neck. A shiver ran right from the place he touched me, down through my entire body. I dragged him closer. "Wanna do it in the ambulance? You'll be my sexy dirty cowboy, and I'll be your sexy dirty...detective."

He snorted on his laughter. "Oh boy. I can't wait to tell you all about this when you're not high as a kite."

EPILOGUE

WHITNEY

Six Months Later

"So, do you want the good news or the bad news?"

I lifted my head and peered at Mia over the pile of paperwork I was trying to get through. She leaned on her cane, but that was the only remaining evidence of the trauma she'd suffered. And it wouldn't be long until she was free of that either.

"Is the good news that you killed it at therapy today and they're letting you ditch the cane?"

She pretended to think about it for a moment. "I did slay today. But no, still stuck with that thing and this desk for a few more weeks."

"I can't wait to have you back with me. Torlane is nice and all, but he's not you."

She smiled. "I know. I'm irreplaceable."

She was joking, but I wholeheartedly agreed with the

statement. "Okay, so if that's not your good news, tell me what is?"

"Um...Karsten is still in jail?"

I frowned. "That's not news. He's going to be there for a long time. People don't normally get sentenced twenty-five to life and then get parole after six months."

Mia's lips pressed into a line. "Yeah, I know. But the thing is, I didn't actually have any good news. So I was stalling."

"You're being weird. Spill it."

"I don't want to rain on your parade. It's been awfully sunny in Whitney World for the past six months, ever since you and Rem shacked up."

I grinned at the mention of his name. Fuck, I loved that man. We'd moved at breakneck speed, moving in together almost as soon as I was released from hospital. He'd been away a lot, once he returned to the rodeo, so it wasn't like we were living in each other's pockets, but it had seemed ridiculous to keep his horrible little apartment when he spent all his home time at my place anyway. We'd already talked about babies. Both of us wanted them. Soon.

"I like the sunshine," I admitted.

Mia grimaced. "I like watching you sunbake in it. Truly, I do. You know I love Rem."

"But..." I totally sensed a 'but' coming.

"Don't shoot the messenger, okay?"

"Mia! Talk!"

Mia squeezed her eyes closed, took a deep breath, and in a rush of words said, "Remgotarrestedandisdown-stairsinthelockup."

I shot to my feet, my eyes bugging out. "Excuse me?

Did you just say Rem got arrested and is downstairs in the lockup?"

Mia winced. "Yes?"

"Please tell me you're joking."

The look on Mia's face said she wasn't joking.

"Un-fucking-believable. I'm going to kill him." Like a woman possessed, I stormed toward the elevators that would take me down to the ground level. Mia and her cane hobbled after me, and I whirled on her while I waited for the elevators to arrive on our floor.

"What the hell did he do this time?" I fumed. "Please don't tell me this has something to do with the Kings of Chaos again? I thought we'd put all that to bed."

Mia shrugged as the elevator doors slid open. I jabbed the ground floor button.

"I don't know," Mia admitted. "Shellie down in processing called me about it."

The elevator began its descent, and I folded my arms across my chest, my anger rising. "Why did she call you and not me?" I demanded.

Mia raised one eyebrow. "Perhaps because she likes her eardrums intact? She would have had serious hearing loss if you'd picked up that call."

I shoved my hands on my hips.

"Oh stop. You know it's true."

"I'm going to kill him."

"Yeah, I figured as much."

The elevator doors slid open again, and I stormed past reception, using my key card to get through the door that led to the holding cells. "Which one is he in?" I asked Mia.

She leaned back against the door we'd just come through. "Cell A."

A sense of déjà vu washed over me. "Fuck," I muttered. "That's the same cell he was in last time." My chest squeezed. I hadn't been back here since that night.

"He's the only one in that cell. They separated him from the others so you could talk to him. I'll wait here so you can have some privacy."

I nodded. "Thank you."

I strode down the hall to cell A, the only cell in that row. "At least there'll be no witnesses when I kill him," I mumbled to myself. The hall got progressively darker as I reached the end, and I glanced a look up at the ceiling, noting to put in a maintenance request to get the busted light fixed. The sounds of the other cells were muffled back here, and it was oddly quiet. No other officers hurried past. No janitorial staff mopped the floors.

Something red on the middle of the scuffed concrete floor caught my eye, and I stooped to inspect it. "What is that?"

I scooped the soft object of the floor and ran my fingers over it.

"Whitney."

Rem's hand dangled through the bars of the cell just ahead. That was all I could see of him. But I knew it was him. He had a chunky gold rodeo ring sitting on his finger. Forgetting the oddly placed flower petal, I took the final three steps toward cell A and stopped dead.

"Surprise," Rem said from behind the cell bars.

I blinked. The cell was filled with red rose petals. Tealight candles formed a love heart shape around the spot Rem stood. My gaze rolled up his denim-clad legs, taking in his short-sleeved T-shirt that clung oh so deliciously to his abs and biceps. A cowboy hat sat on top of his dark hair. His ever-present grin, that had always charmed the pants off me, was plastered across his face.

I gaped at him. "What the hell?"

He pushed the cell door, and I watched it swing open. He held his hand out to me, and I took it. He led me gently into the circle of candlelight, maneuvering me so we stood face-to-face, our hands joined.

Then he dropped down on one knee.

I burst into laughter. Great belly laughs fell from my lips. Partly from the absurdity of what was going on here, partly from relief because he obviously wasn't under arrest. "Only you, Rem. Only you."

He squeezed my hand. "I hope you mean that. Because that's exactly what I want. I want it to be me. Only me. I want to be the man you come home to every night, Whit. I want to be the man who gets to hold you, and love you, for the rest of our lives."

I raised one eyebrow. "And you thought asking me in a pimped-out jail cell would be the right way to do it?"

He shrugged. "This is the first place I ever saw you. It's the place I first realized how special you were."

"It's the place you first beat someone up for me."

He chuckled. "That, too."

I bit my lip to keep from laughing. Rem's smile faded, and he squeezed my hand. "I love you, Whit. I want to marry you. I'm going to ask you here, right now. But if you don't like this proposal, then I'll ask you again tomorrow. And the day after. I'll ask you every day for the rest of our lives if I have to. But I'm going to keep asking until you say yes. Because you and I were always meant to be. I knew it from the moment I stood right here, months ago. I hope, now, you know it, too."

Tears welled in my eyes. "I know it," I whispered back.

He took a deep breath and let go of my right hand. He shoved his hand into his front pocket and produced a ring. It was simple and sweet. A single diamond on a white-gold band. No ring box. No fuss. Just like him.

"Whitney Winona Nicholson, will you be my wife?"

His expression cracked my heart wide open. It didn't matter where we were. We could have been on the most beautiful island in the Bahamas. We could have been on a snow-capped mountain. We could have been in a dingy jail cell, with the faint echoes of an inmate brawl somewhere in the back of the building. It didn't matter, because in that moment, it all faded away. All that remained, was him and me. And a love that would last us a lifetime. Of that, I was one-hundred-percent sure. I'd never loved anyone the way I loved him. And I wanted nothing more than to be his wife.

"Yes," I whispered, a tear slipping down my face.

His smile was heartbreakingly beautiful. And then— "Oh, thank God you said yes, because there's something wet underneath my knee, and I'm really scared it's somebody's urine."

I choked on a laugh as he pushed to his feet. The ring fit perfectly, and I threw myself at him, avoiding his wet knee, because the chance it was somebody's urine was all too possible in a jail cell. I kissed his lips, and he lifted me from the floor in a hug so fierce it could have cracked ribs. Not that I'd have minded. I hugged him back just as hard.

When he set me down, his lips landed on mine. The

kiss was soft and slow and sweet. I had a lifetime of these kisses ahead of me, I realized. A lifetime of kisses with my husband. Girlish butterflies took flight in my stomach, but I relished the feeling.

"I can't wait to be your husband." His warm breath ghosted over my lips.

"I can't wait to be your wife. But I do have one condition."

He groaned. "It begins already, huh? The wifely nagging?"

I punched him in the arm.

He held his hands up in mock surrender. "Okay, okay. What's your condition? Because I love you so damn much right now, I'm gonna agree to anything."

"I plan the wedding," I said with conviction. I cast an eye around the jail cell and wrinkled my nose. "Because you have some funky ideas on romantic settings."

THE END

Keep reading for the Dirty Cowboy series bonus epilogues! Bowen and Paisley, Kai and Addie, Rem and Whitney, Deacon and Stacey, and Isabel and Johnny are all back, with updates on kids and their futures together.

Note from the author:

You want to know what happened 'that night' with Dane, Scout, and Ollie, don't you? Yeah, I did too.

Ha ha. So I wrote it! Download it from the bonus section of my website, but be warned, it's five flame hot!
www.ellethorpe.com
Happy reading!
Elle x

DIRTY COWBOY SERIES BONUS

BONUS EPILOGUE

PAISLEY

I loved the way he still held my hand. I couldn't remember a single day in the past twenty-something years we'd been together where he hadn't. Everywhere we went, his fingers between mine were a constant reminder this gorgeous man was mine, and I was his. And that I was the luckiest woman in the world.

I followed him through the bustling Sydney airport, threading between families saying goodbye, groups of friends boarding for overseas holidays, and businessmen ready to work the long flight away. But my gaze kept coming back to Bowen's broad shoulders, his narrow waist, and that ass that looked almost better in jeans than it did naked.

He glanced back over at me. A tiny grin played around the corners of his mouth. "I know what you're doing back there."

I gave him a flirty smile. "No, you don't."

But he did. We both knew it. I never got sick of looking at him and I checked him out constantly. His hair might have been greyer than when we met, and he might have had a few more lines around his eyes, but the attraction to him had only grown in the days that passed. He worked hard on our ranch, and the physical work left his body in top condition.

It wasn't my fault he was so damn delicious.

Bowen tugged my hand. "Come on, slow poke. Quit gawking. We going to miss our flight."

I grudgingly walked a little faster, so we were side by side instead of me slightly behind him. When he gave me that million-dollar smile I'd fallen for the minute I'd met him, I remembered there was nowhere else I wanted to be than by his side.

We made our way through to the international departures lounge, walking straight through it with no time to stop. The overhead speakers buzzed with a final warning for passengers on Flight 507 to board, and Bowen handed over our tickets to the steward by the entry ramp. The woman smiled, motioning for us to go ahead.

Bowen grabbed two pairs of disposable headphones wrapped in clear plastic from a bin by the entrance to the plane, and handed one to me. "Did you find out which flight Deacon and Stacey were taking?"

I took a pair from him, popping them into the pocket of the breezy, ankle-length skirt I'd picked for travelling. It had an elastic waist to allow for maximum food consumption, and was long enough that I could sit however I wanted for the long trip to Wyoming. "They left this morning. So they'll beat us there by a few hours. I talked to Isabel, too. She said Kai and Addie will be there tonight, and Rem and Whitney are only around the corner, so we'll probably get there last."

Bowen walked close behind me as we moved down the plane's narrow aisles, searching for our seat numbers. "Nothing like being fashionably late. Party won't start until we're there, anyway."

His deep chuckle told me he was joking, even though I wasn't looking at him.

"I know. I'm just excited to see everyone. Damn this stupid long flight. It's been years since we were all in the same room together. Messages and phone calls just aren't the same."

"I miss them too." He stopped me to put his arm around my neck and pulled me in so he could drop a quick, sympathetic kiss on my head. "This reunion is well overdue."

I couldn't agree more. There'd been visits back and forth over the years, and Deacon and Stacey were local, so we saw them the most, but with most of Bowen's old WBRA friends across the other side of the world, all five couples hadn't been together in the one room for at least ten years.

But oh, were our group chats ever epic. We'd become pros at those.

I found our seats, two side by side, with a window view. I already knew Bowen would insist I take it. We hadn't been on a lot of flights together, mostly preferring to stick close to home once he'd retired from professional bull riding. We'd watched our kids grow, gone to Saturday morning football games and end of year dance recitals. Bowen had been there by my side for all the parent-teacher interviews, all the kids' birthdays, and for first boyfriends and girlfriends. More recently, we'd been together to watch the older ones fly the coop, and start their own lives.

But on the few times we had flown together, just like the first time, he always insisted I take the window seat.

I settled in and watched Bowen's biceps pop as he hauled our small carry-on suitcase into his arms, and then up into the overhead compartment. His T-shirt rode up, showing off a sliver of his abs above a shiny rodeo belt buckle. I bit my lip, fighting the urge to grab him by it, pull him closer, and press my lips against that tiny strip of flat stomach.

"You gotta stop looking at me like that." Bowen closed the overhead compartment, and sank down into his seat, his hand landing on my thigh. He squeezed it gently.

"Can I help it if it's been a while since you and I were alone, kid free? And anyway. You're my husband. I'm not allowed to look at my husband like that?"

The hostesses walked by, instructing everyone to put their seat belts on as takeoff was imminent.

"You are. Problem is, it makes me think of that first plane ride we shared together." He latched his seatbelt. "Do you remember?"

Oh, I remembered. The things he'd said to me, and the way he'd made me feel that day, weren't things a girl forgot easily. Not even decades made those sorts of memories fade. I flushed hot just thinking about it. "I remember."

The plane started its slow taxiing down the runway, which was normally my favorite part of flying. I normally loved staring out the window, watching as the terminal zipped past, and the plane made that slow, graceful launch from the ground into the air.

But Bowen's hand on my leg was too distracting to think about anything else.

His thumb massaged a pattern into my thigh, just the way he had that first time. "I remember, too. We'd really only been on a couple of dates. I don't think we'd even slept together yet. But all I'd been able to think about was how badly I wanted you." He twisted his body, so his back was to the rest of the plane, giving us a tiny bit of privacy behind the seats in front of us. His eyes flashed bright, and just like it always did when we were alone, that tension crackled in the air between us.

I sucked in a deep breath. Because I knew all of his looks, all of his expressions. I knew exactly what that look meant. "What else do you remember?"

"Leaning in and kissing you right here." His lips landed on my neck, the touch barely there, but that didn't stop me from feeling it all the way down to my toes. An expectant shiver rolled down my spine.

His hand moved higher up on my leg, fingers making their way between my thighs. It was a barely respectable distance from where a beat was starting up at my core.

"I remember doing this with my hand, too. Inching it higher and higher up your leg, wishing I could go farther, but not knowing if that was actually what you wanted."

I stifled a laugh. "Oh. I'd wanted it. But I remember it a little bit differently."

The plane soared high above the clouds the low drone of the engines barely noticeable beneath the quiet chatter of the people around us. The seatbelt light turned off, and the hostesses started moving around again.

Bowen raised an eyebrow at me. "Oh, yeah? Tell me then. How do you remember it?"

"I remember your hands being a bit less respectable to start with." I laughed as he crept them higher, his fingertips a mere inch from where I was really starting to want them.

"About here? That right?"

I bit my lip and nodded. "But what I really remember is what you said to me."

Bowen cocked his head to one side in question. His forehead furrowed, like he was racking his brain for the memory but it wasn't coming easy. "What did I say?"

A flash of disappointment rolled through me. "You really don't remember?"

Bowen's grin became sly. He leaned in closer, lowering his voice until it was barely more than a whisper, a sexy grumble in my ear. "Of course I remember. I remember how hard your nipples were, poking through your bra and shirt. I remember how hard I was the instant I noticed. And I remember all the things I said to you, all the things I wanted to do to you." He glanced over his shoulder toward the back of the plane. "I still want to do them. I never got to back then, and every other time we flown, we've had a kid with us."

My breath hitched at his roving fingers that promised a good time. It had been so long since we'd gotten to be just us. The Bowen and Paisley we'd been before kids and the ranch had become our lives. "There's no kids with us now..."

"I noticed. And your nipples are hard again."

He wasn't wrong. They strained at the fabric of my bra, just begging for his attention. The pulse between my legs became a needy beat, wanting, never getting enough of him.

His gaze bored into mine. "Go to the bathroom. This is a twenty-four-hour flight. There's no way I'm making it that long without making you come."

We'd literally only been on the plane twenty minutes, but I already knew he was right. Little electric pulses shot through my body at the thought of my man wrapped around me, inside me, making me scream, with a plane full of people just feet away.

I stood so quickly I practically fell over, immediately missing his touch on my leg as his hand fell away. I squeezed past him and made it into the aisle, heading for the back of the plane. I practically ran, the need inside me building with every step, anticipation for what was about to come only taking me higher. In my head, I was transported back to that woman I'd been, giddy with new feelings for a man who seemed too good to be true. I knew now that he wasn't. He proved that to me every day, over and over again. He was a dream man and somehow, he was mine.

I'd barely gotten open the bathroom door before Bowen was behind me, his chest firm against my back. He pushed me forward, enclosing the two of us in the tiny space.

He didn't even give me time to comment on the fact that the entire plane would have seen him chasing me down the aisle. And that they probably now all knew exactly what we were doing back here. He spun me around, pushing me up against the wall, claiming my mouth like he had so many times in the past. There was nothing soft and gentle about this kiss, even though I knew how good he was at those, too. But this kiss was hot and hard. A kiss full of promise and demand. Our tongues tangled, my arms snaking around his neck and up into his hair as he pulled me tighter.

"Turn around," he commanded, voice husky, his stubble grazing over my lips. "I promised you once that I'd bend you over that basin, drag off your underwear, and watch you in the mirror as I took you from behind. I'm not missing my opportunity to make good on that promise."

I couldn't help the moan that slipped from my mouth. Wetness instantly pooled between my legs, readying me for him. I spun around, grasping the tiny sink with both hands, while Bowen made short work of lifting my skirt so it fell around my waist.

His palms traced over my ass, squeezing and slipping beneath the flimsy fabric of my underwear, before he dragged it down.

"Oh, God." I knew exactly how on display I was for him, with my legs spread, ass in the air. There was no shame, no embarrassment. This man had never made me feel anything but a goddess. Even without looking at his reflection in the mirror, I knew his eyes would be filled with desire.

"I want you so bad." He fumbled with his belt buckle, getting it undone and tugging down his jeans only just far enough to free his heavy cock. He palmed it, sliding his big hand over his length, lining it up with my center.

The head of him swiped through the wetness between my thighs, just brushing over my clit, eliciting another moan from me. "Hurry."

If Bowen was worried about how long the two of us were taking in this bathroom, he didn't let on. He teased me, his dick sliding between my legs, nudging at my entrance, coating himself in my arousal. He leaned over me, kissing the side of my neck, his lips just below my ear. "Told you. Want to make you come." He reached around, finding my clit with his fingers, and starting up a slow rub that instantly had me on edge.

"Bowen," I moaned. "I need more."

But this man knew my body. He knew it even better than I did after all the years we've been together. He lined himself up with my entrance, holding my hips still with one hand, while he pushed inside me.

His groan of ecstasy made me want him all the more.

"Look at me, Paisley. Watch."

Our gazes collided in the mirror, and I watched as he worked himself in and out of my body. Fingers on my clit, he drove me higher and higher with every thrust.

I held his gaze as long as I could, but when he sneaked one hand around my throat, his thumb stroking along the side of my jaw, I let my head fall back and my eyes flutter closed, giving in to the roaring sensation building inside me.

Bowen's hips moved faster, harder, and I gripped the porcelain sink so tight it should have cracked. The pleasure built inside me, coiling so tight I was sure I'd explode.

"I love you," he whispered.

I fell over the edge, barreling into my orgasm, yelling out his name, not caring who heard. His fingers worked my clit harder and faster, relentless as his hips crashed against my backside. He found his own orgasm with a roar, me clamping down around him and reminding him I loved him, too.

Always.

That was how we stood, in that tiny bathroom, needing each other now just as much as we had back then.

Slowly I opened my eyes, focusing on his reflection in the mirror once more.

He smiled that devastating smile that took my breath away. "We should fly more often if this is what the in-flight entertainment is like."

I poked my elbow back into his midsection, making him laugh, then twisted in his arms, and pressed up onto my toes to kiss his lips. "I needed that."

He let out a contented sigh, putting his lips to my temple. Then he wriggled his eyebrows suggestively. "We've still got to fly back next week, you know. Maybe I can persuade you to need it then, too?"

I never had been able to say no to my dirty talking cowboy.

BONUS EPILOGUE

KAI

"*W*hat are Whit and Rem's kids' names again?"

Addie gave me an exasperated look. "Leor and Avalon. Seriously, Kai, they're practically grown adults and you still can't get their names right?"

I shrugged. "I try. But they're hard names. It's not like I forget Henry or Lily or Dominic."

My wife just shook her head like there was no hope for me. She was probably right. I sucked with the kids' names. In my defense, between us, me and my friends had a lot of them. For a few years there, it had been like a competition to see who could add the most offspring to our circle.

Addie and I had contributed three daughters, Johnny and Isabel three sons. Paisley and Bowen had gone all-out with their his, hers, and ours mixture. Everyone had been a little surprised when they'd added a baby boy not long after they'd gotten married, bringing their dependent total to four. Rem and Whit's pair brought the group total to twelve. Deacon and Stacey had taken one look at the rest of us popping out kids, elbow deep in diapers and hyperactive toddlers, and decided to never have any of their own. Though plenty of photos of them with Bowen and Paisley's kids came through the group chat, so they took their godparent duties seriously.

Well, as seriously as Stacey took anything.

Addie peered through the dark night surrounding our truck. "Are we nearly there?" Her gaze slid to the clock on the dashboard, lit up in neon green. "I don't want to miss any of Summer's rides."

I paused at an intersection, waiting for another car to pass, then made the turn. "Her first ride isn't for an hour. We have plenty of time. So much of it, in fact, I could probably pull this car over on the side of the road and take a half an hour nap, and still make it there with minutes to spare."

She scoffed at that. "You old man. We only just stopped not that long ago. You couldn't possibly be tired."

I side-eyed her. Her soft dark curls fell around her face in a halo, her pretty lips curving slightly at the corners, as if she were amused with me, despite her exasperation. Her eyes were still as deep and brown as they'd always been, full of intelligence and wit. My heart squeezed a little every time I looked at her. She was the mother of my children. My best friend. The love of my life. And I had literally no idea what I'd done to deserve any of it. Like I did many days, even now, more than twenty years after we lost him, I said a little thank-you to Sunny for bringing her to me.

"I don't want to sleep. But I could think of other things that we could do in the back seat of this truck..."

Addie fluttered a hand around her mouth, like she was out of some 1800's romance. "Oh, Kai. How scandalous. On the side of the road? We're parents. What would the children say?"

I grinned at her. "Who cares? They aren't here. Want to do it?" I chuckled because we both knew we couldn't. Even if I was getting semi-hard over the idea of taking her in the back seat, we were already passing the pastures of Johnny and Isabel's ranch. But I made a mental note to spontaneously pull the truck over next time we were alone.

It had been way too long since I'd had my woman on the back seat.

I steered the truck into the long driveway of the Wests' ranch, bumping down the road in the darkness toward their softly glowing farmhouse, lit up from within. I parked the truck, and hustled around it to Addie's side, opening the door for her before she could do it herself.

She swung her legs out the door, but to my surprise she didn't jump straight down. Instead she leaned in, putting one hand to the side of my face, and pressing her lips against mine.

I kissed her back, letting my tongue dance with hers, loving the way she fit in my arms so perfectly. Just like she always had. That would never change.

She pressed her still perfect tits against my chest and let out a breathy sigh. "I kind of wish we had stopped now."

The sounds of laughter and music came from inside the house, but it was suddenly like the two of us were back in our own little world. I let my forehead rest against hers. "I really want to see the guys. And everyone else, too. But you know I hate crowds." I pulled back and gave her a sly grin. "Can I claim introvert tendencies in about an hour to get us out of there?"

She laughed, slapping her palm against my bicep. "We're here for a week. We didn't drive all this way for you to go hole up in our cabin watching old rodeo replays."

She slid from the truck, but I wasn't quite ready to let her go. "I could make it worth your while..."

She groaned and pushed lightly on my chest. "Stop tempting me. There are always so many people at our place, we never get the chance to be alone."

I slid my fingers between hers, and we started walking towards the house. "Downside of running a bull riding school and boarding twenty cowboys at a time, I guess. Not to mention the girls and their friends. And then there's the bulls, the dogs..."

She sighed wistfully. "If you could go back to when we met, would you choose differently?"

I stopped abruptly and waited until she looked up at me. I let my gaze bore into hers. "I wouldn't do anything differently. Not one second. This life is what I've always wanted. *You* are what I've always wanted. I know I don't say it enough, but you know that, right?"

Addie laughed, the lilting notes washing away in the night air. "So serious," she teased. She brushed a kiss over my lips. "But for the record, of course I know that. I don't need you to tell me. I see it constantly in the way you act around me, around our girls. I love you, too. And I love our life. I wouldn't change it either."

With that settled, Addie moved to the door, not bothering to knock since the music was blaring and nobody would hear us anyway. As soon as we walked in, a chorus of cheers went up.

"You're here!"

"Even we beat you, and we came all the way from Australia."

"Somebody get the man a beer."

Introvert tendencies and all, I couldn't help but grin at the roomful of familiar faces. Addie flew into Paisley's arms, Stacey diving on top of both of them, her wild Afro of curls bouncing crazily around her. Johnny slapped hands with me, but we'd seen each other only recently, so this was no big reunion for us. But then Bowen was there in front of me, still staring down at me like I was the kid I'd been when we'd been on tour together. He didn't say anything, just pulled me into a bear hug, slapping me so hard on the back I was sure it left a mark. I did the same thing with Deacon, and then Rem.

When I pulled back, I was surprised to find the beginnings of a lump in my throat.

Bowen looked like he might have been having the same problem. "Missed ya, kid."

I nodded, because twenty years hadn't made me any better with words. But I was feeling it.

Johnny handed me a beer. "Speaking of kids, how's mine? I thought he might have come back with you."

Johnny's eldest son, Dominic, was currently visiting our ranch, hanging out with my eldest daughter, Summer, and her friends. "Nah. Summer's big rodeo is tonight. Dominic is driving in with her and Austin. Hallie, my ranch hand, and her boyfriend, Nate, are going too." I looked at my watch. "Speaking of, can we put it on?

I can cast it from my phone to the TV so everyone can watch. It's about to start."

Johnny gave me the go-ahead, flicking on the TV. I fiddled with my phone, getting the right app up, and connecting it so it would wirelessly stream.

The conversation continued around me, everybody catching up, swapping stories, mostly about our kids, and what they were doing now that they were all getting so big. But there were also stories from the good old days, when we'd been travelling around Australia and the States together, living out of suitcases, riding badass bulls, giving everything we had for a shiny bit of metal and a fat paycheck.

Happiness swept over me. These were my people. My family. It didn't matter that years would pass between seeing each other in person. The minute we were back together, it was like we'd never been apart. That was the true meaning of a family. They were the people you chose, the ones you never let go of, no matter how great the distance between you.

The announcer called up Summer as the next rider, and Addie shushed everyone, her excitement palpable and rippling through the group. Everyone hushed.

"She could make history tonight!" Stacey squealed. "She's sooooo your daughter, Frost. Through and through."

Addie's hand slipped into mine, and I sucked in a deep breath, using it to calm my nervous system. Summer wasn't just my daughter, she was my protégé. And she was so damn talented. More than I ever was. She could make the pros tonight. All she needed was a handful of good rides and she'd be the first woman to qualify. I hated that I wasn't there in person, but this was one of only a couple of rodeos I'd missed in her entire life. I'd had plans to come visit with Johnny this weekend to look at some bucking bulls. But I'd put that in the group chat, and then Bowen had mentioned wanting to take a trip, and suddenly everyone was coming. This reunion and the new direction I was thinking of taking for our ranch was important. I needed to be here to see my friends and to do my research. But in this very minute, I was desperate to smell the sawdust, to hear the crowd cheering her name.

Everybody wanted this for her. But me most of all.

The camera panned to the crowd, and Isabel shouted when she saw her son in the front row, next to Summer's moron boyfriend, who I couldn't stand, and Summer's best friend, Hallie. But I was impatient for them to focus back on my little girl.

Even all grown-up, she'd always be my baby. The little girl I'd put on the back of her first bull when she was about four.

I needn't have worried. When they switched to the chute cam, Summer had the entire thing handled. There wasn't one thing I could have coached her on, even if I had been there. She was the most competent rider I'd seen in a long time, settling perfectly on the back of the bull, just like she always did.

Pride swelled in my chest. I couldn't keep the grin off my face.

The gate flew open, and the bull exploded from the chute. It spun in dizzying circles, and Addie pressed her fingernails into my palm so hard I was sure they'd leave marks.

"Oh God. Hang on. Hang on." Addie alternated between jumping up and down and slapping a hand over her eyes, unable to watch.

But I watched every second. I watched Summer's form and the way she rolled with the bull, balancing her weight perfectly on his back. All in the space of seconds, I checked her arms, her legs, the way her shoulders dipped, the way her back arched, all in an effort to keep the bull from bucking her off. The timer counted down while Summer owned that bull like she'd been born to ride him.

A hush fell over the room when a hard kick had Summer listing to one side. Paisley let out a small gasp. I think I stopped breathing.

The seconds slowed down, each one seemingly taking an hour.

Then the buzzer sounded, and just like when I rode, it was the sweetest sound ever.

Eight seconds to glory.

A cheer went up from the crowd in the living room that rivaled the one made by the crowd at the rodeo on the TV. Addie cheering the loudest of them all.

We were so engrossed in our celebration that I almost missed Summer's bull kick out one final time.

I almost missed the way her body sailed awkwardly through the air, no longer able to hold on.

But I didn't miss the shriek of pain. Or the scream of complete and utter agony as the bull's hooves came down right on top of her.

The story continues with a new generation of dirty talking cowboys. The above scene leads right into Buck You, Summer and Dominic's story.

But to see where their relationship really begins, start the series from the beginning in Buck Cowboys.

WANT SIGNED PAPERBACKS, SPECIAL EDITION COVERS, OR MERCH?

Check out Elle's new website store at
https://www.ellethorpe.com/store

ALSO BY ELLE THORPE

Saint View High series (Reverse Harem, Bully Romance. Complete)

*Devious Little Liars (Saint View High, #1)

*Dangerous Little Secrets (Saint View High, #2)

*Twisted Little Truths (Saint View High, #3)

Saint View Prison series (Reverse harem, romantic suspense. Complete.)

*Locked Up Liars (Saint View Prison, #1)

*Solitary Sinners (Saint View Prison, #2)

*Fatal Felons (Saint View Prison, #3)

Saint View Psychos series (Reverse harem, romantic suspense. Complete.)

*Start a War (Saint View Psychos, #1)

*Half the Battle (Saint View Psychos, #2)

*It Ends With Violence (Saint View Psychos, #3)

Saint View Rebels (Reverse harem, romantic suspense. Complete.)

*Rebel Revenge (Saint View Rebels, #1)

*Rebel Obsession (Saint View Rebels, #2)

*Rebel Heart (Saint View Rebels, #3)

Saint View Strip (Male/Female, romantic suspense standalones. Ongoing.)

*Evil Enemy (Saint View Strip, #1)

*Unholy Sins (Saint View Strip, #2)

*Killer Kiss (Saint View Strip, #3)

Dirty Cowboy series (complete)

*Talk Dirty, Cowboy (Dirty Cowboy, #1)

*Ride Dirty, Cowboy (Dirty Cowboy, #2)

*Sexy Dirty Cowboy (Dirty Cowboy, #3)

*Dirty Cowboy boxset (books 1-3)

*25 Reasons to Hate Christmas and Cowboys (a Dirty Cowboy bonus novella, set before Talk Dirty, Cowboy but can be read as a standalone, holiday romance)

Buck Cowboys series (Spin off from the Dirty Cowboy series. Complete.)

*Buck Cowboys (Buck Cowboys, #1)

*Buck You! (Buck Cowboys, #2)

*Can't Bucking Wait (Buck Cowboys, #3)

*Mother Bucker (Buck Cowboys, $#4)

The Only You series (Contemporary romance. Complete)

*Only the Positive (Only You, #1) - Reese and Low.

*Only the Perfect (Only You, #2) - Jamison.

*Only the Truth - (Only You, bonus novella) - Bree.

*Only the Negatives (Only You, #3) - Gemma.

*Only the Beginning (Only You, #4) - Bianca and Riley.

*Only You boxset

Add your email address here to be the first to know when new books are available!

www.ellethorpe.com/newsletter

Join Elle Thorpe's readers group on Facebook!

www.facebook.com/groups/ellethorpesdramallamas

ACKNOWLEDGMENTS

Okay, so hands up if you want to claim Rem as your book boyfriend? *waves hand in the air like a maniac*

I seriously loved writing this book. I love all my heroes, but the funny ones are my favorites. Rem, Johnny from 25 Reasons to Hate Christmas and Cowboys, and Damien from Only the Truth round out my top three funny men. How about you? Who's your favorite Elle Thorpe hero? Shoot me an email at elle@ellethorpe.com or come join my readers group and let me know! I love hearing from you guys.

On to thanking the amazing people who help me bring these books to life.

Firstly, a big thanks to my readers. Rem broke a record for my most preordered book, and breaking my own records makes me so happy. Thank you for loving these men the way I do. I can't wait to bring you a whole new crew of sexy dirty cowboys, as well as some familiar faces, in Buck You!

Thank you to Jolie Vines, Zoe Ashwood, Emmy Ellis and Karen Hrdlicka who make up my stellar editing team. And an extra thanks to Jo and Zoe for being my author besties too! Thank you to Sara Massery for the chats, sprints and graphic design advice. Thank you to Shellie, Ally, and Dana for beta reading!

And as always, a huge thank you to my family. To Jira, Thomas, Flick, and Heidi. You four are the loves of my life and I couldn't do any of this without you.

Love, Elle x

ABOUT THE AUTHOR

Elle Thorpe lives in regional Australia with Mr Thorpe and their three kiddos. When she's not at the local cafe writing stories full of kissing, you'll probably find her throwing a ball for her slobbery dog Rollo, or chasing one of the seventy alpacas on the family farm.

You can find her on Facebook or Instagram(@ellethorpebooks or hit the links below!) or at her website www.ellethorpe.com.

If you love Elle's work, please consider joining her Facebook fan group, Elle Thorpe's Drama Llamas or joining her newsletter here. www.ellethorpe.com/newsletter

f   facebook.com/ellethorpebooks

o   instagram.com/ellethorpebooks

g   goodreads.com/ellethorpe

www.ingramcontent.com/pod-product-compliance
Lightning Source LLC
Chambersburg PA
CBHW050011120726
47903CB00006B/1725

* 9 7 8 0 6 4 8 3 8 1 4 8 8 *